# DUES

# DUES

## A Novel of
## War and After

———————

Michael H. Cooper

CURBSTONE PRESS

Printed in the U.S. on acid-free paper by BookCrafters
Cover design: Les Kanturek

Curbstone Press is a 501(c)(3) nonprofit publishing house whose
operations are supported in part by private donations and by grants
from ADCO Foundation, J. Walton Bissell Foundation, Inc., Witter
Bynner Foundation for Poetry, Inc., Connecticut Commission on
the Arts, Connecticut Arts Endowment Fund, Lannan Foundation,
LEF Foundation, Lila Wallace-Reader's Digest Literary Publishers
Marketing Development Program, administered by the Council of
Literary Magazines and Presses, The Andrew W. Mellon Foundation,
National Endowment for the Arts, and The Plumsock Fund.

**Library of Congress Cataloging-in-Publication Data**

Cooper, Michael H., 1951—
    Dues : a novel of war and after / by Michael H. Cooper.— 1st ed.
       p.   cm.
    ISBN 1-880684-19-5
      1. Vietnamese Conflict. 1961-1975—Veterans—United States—
Fiction.   2. Homeless persons—United States—Fiction.  I. Title.
PS3553.0615D8   1994
813'.54—dc20                        94-26056

distributed by
InBook
Box 120261
East Haven, CT 06512

published by
CURBSTONE PRESS
321 Jackson Street
Willimantic, CT 06226

# ACKNOWLEDGMENTS

I owe a lifelong debt of gratitude to many people. Most importantly, to Fred Pfeil, whose untiring devotion, imagination, inspiration, expertise and comradeship laid the cornerstone for this novel's inception, revision and publication. My appreciation also extends to Kerry Ahearn at Oregon State University, whose love of literature and devotion to teaching inspired me; Allison Rose-Gold for reading the first draft, being a friend and holding my hand in Corvallis, Oregon where it all began; Andrew Robertson for reading endless drafts and, with Amy Robertson, providing comfort, love and a place to live during those harsh winters in Skagway, Alaska; John Hoben for giving me shelter in Hamilton, New York; Paul and Marybeth Hilburn for giving me support and the opportunity to work near Captain Cook, Hawaii; James Gavin for providing humor injections and putting up with a typewriter on those long summer days in the Valley of Ten Thousand Smokes; Glenda Choate for providing a wonderful home, support and friendship in Skagway; Tom F. Walker for reading drafts, coaching me into wordprocessing, and providing eternal friendship and a home through the dark, cold winters in Eagle River, Alaska; Kathy Coghill for reading and extensively editing the manuscript while we lived in Logan, Utah, and for her love, even when it went unanswered at the time; John Reale for the room in Hartford, Connecticut where the final draft was completed; Ann Augustine for being so tolerant of my demands on Fred's time during this last push; to all those friends in all those places mentioned, who put up with my dogged preoccupation and forgetfulness, especially those in Skagway and Corvallis, Oregon (First Street House, rest in peace); and finally, to my family for standing by me through my endless travels, changes in forwarding address, and infrequent communication and visits. I thank and love you all.

*To those who have abandoned self-punishment*
*To those who've forgiven*

# DUES

a Novel of War and After

# CHAPTER ONE

Would you just go take a bus? It's dark for Christsake. You got the money. There's no sense in freezing your ass off. It can't cost that much, so stop being such a geek.

He rubbed his hands together and stamped his feet on the hard shoulder of the highway. He was tired of standing here, ten odd miles south of Washington, DC, peering through his frosted breath at the cars zooming north to power and wealth, leaving him and his small knapsack to die. And what would they find to help identify his frozen carcass? A knapsack filled, if you could call it full, with a note pad and pen, a pair of old sneaks which he should have left behind, and an apple, bitten twice, nibbled once and now brown as hell. And in his wallet? Some money (enough to buy a bus ticket), a photo-booth picture of his sister and her first baby, and a New York driver's license. In other words, not a whole lot.

Yep, he should have stayed in Miami even if he had dropped out of college. Why go home to the land of snow and ice? Wasn't the blizzard of '66 enough for one lifetime? With his luck it would happen again, a world record two years in a row.

"Pick me up, please," he begged. "I'm freezing to death!"

Didn't work. Never did. Oh well, sleeping under a bridge again would be fun. It had been so far, especially that night in South Carolina when the spooky shadows gave way to some real boogie men. He still didn't know what it'd been about, but he was sure glad the men shuffling from car to car hadn't seen him, those silhouettes he'd made out against the lights on the highway, passing that bottle from hand to hand and muttering and laughing how they were "gonna kick some ass" later on.

In any event, he couldn't worry about that now. He was more likely to die of exposure due to wearing only a nylon wind-breaker and tee-shirt, not to mention living on candy bars and an apple that tasted like cardboard mush. He should have told his parents he never wanted to attend college. It would have saved some time and money. And it wasn't like it'd been a fabulous opportunity or anything. People dropped out of school every day. Why should he be different? Just because everyone thought he was smart. Besides, it all led to the same rat race anyway. So why cry about it?

Speaking of the rat race, it kept driving by. On their way home, dinner waiting, warm and paid for.

"I hope you all crash."

Not really, but it was an idea.

Guess it was time to take a bus.

The bus arrived in Syracuse at a quarter after midnight. It was cold and windy even for late September. In any case, bad enough to make him hesitate to walk the eight miles home. He could wait until morning he supposed, or call, but his father was at work and his mother didn't drive and wouldn't have the car anyway. Besides, he didn't want to go home. When he told them he'd dropped out, all hell was going to break loose.

Oh yes, let's hear the hard luck story one more time. He had worked too much as a kid, that is, he was thrust into an early adulthood, and after all that, now he has discovered beyond any doubt the fact he is stupid. Yes, it was a sad story indeed. He was sure everyone would lend him sympathy, but in the meantime he needed to find a place to sleep.

It didn't take long to find the bridge of his dreams, especially at the pace he was walking: fast to keep warm, and faster still to keep the boogie man away. It was a functional overpass next to a brick warehouse that shielded him from the wind. There was also some light from a Coca-Cola billboard. All in all, the real thing in outdoor living. He just hoped no one would decide to hold Chinese fire drills the way they had in South Carolina. But as before when his nerve seemed weak, he had an answer.

"Nothing up my sleeve," he said, pulling the marijuana joint from his arm and carefully unwrapping the cellophane. There in the faint darkness of his new abode lay his salvation for tonight. He daintily plucked it from the wrap and ran it under his nose like a good Havana cigar. He settled deeper into the recesses of the concrete sill, further into the darkness. Cold as it might be, life was just a good joint away.

He held the first inhale for seventeen seconds. That supposedly gave the body the maximum effect. When he finally let it out his eyes watered. Then his nose tingled and his throat felt sore. His head was balloon light. Even his lungs felt inflamed. But that was what being high was all about, so he took another hit and leaned his head against the wall.

Of course he wished he had never started with dope, probably the same way people wished they had never begun with cigarettes. But three years ago he had gone to a motorcycle gang party with a friend. There was all that beer to start with, and then when a woman offered him a joint he took it. The rest was history, though during his short stint at college he had managed to keep clean.

So he wasn't a complete basket case, but what the hell was he going to tell his parents? God, it was strange to think his parents believed he was a thousand miles away doing his homework, when he was under a bridge right here. And stoned. His mother would be doing the dinner dishes, stacking them high in the drainer before wiping them dry. She'd also wipe down the stove, the refrigerator, the table and all the counters before she was done. She'd place the tablecloth and a plastic flower centerpiece on the dining table. This time of year it would have an autumn theme: bright reds and yellows with needles and pine cones. Then she would give a last check to see if the salt and pepper shakers were in their place, the tea kettle on the stove, the dish rack under the sink and the dish towel hung to dry properly. Finally she would give the dog fresh water. But she wouldn't be doing that now. She'd be in bed.

Ah, yes, and his father would be on his way home from work, maybe pulling up right this minute. Let's see, what would he do first? Unload the junk he brought from the warehouse, all the broken crap and scrap lumber the business threw away. His father would have him pull out all the nails, but that was another story.

Then his father would go inside, turn the kitchen and porch lights on and let the dog out. While the dog was out his father would read the note Mom had left and maybe scribble something himself, though most times not. Next it was a snack. After that a long arm reach under the sink for the bourbon. At least two shots down. By this time the dog would want to be let back in.

Now to the bathroom to smoke his pipe and read the paper. After that back to the kitchen, feed the dog a snack, give her more water, lock the door, gobble two aspirin, then back to the bathroom to brush his teeth, gargle with mouthwash, cough a bit, and finally upstairs to sleep a few hours, till it was time to get back up to drive the school bus.

A simple life for a simple kind of guy.

If his father knew he was here he'd kill him. On second thought, though, he probably wouldn't do anything.

In any case, he had to think about what to do. It was 1967 and the world was changing fast. What had he heard on the news the other day? Something about legalizing abortion? Something about black unrest in the cities? Something about draft dodgers fleeing to Canada, which led to the next news item about the Ho Chi Minh Trail, also known as the Vietnam conflict? President Johnson was sending more troops overseas. The draft board would be very interested in his brand new status. He'd be 1-A, the first to go.

He should have stayed in college. What did it matter if he was a C student instead of a B or an A? So he wasn't as smart as he had believed, or as anyone else had thought. The question was, why had he thought he was smart? Because he had been an A-minus student in high school? All he could think of was high school had ill-prepared him, given him the false impression he knew something. Why else in college would he get a D in English, an F in chemistry and a C-minus in computer programming? He didn't know. He couldn't even figure how he'd got an A in calculus when he'd never completed a homework assignment. The professor must have confused him with someone else.

He still didn't know why he'd attended such an expensive university in the first place, except maybe so he'd be far from home if he failed. He wasn't sure he could've afforded the second term even if things had worked out. He would have had to borrow more money for food and books, and even then he still would have been short. His parents said they were willing to mortgage the house, but he couldn't let that happen, not with his father already working three jobs. Maybe his dream of rising up and being the first in his family to attend college, first to make money and not be a farmer or a factory worker, not have to work all the time, not have to worry about the car breaking down or the roof leaking, not have to scrounge around the dump on Saturday mornings, was a little too far-fetched.

In any case, tomorrow was another day. Today he was already stoned to the bone. He squashed what remained of the joint. Didn't need to get too high and start thinking too much. The last thing he wanted was to feel sorry for himself. After all, he'd made his choice.

# CHAPTER TWO

"I don't understand," his mother said. "You did so well in high school."

His father was quiet. He had expected that, but he hadn't thought his mother would insist on rehashing it over and over. He had already told them he had found his level of incompetence. That was it, period. Why he did so well in high school was because all he had learned was the mechanics of things. If given the steps and the format, and pointed in the right direction, he could plug them in and make it work. Asking him to conceptualize or discover was a different ball game. In other words, he was lost.

"I mean, to me it's like I said. High school is pushing buttons. College, you need to be able to think beyond the buttons, and I'm not good at that."

His mother shook her head. She still didn't believe him. She didn't want to.

"Listen," he said. "All I want to do now is put it behind me. I failed and that's it. I can't sit here and feel sorry for myself."

"Why don't you live here until you get your feet back on the ground?" his father asked.

"I appreciate your offer, but if I live here it'll be too easy for me. You'll support me and I'll sit here and feel sorry for myself. But if I throw myself to the dogs I'll get off my ass and do something. I need to feel like I can accomplish something, and what can do that better than trying to earn a living and supporting myself?"

"Well, don't expect it to be all gravy," his father said.

"I know it won't be. I've already had my taste of work."

"You should consider seeing what they offer at the community college," his mother suggested. "Leslie's kids are learning a trade."

He knew she was thinking about the draft and the war in Vietnam. Leslie was always ranting about it and how the government wouldn't take her sons, not to fight some dirty war. But he wasn't ready to run into the ex-schoolmates who had made such a big deal about his going to college so far away. And right now, the last thing he wanted was school.

"I'll think about it. Maybe I'll go to night school. But first I need to settle into a job so I'm not a burden on anyone."

"You wouldn't be a burden on us," his mother said.

"I know," he said. "But I still want to do it on my own."

"You'll let us help you, won't you?"

He did and he didn't.

"Sure, Mom. In fact I'll need some kitchen stuff and maybe some sheets and blankets."

"We have plenty of those," his father said.

He couldn't be fussy with what little refund he got back from the college, so his apartment wasn't exactly what you would find in *Good Housekeeping*. It was over an electrical wholesale store in a warehouse area. The kitchen window above the sink overlooked the warehouse roof and provided a partial view of the northwest factory area, smokestacks and all. The living room window gave him a good view of the street, even though all except three panes were cracked and held together with masking tape. But he figured he could still spend his nights watching the Italian girls stroll by on their way to the neighborhood bars. The bedroom window, on the other hand, was so dirty it was near impossible to see anything out of it. But since it only overlooked the roof and nothing else he figured he wasn't missing a thing.

Of course, now that he had paid the rent he realized why it was so cheap. It was like a dungeon in here, and the condition of the furniture made it seem as if violence had been a way of life for the former residents. The couch and end tables had long deep gouges, like tic-tac-toe games had been played on them with a butcher knife. The lamp shades were shredded and the crumpled ones looked like they might have been hit by the missing leg from the dining table, as did the holes in the walls. But the *coup de grace* was the blood-like stain that'd soaked all the way through the mattress. Of course it could have been a coffee stain. But it would've taken a hundred or so cups to make such a large splotch.

But still, for eighty-five bucks including utilities he was here, about to re-enter the rat race, like it or not. There was no crying now and it wasn't the end of the world just because he had to drop back and punt. If he couldn't be a scientist or make loads of money it didn't mean he was worthless or stupid. He just needed to pick his time and place more wisely next time around.

So in celebration of his new beginning he went out for dinner and when he came back at dusk he decided to sit on the couch to watch the neighborhood. But after a mix of old winos and several overweight women had passed, the streets remained empty as though everyone, like him, had decided to stay at home.

So he decided to do something he rarely tried: read. It was part of his plan to change himself, to overcome his deficiencies and be a better, more informed person. But when he turned on the lamp the bulb was bad and so were the ones in the overhead light. The kitchen and bathroom both had only circular fluorescent lamps. Last chance was the bedroom, but there too the bulbs in the overhead light were missing or burnt out. And here he was living over a warehouse where hundreds of light bulbs of all sizes must be sitting in their boxes waiting to be used.

But hey, who was complaining? He had a whole lifetime ahead. So he went back to the couch and as luck would have it two Italian women were strolling across the way, joking and laughing with each other, probably on their way to the tavern around the corner. He thought he should go too and meet them there. One of them might be interested in him. But as he chose the one he wanted a car pulled up to the curb and the women jumped in.

He guessed it wasn't his night, but all was not lost. He had managed to scam some dope from his old supplier. So he rolled a joint and smoked it pretending to be beach combing in the Florida Keys. In a way that was ironic: on Monday, two days away, he would start his new job at the factory and already he was dreaming of a vacation. Maybe he should have stayed in college. Maybe he should have matured enough to accept ridicule, since getting bad grades was a lot less humiliating than getting a bullet in the head.

He raised his hand and studied the smoldering joint between his thumb and forefinger. Maybe, just maybe, he ought to try giving up smoking again.

# CHAPTER
# THREE

"Have a seat," Stanley offered, nodding towards a metal folding chair in the corner.

"Thanks."

Stanley was a medium-sized, broad-shouldered person who filled his work shirt as if it had been tailor made. His sleeves were rolled back in wide, equal folds without a wrinkle. His black hair was cropped short and as meticulously trimmed as the border around a flower garden. And yes, he was a black man, just as the front office had suggested.

"Don't thank me," Stanley said. "It's a free country, and I'm not your boss."

Sorry. He just wanted to do his job. That was why he'd applied and accepted the offer. He was just glad he'd found it in less than a week. He was broke from buying his car, securing his apartment and stocking up with food, not to mention the gas and electric deposits.

"And just for your information," Stanley continued, "a utility man is the worst job in this place. You get to do everything, but you got to do it better and faster than anyone else, and no one's going to pat you on the shoulder for doing so."

Stanley grabbed a marker from the desk drawer and went over to one of the lockers next to the door. He crossed out the bottom name and added a new one to the list: David Thorne. "There's no keys so I advise you not to keep anything of value in it."

"Including my lunch?" he said.

Stanley smiled for the first time, which was a relief. He'd been starting to think he would hate this job.

"Let's go," Stanley ordered. "I'll show you around."

First they got him a time card, then his parking permit, and then the company handout, the union handout, the safety handout, the savings bond handout, the supplemental company handout, the supplemental union handout, and finally the revised company handout and the revised union handout.

"The rest," Stanley added, "you'll have to find out as you go."

"I guess," he shrugged.

"We'll go back to the office first and then go to lunch. We got some time to kill."

"Sure."

Back at the office Stanley stopped to talk with a foreman. It didn't seem to be about anything that concerned him so he went inside the office to look around. Right away he found something he hadn't noticed before, which surprised him since there wasn't much in the place to discover. It was a calendar hanging behind the door, with a large picture of a naked blond woman holding a lever that rose up between her legs from a floor full of gears. It cleverly covered her vagina though he was sure he could detect a little hair off to one side. And, of course, she had extremely large breasts and not an inch was hidden. The picture was signed by Greta.

"Looking for the date?" Stanley asked as he entered.

"Yeah," he said, noticing the calendar was two years old.

"Well, it's lunch time," Stanley said, shrugging and turning away.

He took a last look at the blonde. "I'm hungry," he said. "In fact I'm starving."

Starving for a big tit in the face.

The cafeteria looked more like a gymnasium. It had a wood floor, a half round ceiling with windows at roof level, and a steel beam superstructure whose cables suggested basketball backboards had once hung there. His sneakers even squeaked on the floor and the sound echoed back from all directions. But no matter how it looked or felt, or whatever it had been before, now it was a cafeteria full of tables and the smell of food. The seating arrangement was like high school too. The suits and ties sat up front at the round tables, and had tablecloths. The plain white shirts and light blue ones sat at the next set of tables, with place mats. The women sat at the tables across from them. They had a tablecloth and a flower centerpiece. The next tables were long rectangular ones. Everyone else sat there—the khaki and flannel shirt crowd. These tables were bare.

"Don't eat the soup," Stanley advised as he picked out a cottage cheese dish and two chef salads.

He wasn't into soups and he wasn't into the day's special either: roast beef, mashed potatoes and corn with coffee. That seemed more like dinner to him, even if it was only a dollar and seventy-five cents. What he wanted was a peanut butter sandwich, but no such critter existed so he grabbed an egg salad sandwich and an apple.

"How's the soup today?" Stanley asked the woman cashier.

"Oh, it's real good today."

"Yeah, real good I bet."

The woman didn't catch the sarcasm and Stanley didn't help her out. He paid and went off to the condiment table.

He smiled at the cashier.

"That's a dollar," she said.

"Thank you," he replied for some stupid reason.

She put his dollar in the register and looked up at the next person.

He wondered if he should ask Stanley if he always sat in the back away from everyone else, even from the other blacks. He wondered if the table was for the exclusive use of the utility staff, they being such a rare and tough breed. But no, it was better to eat and shut up, mind his own business and do what Stanley had told him earlier: learn as you go.

For instance: Stanley picked out all the black olives from his chef salad and placed them in the corner of his tray.

For instance: Stanley didn't use dressing on his salad.

For instance: Stanley ate quite fast.

22

He'd better hurry himself. He had almost forgotten. He had to work now. This was his first day, but already he was thinking he wasn't going to like being a utility man. Stanley didn't seem the type he'd work well with. But they said in the front office there were lots of jobs to do and he'd most likely be working by himself.

"It's simple," the foreman said. "You got good clamps and you got bad clamps."

A good clamp had holes drilled in the center of its wings. The bad on the sides. Altogether there were five barrels, maybe two day's work.

"Make it three," Stanley told him after the foreman left.

Actually he didn't think it would take more than an afternoon. But by the time he arranged the heavy barrels and found two empty ones to start the process, he had already wasted an hour. To make matters worse he had accidentally ruptured one of the cardboard barrels. He hoped it wasn't important. None of them were in good shape anyway. He could always say it was that way when he had started.

Well, get to work, slowpoke.

He centered the 'to be sorted barrel' between his legs and picked up the first clamp. The holes were slightly off center but plenty of good metal was left on the sides. Still, it wasn't exactly centered the way he had been shown. After a quick scan of the barrel none of them seemed as perfect as the one the foreman had picked.

"Hmmm." Well, they could only fire him. So into the good barrel it went. The good barrel being the one on the right. Right? Right.

At the end of the day Stanley wasn't at the utility office. So he nosed around, searching the desk drawers for anything of interest. All he found were scraps of paper with names, times, numbers and places scrawled on them. One larger piece had a woman's name and possibly the name of a bar. Some had dates that went back four years, and no two looked like they'd been written by the same person. Under the desk were piles of oily rags, a black top from a thermos bottle and a few short pencils without erasers.

On the other side of the room was the sole filing cabinet. In the top drawer a dozen unused manila folders lay flat on the bottom. In the back were four greasy machine operator handbooks. On top of the books were some party napkins, all with the same cartoon. It showed a drunk standing at a doorway ready to knock while a young, big-bosomed woman clad in a sheer negligée stood innocently holding the door open. The caption read: Now there's a great set of knockers! The woman's breasts were distinctly shaped like torpedoes and her large nipples were inked in red. The other drawers were completely empty.

On top of the filing cabinet sat a brown lunch bag. A curled black banana peel and a pack of ketchup were inside. He put the bag back in the exact same spot, where it wasn't dusty. He was beginning to get the feeling that it was best to leave things alone.

*Well, toots,* he said to Greta, the big blonde on the calendar. *It's been one hell of a first day. I'll miss you, but I'll be back to see you in the morning. Rest assured that I'm your one true love.*

He threw her a kiss and closed the door behind him.

God, he would love to fuck her.

# CHAPTER
# FOUR

He rolled up his sleeves, following Stanley's example. Now he
wished the clamp job had taken longer. Not that he minded
cleaning two filthy mammoth tappers with a solvent solution. It
just wasn't the most fun thing in the world to do. The machines
were quite impressive though. They looked like huge microscopes.
So he guessed he could imagine himself as a scientist, the one he
had thought he always wanted to be. It was just too bad they hadn't
been cleaned in over a year.

"It should take us until Friday to finish," Stanley said.

"How nice."

"What's the matter? You don't like getting dirty?"

"No. I love getting dirty."

"Well, we'll see who gets to clean the sump hole. Winner gets
the hole. Pick a side," Stanley said as he waved a wrench. "Dull or
shiny?"

He looked first at the hole. "How deep is it?"

"Deep."

"I'll take the shiny side."

Stanley bent over and spun the wrench on the tip of its handle.
It fell over onto the dull side. The shiny side up.

"Beginner's luck," Stanley smirked.

"I might as well get used to it. I got a feeling I'm going to be
doing this a lot."

"If you get used to it," Stanley said, "you can do it all the time."

"Thanks."

He knelt down next to the hole and rolled his sleeves up a little
more. In fact it might be a good idea to take off his shirt and just

wear his tee-shirt. But then he'd get that dirty and wouldn't have anything to wear at home.

He dipped his rag into the solvent bucket and wrung it out. The solvent instantly bit every pore of his skin like a million starving ants. Within seconds his skin turned powdery white. It looked like he had a dandruff problem.

But that was the least of his problems. He had to dip his hand into a black hole where no hand had ventured for a year or more. The damn thing looked like a likely spot for some creature to be waiting not to shake his hand but bite it off, eat it, then lick its lips for more. Maybe it would pull him all the way in.

"You don't need that arm, do you?" Stanley asked.

"Very funny."

He reached down into the hole, sliding his arm deep into the dark syrupy oil. It reminded him of the time he saw his uncle reach into the rear end of one of his dairy cows, how that and the slick sound of it almost made him faint. He was feeling a little lightheaded now. Maybe it was from the strong smell of the solvent. It certainly made his eyes burn. But he couldn't faint now, not in front of everyone. And he wouldn't faint anyhow, he knew that. He was just fucking with himself, making it harder than it was. Speaking of harder, there were several hardened clumps sitting on the bottom like little spiny sea urchins. Below them was one mother of a clump, hard as nails. No way was he able to dig into it. He needed a jack hammer or a stick of dynamite, no use tearing out his fingernails. They weren't paying him enough for that.

When he turned his head sideways he discovered the shop foreman staring at him from the aisle. He had his arms crossed on top of his plump belly, standing silently like he was expecting something to happen. And the man didn't have all day.

He settled for retrieving a spiny clump or two. Maybe it would be enough to satisfy the foreman so he would leave. He couldn't stand bosses watching over him, or anyone else for that matter, but those floating clumps weren't exactly easy to catch. They scurried around just ahead of his grip, squirting out whenever they could. Finally he caught a small one. He squeezed it hard so the tiny spines embedded into his palm.

"Nice stuff," he said to the foreman as he brought it out for inspection.

The foreman nodded.

"A little hard down there?" Stanley asked, holding something behind his back.

"Just a little."

"Use this."

It was a length of pipe that had been flattened on one end. It was just what he needed to loosen the big one at the bottom. He decided it was best to retrieve the floaters first, get all the easy crap out of the way and then go for the hard one. Besides, the foreman was waiting, his hairy arms still crossed over his chest, looking like a drill sergeant with a greasy brush-cut.

He pulled out three more clumps and each time the filthy oil dripped off his arm onto his shirt and pants and all over the floor. Now the little metal slivers the oil was filled with were digging into his skin like prickers. One cut by his wrist was bleeding and burning from the solvent and oil. In fact, college was looking better by the minute.

It was time to switch to the pipe, try something else for a while, make it look like he was progressing. He eased it into the hole then stabbed the clod on the bottom. He felt it budge and it seemed like he had a good bite. He brought the pipe to the edge and wrenched on it, using it like a lever, but it went nowhere. So he placed his body weight over the end of the pipe and pressed down, until suddenly the bite gave way and he went crashing down to the floor as the oil splashed up into his face.

"Shit," he said, regaining his balance, squeezing his eyes tight to force out the oil.

"You get solvent in your eyes?" Stanley asked.

"No, just oil I think."

"Use this. It's clean."

He reached blindly for the rag and wiped his face and eyes. It didn't burn much but felt funny, like slime was coating his eyeballs. His sight was filmy but with each blink it became clearer.

"Got to watch out for that stuff," Stanley said. "It'll eat your eyeballs out."

He had just discovered that.

The foreman dropped his arms and walked off. So much for impressing the guy. Not unlike how well he'd done with his English professor, the S.O.B.

"Don't worry about him," Stanley said. "He's an asshole. He'd back-stab you if you were the best worker in this place."

"I can work just as good as anyone else," he came back. "And I don't care about anybody's opinion."

Stanley stopped wringing out his rag, looked across the room and then returned to wiping down the machine. He guessed his reply had too much bite in it, though he hadn't meant it to be aimed at Stanley. On the other hand, he did have a feeling that cleaning the sump was partly a haze job. Maybe Stanley could make that wrench fall on any side he wanted. Still, running away from college didn't exempt you from paying your dues somewhere down the line.

# CHAPTER
# FIVE

"How old are you anyway?" Stanley asked.

"Eighteen, going on nineteen."

He was surprised Stanley was asking so many questions, almost as if he were still applying for the job. But it was a welcome change from yesterday when they hardly spoke at all.

Or of course, it might also be an attempt to remain sane after three days of shit work. He looked down at the black grime imbedded in his fingerprints and every other line or crack in his palm, not to mention enough gunk under his fingernails to re-oil the machine, or the red, puffy cuts stinging like a swarm of wasps had attacked him. No, this wasn't the time to be thinking about those warm, sunny, clean classrooms again, full of all those fabulous young coeds just itching to find a man. Not that he was the answer to their dreams even if they were.

"Why aren't you in college?" Stanley continued. "All the other smart kids are."

"Who says I'm smart?" He raised his hands for Stanley to see. "I'm here, aren't I?"

"You chose to be here. Why?" Stanley asked.

"What's that got to do with anything?" He was becoming a little perturbed here. It was coming clear why Stanley ate alone in the back of the cafeteria. Maybe he should do the same.

"Two days ago, when you got mad."

"I didn't get fucking mad," he said.

"You sure acted like it. It made me think this was the last place you wanted to be and that didn't make me feel like the King of England. I see enough of you college boys coming through here thinking they're hot shit, but they don't know shit. They're on their way to a fat career, not a fucking job like this. So don't try to fool me by saying you like this shit, because I won't believe you one bit."

He stared eye to eye with Stanley but had absolutely no idea how to answer. So he reached down for his rag and, Goddamn it, felt his eyes heat up and start to blur. Now he wasn't wanted in a fucking factory. Where in hell was he going to go next?

Stanley dropped his rag into the solvent bucket and stared briefly at his fingernails. Then he reached into his pocket and pulled out his watch.

"Meet you back at the office when you're finished. Then we'll go out for a beer. Okay?"

"Sure," he replied, wringing out his rag.

After Stanley left he realized there was more than 'finishing up' left, but there was no use in crying about it. He had chosen this job just like Stanley'd said. But if Stanley, his parents, his professors or whoever didn't like it they could go fuck themselves. He had his plan and it was only a matter of time before he would never need to rely on anyone again.

Back at the office Stanley was filling out a weekly report and didn't bother to look up. After he sat down Stanley glanced at him but then they both looked away. When his gaze caught on the calendar hanging on the back of the door, he started wondering if Greta made enough money to support herself. He guessed he could become a photographer. He could teach himself.

"You can take that home if you want," Stanley said.

"Nah," he said. "Then I wouldn't have anything to look forward to when I came to work."

Stanley made a face and a noise close enough to a laugh. After all, no matter what their differences they were both hard workers. Maybe, just maybe, he should have told those professors to kiss his ass.

The bar itself was small but a larger room in back held several pool tables. The décor was simple tongue-and-groove knotty pine. Nothing on the walls, not a beer sign, not a nail to hang one on, not even a black velvet painting of a nude lady. In fact, no sign out front, the bar didn't even have a name. But a poster taped to the cash register announced a name contest in progress, and there was a jar with a pad and pencil set on the bar.

"You want to enter the name contest?" the black bartender had asked after Stanley introduced him.

He shrugged his shoulders.

"Don't listen to him," Stanley warned. "The contest has been on for years."

"It don't cost anything, though," the bartender said.

"I'll think about it."

"You see?" the bartender said to Stanley. "Some people care."

At first he'd been afraid he'd be the only white guy in the place but it turned out okay. There were other whites, most of them in work clothes like his, all dirty and drinking the week away. Even two white ladies were there, both redheads. They sat at different tables talking with a couple of black women and some Oriental ladies, all the women looking sexy and beautiful with their flashy wardrobes and chic hairdos.

"You play pool, you said?" Stanley asked.

"A little."

"We'll play partners, okay?"

"Sure. As long as you don't mind losing."

In the back it was even more smoky, enough to make his eyes burn like the solvent did. But he was up for it. It was good to get out and finally enjoy himself. No more being stuck inside his apartment. Now he had a friend, and more friends on the way.

They lost the first couple of challenges but after a few beers began loosening up. On the third they allowed the competition only one shot, which they missed. Now people were challenging them and Stanley had started ordering shots of whiskey along with the beer. It didn't take long for the hard liquor to hit him, but he wasn't about to end the fun. So he drank on and it became harder to concentrate but the balls kept falling and the drinks kept coming and then it was ten o'clock and then it was eleven, then midnight and the smoke didn't bother him anymore.

"You tired?" Stanley asked him after he finished yawning.

"No. I'm just used to going to bed at about eight."

"We can go home anytime you're ready."

He wanted to go home but Stanley had begun winning bets on the side so he didn't want to upset the streak. He would stay and do what he could though it was Stanley who was winning the games. At best he kept them afloat by making a few and not screwing up. In fact he was making some very difficult shots. Too bad he couldn't make the easy ones.

Stanley brought over more whiskey and beer.

"No more for me after this," he said. "I won't be able to stay on my feet."

"Looks like you're having trouble doing that now," Stanley said.

"Yeah, no kidding."

"You break this time."

He watched the black guy racking the balls. He was at the point where he was forgetting how to play the game. He felt more like a spectator, way up in the bleachers, barely able to see the game, let alone focus on it. But it was only a game and if they lost because of him, well, they lost because of him. He'd pay Stanley back if he had to.

Stanley offered him the privilege. He accepted.

It wasn't easy pretending he was cool when he truly was fucked up. When he leaned over to break the rack of pool balls his chin smacked the end of the table, and he blacked out for a sec. Then he accidentally knocked the cue ball off to the side. After he lined it back up he missed it completely. When he did manage to hit it he sank it in the far corner pocket, and the rack itself hardly broke up at all.

"Sorry."

"Don't worry," Stanley said. "The game ain't over yet."

While Stanley was making his shots one of the redheads from up front sauntered over to the tables. She stood next to him and watched Stanley sink the seven. He tried to ignore her, giving her only a slight smile and nod. She smiled back.

"Hi!"

"Hi," he replied nonchalantly.

She had a cute freckled face like a little girl. But something was wrong with her hair. The color was okay but the hair itself was too thin. The way he could see her scalp made her look almost eerie, like she was wearing a mask. Fortunately, she was on her way to the ladies' room. Besides, Greta, the blond bombshell, was his girlfriend. She was waiting for him back at the office.

But when it was his turn to shoot, the redhead came back out and watched him. It made him nervous because he had a relatively easy shot but a lot of green was between him and the ball and if he missed it, the challengers would have an excellent chance to win.

He aimed and then re-aimed. He made sure he wouldn't scratch. He aimed again, positioned his hand, set the cue in it, aimed at the cue ball, pulled the stick back, slid it back and forth a few times, pulled it back for the last time and careened it off the cue ball when he shot.

Nice!

"Hi! Again."

He looked over at Stanley but he was busy studying the table. Stanley didn't seem mad but he didn't seem happy either.

"You come here often?" she asked.

"It's my first time," he said shrugging his shoulders, trying to ignore her.

"Mine too."

Oh, great. They had something in common.

"I'm not sure I like it. It's awfully smoky in here."

"Yeah," he sighed.

"You guys are good."

"Not bad," he shrugged.

The opposition was making a run now. All that was left was a combination and then the eight ball. If the guy made the shot it would end a monumental winning streak by Stanley and him, but at this point he wouldn't mind. Maybe they would go home then.

The black made the combo. "Oh, you can do that?" she asked.

"If it's your own balls," he said.

She smiled, her mouth growing wide and long enough to expose her crooked teeth. She looked much better with her mouth shut.

The black dude quickly sank the second ball and then the eight ball, ending their streak.

"Come over for a drink if you like," she invited.

"Yeah, maybe. We might play some more."

"Okay. Maybe I'll see you later then."

"Yeah, sure."

God, he was glad that was all over. He was glad everything was over.

"You go for redheads, huh?" Stanley said when he came over.

"Some of them." He was glad Stanley didn't seem perturbed about losing, especially since it was he who had blown it.

"Well, let's go home," Stanley said. "I've had enough for one night."

"Me too."

Just for the hell of it he said goodbye to the redhead and the other girls. The redhead waved and smiled, exposing those crooked teeth again.

Outside, the cool air opened his nostrils, which he hadn't realized had been stuffed, and split his headache down the middle, something else he hadn't know he had. Then he realized he had to piss, maybe since yesterday.

"The car's this way," Stanley motioned.

"Yeah," he chuckled. "I was just checking you out."

Before he got in he decided to piss. It was a good idea; as soon as the pressure was released he felt distinctly less drunk and his headache seemed to subside, at least temporarily. Now he wished the redhead were holding it for him. She'd love it. It was taking long enough. So long she might still have time to get out here and do it. Maybe the bar would close before he finished. God, the tip of his dick was cold. So why was he laughing?

"You all right, man?"

"Yeah," he yelled back. "I'm fine." He zipped up his pants and jumped in.

"Can you drive, man?"

He closed the door and gazed out the windshield at the lighted street ahead. Sure, he could drive. "Sure, I can drive."

"You got any grass on you?"

Well, well, well, Mr. Stanley. What's this I hear? A dope fiend too? "Yeah, I do as a matter of fact."

"Let's light up then."

He turned and looked at Stanley. Simultaneously they began laughing.

"I was in the army once," Stanley said after finishing his third hit. "Joined when I was seventeen. Got out when I was eighteen. Supposedly I had a discipline problem. But all I actually did was fool around too much. Never took anything seriously. Hard to believe, huh?"

"I guess so."

"Then I came here and that's it. No more excitement. No more nothing. Just seven wonderful years of the same thing. Grinding and drilling holes."

He followed Stanley's example and took another hit.

"If you get drafted or join up and you make it out alive, don't ever come back here. It ain't worth it. But hey, who's bitching?"

"Sounds good to me," he said. In truth, he didn't appreciate the suggestion he wouldn't make it back alive, let alone that he was going in the first place. Lots of things could happen. Maybe the war would end. Besides, where did Stanley get this idea that he was about to be drafted? Did he have some crystal ball or something?

"By the way," Stanley asked, "how come you work so hard?"

"What's wrong with working hard?"

"Nothing," Stanley said. "I was just wondering who put the fear of God in you."

"No one."

"No one?"

"Well, if you're talking about where I got my work ethic, I guess it's from my father."

"Your father a hard worker?"

"You could say that."

"What's he do?"

"He has three jobs. He's a factory warehouseman, a school bus driver and a store detective."

Stanley nodded and looked out the windshield.

"As far as what my opinion is," he continued, watching Stanley hold his smoldering joint near his lips, "if I knew the conditions of a job and accepted it, then I'd better not bitch about it and do my job. Otherwise I should quit. I don't think other people should carry my share of the load."

"That your father's philosophy too?"

"I guess so."

"It's a good one." Stanley took another hit, holding it in for several seconds. "And a bad one."

"What do you mean?" he asked.

Stanley frowned. "It's a whole different story if you *got* to live and work here. You may not think that now, but you will after you leave. And the sooner you leave the better."

He turned and stared out the windshield. Why was Stanley pushing him to leave? Christ, they'd just had a good time together. And work hadn't even been that bad.

"Take me home," Stanley said. "I got work to do."

He started the car and put it in gear, but it stalled and he knew it would take minutes before he could get the cold-hearted piece of shit to stay running. Stanley would just love that. But at least being mad at the car helped pull back the tears. It would have been hell if Stanley had seen him crying again. What the fuck is wrong with you? he asked himself. Haven't you ever bothered to grow up?

At dawn he had a headache and had to pee. At nine o'clock he had the same headache and he had to piss *bad,* but the bathroom hadn't gotten any closer. It was still too far, even with aspirin. He just couldn't move. He didn't want to move. Opening and closing his eyes made his whole body convulse. He couldn't even gather the blankets to cover himself. He would just have to suffer.

He closed his eyes and went back to sleep, but not before the room started spinning.

It was a few minutes after noon when he woke up again. It was bright in the room, possibly a sign of a great sunny day, a day he was missing. But he still had a headache and he still had to piss and it was beginning to leak out the end of his dick and his stomach ached and his back ached and if he would just be brave enough to get up and move around and go pee most of the problems could be eliminated. But no, he had to be lazy. He wanted to feel sorry for himself. He wanted to shoot himself in the head.

Unfortunately being a cry baby was getting him absolutely nowhere. So he got up and bore the pain. He went straight for the bathroom and pissed even before his hard-on was completely gone.

"Yeah!" He loved it. The mentholated sensation streaming through the core of his penis ran circles around his headache. Christ, it was better than aspirin. Too bad he had pissed all over the seat and the toilet base.

He took aspirin anyway, since the headache returned as soon as he had finished peeing. He splashed cold water on his face a couple of times and stared in the mirror. He looked terrible. The bags under his eyes were almost purple. His skin was a pale sickly white. His eyes were red.

"Fuck."

He peered down at the piss puddles around the toilet base. What a fucking bum. Then he backed away from the sink and gazed down at his penis, which was surprisingly getting hard again.

"So what do you want?"

It wanted Greta, beautiful sweet Greta, the Amazon woman. And it wanted her now. It wanted her to shake it, get that last drop off. She could even wash it if she liked. She could slide her hand back and forth, going faster and faster and at certain critical points suddenly slow it down, pull on it, squeeze it, and when everything had subsided she could start again and call up his semen to the tip so it could ooze out, squirt out and fill the palm of her hand.

Yeah!

He went back to bed and gathered the blankets and pillow underneath him. Then he slowly began humping as he kissed Greta all along the neck, even sticking his tongue in her ear. Greta moaned. She twisted. He slid his lips down from her neck and kissed her breasts. Then he tongued her erect nipple. Round and round he went until she pulled on his hair. Then he grasped her nipple between his teeth, biting just a little until she grabbed his hair with her other hand. Then he sucked it up into his lips and kept sucking until he filled his mouth.

"Ahhh!" he moaned.

He fell limp on the pillow, letting the warm sensation fade from his groin. He was so exhausted he didn't care if the blankets were gooey and stained. Greta always did him so good. So he sucked her breast again, taking it all up into his mouth, and she loved it. He started humping again and the goo smeared their bellies and he tried and tried but he just couldn't get it up again.

"Sorry, love," he sighed as he rolled over on his back. The blankets were a bit too scratchy now.

After mopping up the pee, he cleaned the blankets as best he could and hung them to dry. Then to the shower where he and Greta got it on again, but only after they each washed the other's body. Lots and lots of soap! The steam was great for opening his sinuses and sending a tingle to each of his pores, and the fresh air ate up his headache.

Next on the agenda was an eye massage and a neck pinch in front of the mirror. Then he splashed more cold water on his face, brushed his teeth, and took more aspirin, three this time. Finally he grinned. A big, happy one for he was cool. Though a bit ugly. Skinny too.

He wasn't in the mood but he decided he should visit his parents and tell them about his marvelous first week of work. It was such a nice Saturday afternoon too. So there was no excuse not to, unless he called and said he had a hangover the size of Manhattan. But he could also leave early if he liked, using the excuse he didn't feel well.

So he went and was glad he did. It felt great riding along with the window down. It got the blood oxidized and moving. And before he knew it he was there and feeling like a new man.

As he pulled into the driveway his parents came out the side door from the kitchen. It looked like they were going shopping. His mother had her coupon file and his father was already yawning. They looked up but didn't recognize him immediately. Finally his mother waved back.

"We didn't recognize your car right away," said his mother. "Your father thought it was those kids again, driving up and down the street."

"They've been a nuisance lately," said his father.

He shrugged. "So you're going shopping?"

"Your mother wants to get some apples for your grandmother."

"He's the one who wanted to go," his mother said, pointing at his father.

"I am not."

"You said you'd rather get them at the store than go pick them."

"I said," his father loudly said, "I'd rather go to the store if we're only going to get a few for your mother. There's no sense driving all the way out there just to get a dozen or so. Right?" his father asked, looking at him.

"I guess so."

"Your father just doesn't want to go pick them," his mother said.

"If you want to pick them then we'll go," his father said, raising his voice.

"Now he wants to go," his mother said, pointing again.

"Listen," he interrupted. "Just go to the store and buy a dozen. You can go picking some other time."

"That's what I was trying to tell her," his father said, waving his mother off.

His mother turned away from his father and towards him. "So are you going back to school?"

"I have a job."

"You don't expect to work in a factory all your life, do you?" asked his father.

"You could go to night school," his mother added. "Many people do."

He didn't want to go to school, Mom. He was out to make a living for himself, like everyone else, including his father who *had* worked in a factory all his life. So let's drop the subject before the headache comes back.

"It's not that expensive around here," his mother said. "You'd be close to home too."

"Mom," he said. "I don't want to sound as if I don't agree with you. I know it's important to you, but like I said, I can't deal with it now. I got other things on my mind."

As his mother stared at him his headache moved over behind his right eye. Fortunately, though, then she looked down at the ground so he could close his eyes and rub his forehead. Still, he had the distinct feeling that his mother had not given up yet. She had at least one more thing to say, most likely something like his father needed help around the house. That was easy enough to deal with. But suddenly he felt like running to the shed to be with the garbage cans so he could smoke a joint and be by himself. He didn't have any convincing arguments to justify his life. He was just pissed off.

"We'd better get going," his father said. "It's getting late."

His mother quickly wiped her cheek, though he hadn't seen tears in her eyes. He could tell by the awkwardness between them that she was frustrated and in pain. But he still didn't believe he was doomed. There was plenty of time and he had started on his plan. He would find some training, possibly in a technical field. All he needed was money, independence and a feeling of self-worth.

"I was wondering if I could borrow some things?" he asked.

"Your mother's already made up a box for you. It's behind the kitchen table."

"It has more sheets and blankets, pots and pans, some dishes and utensils—"

"Thanks," he said, interrupting his mother, wanting to get out of here as soon as possible.

"You need any furniture?" she asked. "Your father has a whole shed full of junk."

"It's not junk," his father said sharply.

"Antiques, right?" he said. His mother laughed.

"You two don't know anything," his father said, and turned abruptly away.

After his parents left he realized he'd better act more carefully around them. He didn't want to get into any arguments. He knew he'd disappointed them by dropping out of college, especially since they'd had such a hard time just eking out a living. On the other hand, if this was his fate he'd accept it. If he had to serve in the armed forces, he'd accept that too. He didn't want any special privileges or loosening of the rules.

But of course thinking about that now only made his headache worse. He had better things to do, like make his apartment more like home. So he began sifting through the box of goodies his mother had left. It was full of knickknacks, dish towels, cleanser, toilet paper, toothpaste, shampoo, napkins, wooden spoons and other household and kitchen items. As for his own junk, he decided it was time to lighten his load. It would be advantageous if he were going to leave. So he tossed out his plastic airplane and car models and all his high school memorabilia which amounted to a few programs of concerts he had played in with the junior high band and a couple of yearbooks.

Later on, though, he had second thoughts and found himself staring down at the trash pail, debating the merits of sentimentality. Eventually he pulled everything out. The models had been slightly damaged, but they never were that good. He'd always rushed them so that globs and strings of glue showed and his paint jobs were sloppy. So he threw those back in. Then the other stuff proved even more difficult. He had enjoyed playing in the band, especially the marching band when they had traveled around the state. But several months after the motorcycle party he had cut his music career short and stopped buying yearbooks at about the same time. Finally he tossed everything and, just to be sure, carried the pail outside to the garbage cans and, when he dumped it, took a two-by-four and smashed the models. Then he poured food slop over everything and for a clincher added a little used motor oil.

Back at the attic his chest still felt tight and it hurt between his breasts as if he had strained a muscle. He was surprised it had lasted so long, but he knew from experience it would pass. It had passed after the motorcycle party. It had passed after discontinuing his music lessons. It had passed when he had stopped socializing with his friends. Every new beginning had its difficulties.

He looked down at the baseball bat, glove and ball. He had quit baseball too, but that was one area of his life where someone outside his family and friends had complimented him on his ability. Not a lot to be proud of, but it was comforting to know that he was capable of at least one thing.

"You're still here," his mother said, happily surprised.

"Yeah, I got a lot more stuff than I figured."

"Wait a minute," his father said as he went down to the cellar.

"So do you have everything you need?"

"I hope so. I could use a stereo though," he joked. "For Christmas."

"Couldn't we all," his mother laughed.

"Here," his father said coming up the stairs. He had a four foot long picture of a tiger painted in Day-Glo colors. Green velvet provided the background. "How about this for your apartment?"

"No thanks," he snickered, eyeballing it widely.

His mother let out a tremendous guffaw.

"The hell with you two," his father said. "I'll hang it in my shed."

# CHAPTER
# SIX

It was Friday, his sixth Friday of work, his fourth week of working double shifts on Wednesday, Thursday and Friday. He was always exhausted on the weekends. But he was filthy rich, so rich he could afford to sleep all day on Saturday and Sunday.

"So tell me, O Great Mirror," he asked the shop rest room mirror. "What do you see?"

I see the stalls behind you. I see the toilet paper on the floor. I see one toilet paper dispenser empty. I see one seat up. I see the trash can overflowing. I see smudges on my glass. I see you and no one else.

"You don't see me. I'm not here. I'm in college basking in the sun. Remember?"

Little good it did talking to a mirror. Someone would come in and see him and then they'd send him to the loony bin without pay. And wouldn't everybody love that? The whiz kid finally blew his top. The kid who could do everything. The kid who had done everything. Worked in every department, every shit hole, doing every job in the fucking place. People didn't know him by name. They didn't know him by face. They knew him by his filthy maroon shirt, the one that was rotting off his back thread by thread. The women were waiting for his pants to fall off. That was funny, so was he.

"Yeah, right," he sneered.

He let his head drop, then leaned farther over the sink until his forehead met the mirror. First he remained still, thinking but not thinking. Then he began rolling his forehead back and forth, grinding his hair into the glass. When he was tired of that he raised up and touched the tip of his nose to the new smudge on the mirror.

The next logical step seemed to be kissing the damn thing. So for the hell of it he puckered his lips and kissed the glass.

"Ick!" It tasted like ammonia.

He reared up and spit at the mirror. "Take that, you son of a bitch." The gob hit his reflection at the tip of his left collar. "Well, fuck you too."

In any case, he'd better hurry up. Stanley was waiting out in the parking lot—their daily meeting spot where they drank beer and smoked dope, and where all the world's problems were solved. It had become quite the tradition in just a few weeks.

Hey, asshole! Wipe the damn mirror off.

Yeah, he should. The janitor had enough shit to deal with without having his. But did he really care? He was no shining example of cleanliness. His filthy face reminded him of some small kid eating dirt. But the real story lay in his eyes. They were bloodshot and the purple bags under them looked like they had met up with too many doors. In fact maybe he had. He couldn't remember. He couldn't remember a thing. That was why he had to park his car in the same place every day. So he wouldn't forget where it was.

Did that make sense?

He stuck his tongue out at the mirror and left.

"Beer?" Stanley asked.

"Dope?" he offered in return, reaching across between the two cars to make the exchange.

"Thank you."

"Thank *you*," he heartily replied.

"So?"

"So...?"

"Here we are," Stanley said lightheartedly.

"Again!" he cheered.

"And richer for it."

"And dumber too," he added.

"In a good mood tonight, huh?"

"Just like every night. I'm so happy I could die."

"You know when I was waiting for you the guard came over and asked me what I was doing." Stanley took a drag off his dube.

"Really?" he asked. "I didn't know they could walk that far."

"He wanted me to give him a ride back."

"Shit! You're kidding!" He almost choked on that one.

"Don't die now. The guard would have to walk all the way back here again."

"Well," he gasped, catching his breath, "it'll be good for him." He held up his joint and nodded. "This is some good shit, huh?"

"A little harsh, but effective."

He took a swig of his beer.

"I hear they're thinking of working people three shifts now," Stanley said.

"Bullshit," he said. He wouldn't believe that one.

Stanley rested his head back on his seat and blew out a plume of smoke and frosted breath that blurred the view between the cars.

"You working in the foundry on Monday then?" he asked when the air cleared.

"Yeah. Are you?"

"I guess so. I'm a utility man, aren't I?"

"That you are. Need another beer?"

"Sure." He reached out for it, but Stanley held it out just a little from his window.

"Hey," he said to Stanley. "You could reach out a little yourself."

"I am," Stanley teased, pulling it back from him.

"You asshole."

"Ah, what's the matter? Not getting enough pussy?"

"Not getting any pussy."

Stanley handed him the beer. "Yeah, I hear you, man."

Please, don't get into philosophizing tonight. He was tired. He wanted to go home, get some sleep.

"You know," Stanley said. "We should do this between shifts too."

"Yeah, right. I can hardly make it through without doing it. I'd die if I did."

"You'd be surprised what the old body can do when it gets charged up like this."

"My body ain't being charged, brother," he said.

Stanley turned up his radio so the soul music blared out into the dark, virtually empty parking lot.

"It's getting cold out," he said louder than usual.

"It's *been* cold out," Stanley said. "Where've you been?"

In Florida attending college. God, why did that come up again? It had been weeks since he'd thought about that. Just goes to show how working sixteen hours a day can keep your troubles at bay. But he had to be careful not to say anything about school. He didn't want Stanley to know he was a college boy. That would be fatal.

Stanley exhaled another cloud of smoke and breath. It was times like these he feared he might spill his guts. Almost as if Stanley had set him up.

"So did that guard really come over here?" he asked.

Stanley gave him a mean-eyed look. "Yeah, he did. He wanted to know why we parked our cars in opposite directions, and so close."

He took a gulp of beer to avoid Stanley's stare. "What'd you tell him?" he asked.

"We're queer."

He shook his head and paused before taking another sip, still keeping his eyes gazing out the windshield. "I don't doubt it."

"That we're queer?"

"No," he frowned, finally looking at Stanley. "That you told him that."

"He was queer too."

He had to get out of here. This was too much, too crazy, too something.

"Time to head home, huh?" Stanley asked.

"Yeah," he yawned, though it was more fake than real. "I got to do something productive this weekend. I can't keep getting drunk and playing pool all the time."

"Did you hear from the draft board yet?"

"No," he snapped. It disturbed him that he had answered so sharply. It seemed to surprise Stanley too, though in his mind Stanley deserved it.

"Well," Stanley groaned, "I guess it's a good idea to get some sleep for a change. If anything comes up give me a call."

"Sure thing," he said. Unlikely though.

Stanley gunned his car and burned rubber as he did a one-eighty to head out towards the gate. He let Stanley get a car-length ahead and then followed behind, somewhat less dramatically. His car didn't have the guts Stanley's had. But that was okay because Stanley took all the chances while he was just the caboose at the end of the parade. He did do well, though, when they wove their way out through the parked cars. It was his favorite thing to do, swerving back and forth as if in a high speed chase on the freeway. It would be super fun when it snowed.

As usual Stanley fishtailed by the guardhouse, screeching the tires once again. No knowing what the guards thought about their antics but it didn't matter. They were having fun.

Stanley flipped the bird over the roof of his car and went left onto the main drag. He turned right and, as tradition dictated, yelled back at the factory.

"Fuck you double!"

It was great to get off from work.

# CHAPTER
# SEVEN

Saturday, five-thirty in the evening: Let it be known he had finally risen from bed, and let it be known he went directly to the kitchen (after a quick stop in the bathroom) and ate four doughnuts and drank a glass of milk. Then he went to the couch and smoked a joint. Let it be known he hasn't moved since (other than to smoke another joint), and he has done nothing but stare out the window at the somber day with its persistent rain. Greta and he have been married twice, have lived together two different times, have had career jobs, been doctors, lawyers and adventurers, saved the world three times, and managed to survive a natural disaster and an auto wreck. Not to mention, of course, how they've fucked a hundred times in every imaginable position and place.

However, by eight in the evening he was bored. His doughnut dinner was fading in nutritional value. In other words, he was starving. So he decided to call his parents and if he dropped the right hints maybe they would invite him over to see the Saturday Night Movie. Then he could chow down on some leftovers and treats. Of course, that meant walking several blocks to the public phone. But the exercise would do him good. It would wear off his being stoned and he sure didn't want his parents to know he smoked dope.

"Your father's making popcorn for the movie."
Yeah! He could smell it over the phone. "What's the movie?"
*"Rio Conchos."*
Shit. He had already seen it, and not too long ago.
"So where've you been?"
"Working."

"You never come home anymore."

"I'm busy, Mom. They got me working double shifts and everything."

"You sound ill."

"Just tired. Been working too much."

"That flu's been going around."

"Yeah, I know. I'm lucky I haven't gotten it yet."

"You should come over and watch the movie."

"I'd like to but I'm too tired. I think I'll call it an early night and go to bed."

"Your father says there's plenty of popcorn."

"Yeah, I bet."

"Ice cream too, he says."

"I'd love to, but I'm tired. Maybe I'll come over tomorrow."

His mother covered the phone and said something to his father. He could hear the popcorn popper being shaken on the gas burner. He should go over. He hadn't seen them in weeks and he knew he was avoiding them. Maybe because his mind was made up. Stanley was right. He was leaving. He didn't know how or when, but he knew he couldn't last much longer in the factory. He also knew he couldn't go back to school. He wasn't ready yet, but he had to find something somewhere else.

"Your father says he can't guarantee any popcorn being left over."

"That's okay. I'll make my own."

She spoke to his father again, telling him that he would just as soon make his own.

"Your father says phooey on you then."

That was not the way he had meant his father to take it, but it was too late now. "Okay, then. I'll see you soon. I got to go. Someone else is waiting to use the phone."

"We love you."

"I know. Take care."

"Bye."

"Bye."

"Oh!" his mother screamed just before he hung up.

"Yeah?"

"You're coming over for Thanksgiving, right?"

"Yeah."

"I just wanted to make sure. Your father has to order the turkey soon."

"Yeah, I'll be there."

"Well, we're going to get a twenty pounder this year."

"Sounds good to me."

"Well, your Grandmother and Grandfather may be coming over so we thought we should get a big one."

They always had bought a big one. "Well, I got to go. This guy is getting anxious."

"Okay. We'll see you soon."

"Yeah."

Amazingly, for a Saturday night, he was the only one in the store. The cashier was reading the paper. It would be a good time to rip something off, but with his luck he'd probably get caught. A year in jail was all he needed to make his life complete.

He went over to the beer cooler, chose a six pack, then wandered over to the bakery section and picked up the last box of sugar doughnuts.

"Good evening," the cashier said. The guy had a runny nose.

"Good evening."

"How's things?"

"Fine," he replied.

The guy gave him his change then went back to reading the paper. That was okay with him. But as he left, the cashier flipped over the paper. Though it was upside down the photo of the helicopter landing in the tall grass didn't need any caption.

It struck him on the way home he ought to go down to the bar to keep occupied instead of worrying about current world affairs. But Stanley would be there, and lately Stanley had been a pain in the ass, if only because he was on this roll of work, work, work until your butt falls off, then smoke, drink, smoke, drink, smoke, drink until you're blind, then work, work, work until you drop dead. As it was right now they could barely hold a decipherable conversation. Though on the other hand, that eliminated the possibility of an argument.

Ten o'clock: He remembered how he used to climb to the top of the weeping willow tree near his house, sit in one of the crotches and daydream all afternoon. In the distance he could hear the children playing in the streets and the dogs barking. From the nearby airport the planes would soar into the sky and the helicopters from the army base roared and rumbled all around. He would always look down and picture himself falling through the small branches until he careened off the lower larger ones. The last one would flip him over and send him flying like a soaring eagle, wings spread wide open. On the ground he would lie in a pool of blood, his head split open, until he died. But he wouldn't die instantly. First a few dogs would come by and sniff around, but they would be too scared to go near him. If he had a choice he would have this happen during winter, so the blood would stand out on the snow and his last sensation would be of his clothes becoming wet. His final thought would be of his mother yelling for him to come in before he caught his death of cold.

Yeah, right. Fake your suicide once again. When are you going to learn it's a no-win situation? Isn't it better to admit your limitations and failures, then get on with your life?

He rose from the couch and went to the kitchen. He retrieved a beer from the refrigerator and popped it open over the sink. Next to the sink was his carving knife. He picked it up with his free right hand and held it in front of him as if to stab himself.

Yes, sulking was not the answer. He didn't need to hit rock bottom to discover that bit of wisdom.

He poked the knife through his sweatshirt just enough to feel its tip touch his skin. It would be a cold day in hell before he would ever kill himself. He wasn't dumb. He was just a plodder: it took him more time to get where he was heading, but he would get there.

Sure, sure.

# CHAPTER
# EIGHT

It's simple. First you set the box in the jig holder. Then you push the button. The holder clamps down on the box. Oil spurts out on the rotating tappers as they move in from the sides to thread two of the outlets. The box tenses some and squeals like a pig as the threaders enter the holes. When the tappers fully penetrate they retreat, leaving the box full of oil and metal slivers. The box relaxes. The oil stops. The tappers stop and the jig opens up. You turn the box ninety degrees.

Repeat.

Now with your left hand (if you are right-handed) take the completed box and toss it into the finished dolly. Simultaneously grab an unthreaded box from the other dolly with your free right hand and place it in the jig. Then push the button with your right hand. If you are left-handed reverse the procedure.

Rule: never place the box in the jig with one hand and then push the button with the other.

Now that you have the system down you must acquire speed. It's piece work by the hour and that requires and demands speed. Speed is money. Rate is everything.

Rule: never let one hand do all the work. It's too slow.

What you want to do:

Place the box in straight each and every time.

What you don't want to do:

You don't want to strip or break the tappers.

What could happen:

The box could jump out, crack or be cross-threaded.

The box could fly out and hit you.

If you push the button too soon and your fingers are
still in the holder, sorry, no more picking your nose
or jacking off.

Don't worry if you screw up in the first fifteen minutes or so.
You're trying to find that sweet rhythm which will make you a
millionaire. Or as they say in the shop, that split second timing
between having all the money you need and having your fingers.

Don't worry about getting filthy. It will only slow you down.
You can take a shower when you get home. You can buy new clothes
with all the money you make.

It is said that filthiness increases one's speed and efficiency.
Believe it.

If the tappers break or the machine smokes or a box jams or
you just miss your finger, don't stop, don't get mad. On the other
hand, if you get into a groove don't get cocky. If you cut your hand
don't be afraid to suck the blood. A little oil won't kill you
immediately. If you daydream try to keep it in short segments.

Finally, cheat as much as possible. Punch the time clock after
you start and before you finish. Don't worry, everyone does it now
and then.

Absolute rule: never, never, never push the button with your
knee. Your knee is too far away from your head that's somewhere in
the South Pacific spending all your money.

Once again Stanley had managed to punch out before him and
was out waiting in the parking lot. Tonight Stanley's car exhaust was
lingering low to the ground like a snake slithering through the grass.
As he got closer he could see the greenish light from Stanley's radio
through the frosted rear window. Stanley's dark silhouette also
became visible. It looked like he was guzzling some beer and in the
other hand held a burning joint.

He pounded on the trunk as he went by. Stanley rolled down
his window, blowing out a plume of smoke. The music blared like a
full-fledged stereo in someone's home.

"What's happening, man?" Stanley said.

"What ain't happening, man," he grumbled.

"Lighten up, will you, man? When are you going to learn?"

As usual Stanley had parked so close to his car he had to enter from the passenger side. Not that it was a big hassle. It happened every night. But this night, though he had to admit he could lighten up a little, he wasn't in the mood.

He slid across the ice cold front seat and positioned himself behind the steering wheel. He inserted the keys in the ignition and brought his hands together, rubbing them and blowing some warm air between them.

"Come on, Old Betsy," he said pumping the gas pedal. "Don't fail me now. I been working all day to take care of you."

The engine turned over but whined and whined and whined until he put the pedal to the floor. Then it fired up.

"That's a baby."

Stanley knocked on his window and held out a beer.

"Pretty cold out here," Stanley said, shivering.

He rolled his window down halfway. "Yeah, sure is." He grabbed the beer, put it between his legs, and went back to rubbing and blowing on his hands.

"I got a dube for you too. I took the liberty of raiding your stash while I was waiting for you."

"No problem. Long as I get some."

"Turn your radio on twelve-forty so we can have stereo soul."

"Sure." After tuning it in he shoved his hand under the dash to check the progress of the heater. It was warm but not hot. He decided to wait on the beer, though it was freezing his balls off.

"So what the hell you've been working on?" he asked Stanley as he lit his joint.

"Grinding and grinding and grinding. Do I have any teeth left?" Stanley opened his mouth wide, exposing his pearly whites and a good portion of his gums.

"They're all there from what I can see."

"City water."

"Yeah, right."

The conversation seemed to be at a natural lull. Or at least they were both staring out their windshield, music in the background. Stanley tipped his head back, finishing his beer. It was time to catch up, so he took a long guzzle too. There ought to be a law against working sixteen hours a day, but that made him think of the army.

"So what are you grinding?" he asked Stanley when he finished his beer.

"Boxes."

"The four-legged type?" he said. "Same type I been threading all day."

"Yep. You grind those before?"

"No, but I got a feeling I will."

"They're not really that bad."

"Is that so?" he said.

"Well, you sort of lose count, you know. You do three corners and think you're done. But no, there's still one more fucker to go. It seems like it takes forever to get one done. Sometimes you can't even tell where you started."

"Sounds lovely," he sighed. "I can't wait."

"I heard they were making more in the foundry the other night."

"Now who would do that I wonder?" Knowing full well it'd been him.

"I don't know," Stanley said. "But if I find him I'll kill him."

They both laughed and didn't stop laughing until they sounded a little maniacal. Suddenly it wasn't all that funny, especially when he pictured himself being tied to the tapper, surrounded by four-legged boxes, and they were bringing him more, the ones he had forged the night before.

"Fuck me," he moaned as he took another drink.

When he looked over at Stanley he found him falling asleep, head resting against the window frame.

"Well?" he asked.

Stanley's eyes shot open. "Well what?"

"Well, what do you know?"

"What do you want to know?"

"I don't know," he shrugged.

"I'll tell you something. All this shit we're doing?"

"Yeah?"

"It's some big overseas contract deal."

"Impressive," he remarked.

"Military probably."

"All right," he cheered.

Stanley finished his beer then tossed it at him, hitting him on the side of the forehead. The can somersaulted down his shoulder and arm, then bounced off the door onto his lap.

"Thank you," he said.

"You're welcome."

"How come you got cans tonight? I thought you didn't like them."

"They were on sale. Ninety-nine cents a six pack."

"Sounds like my kind of beer."

As he began to guzzle some beer Stanley revved up his engine. That meant going-home time was here. That surprised him. During the good old days Stanley was always the one who wanted to stay until they finished the beer, whether they were talking or not.

"Well, I'm going home," Stanley said. "Where you going to be tomorrow?"

"I think I'll be screwing four-legged things. Or they'll be screwing me."

"I hear you, brother."

"Yeah," he sighed.

"Heard from the draft board yet?" Stanley asked.

"Nope." It figured. Now that they were talking again, the old 'When are you going to leave?' had to come up.

"Knowing the draft board, they'll probably get you right after Thanksgiving or just before Christmas."

"Yeah," he mumbled.

"Still haven't heard anything, huh?"

"Nope." He might just as soon gun his car and get out of here.

"The war isn't exactly ending, you know," Stanley said.

"Hey listen," he barked. "I dropped out of fucking college. Is that all right with you? Does it meet your requirement that I'm not a college boy? If it doesn't, it doesn't matter. I'm leaving in any case, college boy or not."

Stanley took another swig from his beer, but it was empty. So he chucked it to the floor of his car. He had one hell of a blank expression on his face, like a man who had been grinding too long, who needed a beer, some dope, a woman, a shower, a massage and some fresh blood.

"Well, I'm going home," Stanley said.

"You're not mad at me, are you?" he asked Stanley. "I'm sorry I blew up."

"No, I'm not mad, man. Just tired. Might be coming down with a cold or something."

His own legs were twitching, like he was nervous. Like he had to confess something that had been bothering him for years. But his mind just couldn't grasp any specific thought or feeling. It didn't matter either, since Stanley was staring off into space, stoned to the bone or maybe worse.

"You want another joint?" he asked.

Stanley didn't flinch. He didn't know what to do. Go home? Shake Stanley? Leave him alone?

"Yeah, why not?" Stanley finally blurted.

"You sure?" he asked, feeling stupid for asking in the first place. Stanley certainly didn't need any dope right now. He needed rest, some good food and plenty of liquids.

"Why the hell not? I can smoke before I go to bed to put me to sleep."

"Okay." He handed it over to him.

"You only got one life to give to your country, right?"

"Right," he said staring into Stanley's bloodshot eyes.

Just one.

As tradition dictated, he let Stanley go first. But this time Stanley drove slow and straight down the lane without weaving through the parked cars. It must be one of those temporary low periods everyone went through. Besides, the upcoming holiday season was well known for bringing on the blues.

# CHAPTER NINE

He guessed it was an honor to serve one's country, especially for the cause of freedom. On the other hand, didn't the country also need four-outlet conduit boxes? The ones he was expert at forging, grinding and threading?

He set the mailgram down on the coffee table, then leaned back in the chair. He knew at any moment he would start feeling sorry for himself. And if the tightness and wringing sensation in his chest was any indication, he was already in pain. But he didn't want to feel sorry for himself. He didn't want to start making excuses or question why he'd let this happen. He wasn't sure he even knew.

In any event, he had to get out of his work clothes, take a shower and go to bed. It was late and another double shift was less than eight hours away. He knew the key to all of this was to keep busy, not to think of the future, just take one step at a time.

So he got up and did just that. But after taking a shower he put on his sweats and sneaks and walked out to the trash bins alongside the building. Inside the one with a dozen or so broken and oozing containers of caulking he shoved his draft notice in the midst of the gobs of white gel and so far down it would be irretrievable. He didn't think he could sleep with that thing in the same room.

# CHAPTER
# TEN

"Can you believe this snow?" his father said.

"It's pretty weird, that's for sure."

"I hate it," his mother said.

"She hates it," his father said. "She doesn't have to shovel the driveway."

"You don't either. You have that new snow blower of yours. If he can get it started," she added, laughing a bit.

His father shook his head. "Hmmf."

"What I want to know," he said, "is why we didn't have one when I lived here."

His mother chuckled, looking at his father as if saying, "I told you he'd ask."

"Your mother wouldn't let me."

"That's not true. Your father had you, that's why."

"Child slave labor, huh?" he said. "I can't wait until I become a parent."

It was funny how at the same time it was easy and hard to keep the subject from changing back to being drafted. But this Thanksgiving was no different from other times in his family's history when hard stuff came up. He wondered how much would truly change if they did talk about their problems. Certainly his draft status would remain the same, so why bother? But he could tell this line of reasoning was leading to another tale of woe. So he made an oath to himself to quit smoking pot as of now. He would go home later and flush it all down the toilet. He'd even pop all the bottles of beer and dump them down the sink.

He chuckled to himself and a cautious grin stretched across his face. He felt free. He was beginning to respect himself again. He knew now he would make it in any endeavor he pursued. He just needed to take one step at a time. When he got back from the war he would really be ready to attend college. The only mistake he'd made before was timing. He wasn't stupid. He'd just needed more time.

"We're glad you could be here," his mother said as they all sat down at the table.

"Yeah, it looks great."

"Say grace, Father," his mother said.

"You say it," his father said to him.

"Not me," he said. "I just shovel the driveway."

"You say it, Father. It's your responsibility."

"All right."

His father folded his hands and closed his eyes. His mother followed suit. He tilted his head down slightly.

"Thank you Lord for the food before us. Amen."

For a moment there was silence while his mother and father remained with their heads bowed. They weren't very religious people, especially his father, but he could tell they were praying and probably for him. Tears came to his eyes, so he lowered his head back down. He loved his parents and though he knew he truly hadn't disappointed them, he wished it hadn't come to this, for his and their sake.

"May God be with you," his mother whispered.

After dinner he helped clean up. He did the dishes. He watched some football. He helped his father start the snow blower. Later his sister came over after visiting her in-laws. Then they ate the lemon meringue and pumpkin pies with plenty of whipped cream. Again, no one mentioned his leaving, though his sister cried when she had to go.

"I got to go," he said. It was about ten in the evening. "I got to work tomorrow."

"Come back for leftovers," his mother said.

"What?" his father said. "You didn't give him any to take with him?"

"Yes, I did. It's out on the counter. I was just inviting him back."

"Yeah. Maybe I'll be back on Sunday."

"Give us a call."

"I will," he said.

"Happy Thanksgiving," he said again while waiting for his car to warm up. But no one was on the porch waving goodbye. They had gone in. It was too damn cold to stay out there.

# CHAPTER
# ELEVEN

He had an easy job for the rest of his last week. He had to screw two little screws into the cover plate holes of outdoor conduit boxes. Then, after they were painted, he had to remove them. So first in, then out, in, then out, all day long. Plus he had to stand while he did it. That wasn't too different, but the strong lacquer smell was. It gave him a headache and made him feel woozy. But the painters, decked out in their white coveralls with red and green Christmas trim, didn't want to open the windows. They said it would create an overload for the ventilation system. At least that was what he thought they'd said behind their respirators. Which of course, the supply office was fresh out of just now.

"Don't save the screws," the foreman said as he came by. "We have plenty of them."

"That's no problem."

"The paint builds up in the slots. It's harder to get them out."

It wasn't that hard. At least they could be run through a couple of times before they became clogged.

"It's faster using new ones." The foreman was adamant about that.

"Whatever."

Just the same he'd save them to take home to his father.

For lunch Stanley and he went to the cafeteria. It had been weeks since they had done so, thanks to working so many shifts.

Nonetheless he still remembered not to touch the soup or the egg salad.

"So what did Harrison say?" Stanley asked.

"Not much," he said, swallowing his spoonful of macaroni salad. "He told me I wouldn't be working overtime this week. That's all."

"Yeah, he told me they would have a new guy by the end of the week. I'm supposed to break him in."

"Be a little more sensitive this time, will ya?"

Stanley didn't laugh as he thought he would, though it all made sense when for the rest of the meal they didn't utter a word. He was leaving, after all. So he spent his meal turning around to look at the clock each and every time Stanley did the same. It seemed a shame their friendship had deteriorated so far, but he had no idea how to salvage it.

"It's time to go," Stanley said, though they easily had nine more minutes.

He shoved the rest of his salad into his mouth, thinking all the time he could stay and finish it alone. But he guessed he still felt he had to leap when Stanley said frog.

When he returned to the paint shop he found the paper cup of screws he had saved for his father in the waste bucket next to the table. On top of it someone had poured some gooey crap.

The last day of work didn't seem different from any other Friday, except he wouldn't be working a double shift. Otherwise he was still screwing screws, in and out, saving none.

There was one difference though. Stanley was nowhere around. Stanley was off sick for the first time since he had known him. He wondered if it could be intentional, to avoid saying goodbye. Whatever it was he felt funny, not just because he might not see Stanley again, but also because now there was absolutely no one he could talk to. For all he knew, for all he did, it might as well have been his very first day.

"So long," he said to the company sign as he got into his car.

Tears came to his eyes, but he held them in check. Stanley had been right. No one was about to pat him on the shoulder. Still, he would miss this Goddamn parking lot.

He waited until everyone from the day shift left and then carefully wove his way through the remaining cars of the swing shift crew.

Then he went left onto the main drag just for the hell of it. He even flipped the bird over the roof of his car.

# CHAPTER
# TWELVE

It took less time than he had planned to store his things in his parents' attic. Most were his mother's: all the knickknacks, towels, sheets and blankets, pots and pans. So there wasn't much to do but sit at home and watch television and listen to his parents argue about who would drive his old car. But after a while his father fell asleep in his recliner and his mother stayed out in the kitchen making dinner. The only noise came from the TV and the neighborhood kids having snowball fights outside. Needless to say, he was bored, so he went into the kitchen and got his coat.

"I'll be back."

"Don't go far. We're going to eat soon," his mother said.

"How long?"

"About an hour."

"Okay," he sighed.

"David," his mother said. "You know your father and I never wanted you to go, don't you?"

"Yeah, I know."

He left without hugging his mother, though he felt it was what she had wanted. He guessed he didn't want the feeling that it would be his last hug, whatever sense that made.

What made even less sense was that when he got to his favorite tree he felt less like climbing it than he'd thought. Maybe he knew from other times that he would just sit atop it dreaming about his death by suicide, falling through the branches until he hit the ground. And that didn't seem appropriate now. Now he had a much firmer grasp of reality. That was one of the fringe benefits of working double shifts.

# PART II

# CHAPTER THIRTEEN

He's sweating. His shirt is soaked. His pants are as damp as if he'd wet them. For Godsake, where's the oven temperature control? The air feels like boiling water with all the water boiled out of it. Does that make sense? If not, just ask these guys. There's about a dozen to choose from, all wetting their pants too. Not one shirt in this flying sardine can is dry. Not one forehead. Not one pair of socks. Not one of anything. And they call this a helicopter? Helicopters are supposed to be fun, especially with the doors wide open. You know, fresh air you can breathe without water drops forming on your nose hairs. The problem is there ain't no fresh air. Ventilation is a myth. So much for choosing a door seat. By the way, how many guys does it take to fill a helicopter, and how many of them are black?

He's tired. He's fucking exhausted and all he's done is move from the holding area in Saigon to this chopper, this bumpy ride to his future destination. Nothing like embedding rivets in one's ass, or holding onto a tiedown with your index finger to keep from falling out of this can of worms. Now he knows why nobody wanted to sit by the door. Better to be packed like tuna and sweat off a few pounds. Besides, what's a few elbows in your face? And as for everybody's body odor, he can smell it anyway. Or is that just a dead, maggot-ridden cat?

What'd they say back in Saigon? Vietnam is a nice place to visit, but I wouldn't want to live here. Can anyone sleep in this shit? Maybe he was going to have to grow gills.

When he looked back out the open chopper door all he saw below was the same muddy, twisty Mekong River winding through the same flat expanse of tall grass and brush. Plus field after field of flooded rice paddies and trees with umbrella-like canopies along the waterways, like the great elms shading the sidewalks back home. But all of it here had the same stagnant, stinky, smell, like a dump on a hot summer's day. In other words, as far west as Cambodia, the entire area was one big swamp.

Now, though, one big difference from earlier was that the villages were fewer and smaller along the way. It still amazed him people lived in grass huts, like the ones in a *National Geographic* magazine. He'd always thought grass huts were only in Africa. Besides, how in the hell did the thatch keep the rain out? He guessed the sudden sparseness of the population was because nobody in their right mind wanted to live in a swamp. Unless, like him, you didn't have a choice.

He wiped his forehead, squeezing out the sweat-beads clinging to his eye brows. That shit tickled like bugs crawling through his hair. It could drive a guy crazy if he thought about it too much. And there wasn't much to think about except how scorching hot it was and how parched his throat felt. Unfortunately his canteen felt like a basket of freshly baked buns. No way was he going to drink that.

Jesus, he couldn't function in this crap. He was a northern boy, not some crawly thing slithering along the ground. Christ, even his sweat smelled like week-old moldy socks.

But behold! Home Sweet Home!

As the chopper banked to make its approach, they all looked down at the base, built in the middle of nowhere, bull's-eye in an expanse of muck, water and tall grass, with an atmosphere hovering over it like lingering smoke from a small forest fire.

The base was nothing more than a fenced-in boy scout camp, not much larger than two thirds of a football field. At one end of the compound a chopper pad lay complete with metal grating, probably where they would be landing. Scattered elsewhere throughout the camp were various tents and shelters, numerous machine gun and mortar emplacements, and defense bunkers positioned along the perimeter. In the center of the compound, commanding a view of the area, stood a ten-foot tower complete with a wall of sandbags fortifying it, like a turret on a frontier fort. And that was it, except for the mound the base was built on, several feet above the area's natural lie. The vegetation was plowed back a hundred feet or so from the three rings of concertina wire surrounding the base. For extra measure a tall wire fence was inside the barbed wire. It was like the corporal back in Saigon said it would be, the one who'd called it the "Armpit of the Mekong". Still, it made him feel somewhat excited. It was his new home and it was unique. It was where nothing had existed before, where nothing could exist, yet here it was.

"That's it, huh?" the black guy squeezed next to him asked.

"That's it," he nodded.

"Don't look good," the black guy said, shaking his head.

No, on second thought, it didn't. On second thought it looked just as cramped as the chopper, only more like a stockade. In fact, he might just learn to hate the place.

He figured he'd better start taking note of what the hell he was doing if he expected to get out of here alive. This was nothing like boot camp. Someone could be out there. It was dark enough there could be a lot of somebodies out there. And he was all alone. It was like shutting himself inside a closet, and darker yet beyond the fence. Even when he strained his eyes he couldn't tell if what he saw was real or not. It all looked like a brick wall, with another wall farther back and above that. And this was a clear night! Though with no moon, unfortunately. A great night for his first watch in Nam.

But there were a million stars. Somehow that seemed strange, too. What were they doing here? Even the Big Dipper was there, just above the northern horizon. Here he was so far from home, and there were still stars.

Then there were all the chirps and songs of the little bugs and reptiles, and all the not-so-little bugs and reptiles. Like what he could have heard in his own back yard, but ten decibels higher and a whole lot spookier.

And all of this went on and on and on, back and forth along the fence, down the path, looking out into the dark, hoping he hadn't peed his pants, hoping he wouldn't fall flat on his face as he peered out towards the marshlands in search of the enemy. Not to mention his feeling all alone, like there was absolutely nobody on the base except him, which could easily be, since he hadn't seen anything resembling life for a long time.

> Here I walk, rifle in hand
> > Trying to stay awake the best I can.
> > But before the dawn can come
> We must sweat some, and isn't this dumb
> > That my back hurts some, my legs too,
> And so does my thumb on the trigger of my gun.

Gee, he was becoming a poet, wouldn't you know it; he hoped he didn't blow it. And wouldn't it be nice if a VC sneaked up and slit open his throat? That didn't rhyme as well.

He looked back out through the fence and over the rolls of concertina wire to the shadowy reeds where a rifle muzzle could stick out an inch or two and he would never see it. He wished he knew what in hell those dark things were. It looked like a whole squad of VC standing just out of range to test his nerve. If so, it was working very well.

He wiped the sweat off the back of his neck. Now his eyes felt gritty, too. And he had three more hours of the same.

He didn't like this place at all. Not to mention the army.

For the next two weeks it was hot, humid, predictable and routine. He slept at night except when he had a watch. A couple of times he had a late evening patrol down by the river, also known as the 'slapping bugs' watch. Of course, he never heard or saw anything, except rodents and floating branches. In fact he still hadn't seen hide nor hair of the enemy. Some war, huh? But he wasn't complaining. Rumor was saying the war had been transferred from the countryside to the cities. That was fine with him.

When they did patrol the area all they did was parade through the hamlets showing their muscle and firepower. But no one out there seemed very impressed. Most of the people were either very old or very young and were busy working out in the fields anyway. The villages were simple, just thatched huts and animals running around, though in some of the larger villages a few homes were made of cinder block with tin roofs. The people in these houses seemed healthier and better dressed, their kids wearing white shirts and black pants or long skirts like kids from Catholic school back home, and these people usually waved to them too. They were not like the others who never bothered to look for long before bending back down to the rice they were husking, the baskets they were making, the kids they were taking care of.

On the other side of the equation were the work details. It was either cleaning the fifty or sixty caliber machine guns, or, more likely since he was a new guy, digging holes, filling holes, carrying sandbags or burning shit in the half-barrels that pulled out from the latrines. The shit detail would wrench his gut into several granny knots, but so did sitting in the latrine. In any case, to make it burn he had to add diesel—three parts diesel to one part shit. More diesel if there was a lot of piss. But however much fuel he used the black sooty smoke followed him everywhere, and clung to his clothes so he smelled like engine exhaust for days. The same soot also mixed well with bug dope and sweat, so he was always ready to go Trick or Treating. Even the times he took the extra effort to wipe himself clean, next morning he found smudge marks all over his arms and face as if he had been blackened as he slept.

In other words, it was a lot like working double shifts back at the factory, except here he couldn't sit on a couch and stare out his apartment window after work, whatever good that had done. The fact was he was bored then and he was bored now. He guessed he didn't belong here any more than he had in college or the factory. But this time there was no use crying, since there was no way he could either drop out or leave.

# CHAPTER
# FOURTEEN

When he woke up he had no idea how long the mortars had been coming in, but the tent barracks was completely empty and the door was hanging by half a hinge. Helmets, boots, socks and clothes were scattered all over the floor and the debris falling on the canvas sounded like pouring rain. It made him think he didn't want to go out. Still, his best bet for survival was a bunker, no matter how far he had to run.

The whistles were getting louder and the explosions nearer and more frequent. The barracks was starting to feel like a coffin, especially with him all alone. His sweat glands were in full gear now, drenching his collar and sending streams like radiator leaks down his face. And with all that he had to take a dump.

He looked at the doorway at the far end of the barracks. Being able to hear the explosions but not see them made it harder to rise up from his squat and go. It was the idea of that one mortar waiting for him to step out where no mortar had landed before. Which of course, would be pretty ironic, right? But no more so then back on his second patrol when he'd been the point man leading the squad through heavy brush. Back then the idea was a personnel mine, how it could blow your legs off before you knew it. But he'd made it through that patrol and others so this shouldn't be any different. He just had to remember his promise to take only one step at a time.

A round exploded behind the barracks, tremoring it and splattering debris into the wall. He dropped flat to the floor, his face turned away. And nothing more happened, it was quiet for a second or two, before another whistle came zeroing in. The mortar landed outside the door, blasting dirt into the barracks like stokers shoveling coal into a furnace. He covered his head, then, when the blast was over, looked up at all the dirt on the floor, until a second later when he sprang to his feet and finally made it out the door.

"Thorne!" a sergeant was yelling outside. "Go man the sixty!"

The sergeant was pointing to the west perimeter. The whole base out here seemed engulfed in explosions, like some Fourth of July fireworks display. He ran as fast as he could, keeping his head down, feeling, with all the explosions on both sides of him, as if he were running down a glass corridor, one that let in only the smoky smell of the mortars and some of the finer dust. Yet he could feel the ground tremble underneath him, the sweat dripping like rain off his face. The bunker seemed farther than he'd thought, like it was pulling away. But nothing would stop him now.

He reached the bunker at the same time as three other guys. All of them sat down panting against the bunker walls. He was as short of breath as if he'd never exercised a day in his life.

"Go man the front bunker," the corporal ordered him.

He peeked over the sandbags. It was the northwest bunker, the first line of defense. One guy was already there, peeking over the top to see what was out in the swamp. But why him? Why not these other guys, for crying out loud?

"Take the ammo box with you."

He took a deep breath, grabbed one of the handles and started dragging it along. It was one heavy son of a bitch, but they might need every bullet, not to mention a lot of luck. But by the time he had traveled a third of the way there, he was pooped again. So he stopped, slung his rifle and picked the box up with both hands. A mortar came whistling in over his head and landed in front of the bunker he had just left. Instead of ducking or falling to the ground he turned away and made a dash for the other bunker, lunging forward within a step or two of it, letting the weight of the box pull him in. The ammo box dug into his chest like a shovel blade as he went down, but stopped him from burying his face in the dirt.

"Shit," he gasped as he landed on his knees.

The black guy turned around, not at all impressed with his circus-like entrance, and acknowledged his presence with a nod. He was a well-built guy but not big, maybe five ten and a hundred forty-five pounds with a prominent brow, high cheekbones and large eyes.

"Ammo," he said as if the black guy didn't know.

"Yeah," the guy responded as he turned and sat down himself. So he got a look at the guy's name tag. Long, it said, with an inked exclamation mark after it, and above it, also penned in, the name Stanley. Same as Stanley back at the factory. Would this Stanley ask him if he was drafted, too? In any case, he could see Stanley Long had a letter stuffed in his other breast pocket. Mail from home, he thought through the strange daze he was in. He himself had yet to get any mail from home.

"Guess we're the only ones," Long said.

"Yeah," he said. "I guess so."

Long's eyes were bloodshot like he was drunk or stoned. Or maybe he was a heavy sleeper like himself. But he didn't have time to worry about that. He went to the wall and peeked over. The mortars seemed to be diminishing, or at least landing farther back in the camp. Then suddenly one landed in front of the bunker. He ducked but not without first being pelted with dirt in the face and helmet.

"Phew," Long said. "That was close."

"Yeah." He wiped his face with his hand and cleaned out the inside corners of his eyes using his index finger. Then he began spreading two of the top sandbags apart. He used his rifle to make a deeper indentation between the two lower bags, finishing up his little defensive parapet.

"That's a good idea," Long said, and began to do the same.

"Yeah," he said. "No sense getting my head blown off."

Then another blast landed nearby, and the concussion knocked both of them off their feet. Dirt and dust blew through the seams between the bags, spraying them like a sandblaster. Then debris rained down like a load of rocks dumped from a truck.

"*Jesus!*" Long shouted.

He got up off his ass and secured himself against the bunker wall like someone trying to stay out of the wind. This, he thought, was a lot different from burning shit and picking up garbage or even going out on patrol. He was definitely not used to this crap.

He wiped the sweat off his brow again, and happened to look up towards the center of camp just as the mess tent was hit with a mortar. One side of it tumbled in while the other blew out in a whirlwind of lumber pieces and fabric scraps.

There went his cleaning job from yesterday.

"Hey!" Long yelled, dropping back down from peeking over the top. "Look."

He turned around and glimpsed them over his newly made rifle slot like fleas in a dog's hair, his first VC. He had waited a long time, nearly six weeks, for this. He had thought about it every night. He was going to die here. He knew that now. As sure as shit.

Suddenly the incoming stopped. It was quiet for a moment. His ears were ringing. Then he heard mortars being fired from the base bunkers. Then he heard another sound, one he wasn't familiar with. He turned around to look. Off in the distance he saw two growing specks with a long tail of black smoke trailing behind them.

"Jets," Long said.

That they were.

They roared over the base and fired their rockets and the marshlands turned into fire and smoke. The tall grass was being blown to smithereens. Mud was flying everywhere. At times through the smoke and debris he could see the VC running for their lives, bullying their way through the tall reeds as though escaping from a fire in the midst of a crowd. His heart began thumping against his chest. It sounded hollow, and then stopped as quickly as it started. He knew exactly how the VC were feeling. Scared like him.

He ducked back down and looked at Long. "My name's Thorne."

Long looked over at him. "Yeah, I know. The guy who likes to work alone all the time."

What? He didn't like working alone. Burning shit was the detail he was stuck with, like it or not.

"I'm Long." Long pointed to his name tag and then the exclamation point. "At least that's what the girls say."

"I bet," he chuckled.

"My friends call me Stanley." Stanley held out his hand.

He shook it. "Hello, Stanley."

"Hello, Thorne."

They went back to peek over the bunker at all the action, which looked like it was starting to wind down. The VC were out of sight now, and the base helicopters were coming back in. He hadn't even realized they'd escaped. He must have been still asleep. God, that was scary. He could get himself killed some day, blown up in his bunk. But it would be a good way to go if you were going. And he was going to go. He didn't know why, but he just felt it. But maybe he'd just inhaled too much diesel smoke.

"You two!" the sergeant yelled from the bunker behind them. "Keep your post and keep a look out!"

"Sure thing, Sarge!" he shouted back, and looked over at Stanley.

Stanley gave him the same look back. "I guess it's us."

He guessed it was.

A few moments later the shelling stopped. All that was left was the powdery smell of smoke and plenty of holes he'd probably be filling by day's end. Another job he did by himself. But he only worked so the time would go by faster.

"What do you see?" Stanley asked.

"My next project," he sighed. But working was better than what just took place. Look at what happened to the VC, having to run like scared rabbits through the grass, being chased by cold hard steel.

He checked over his rifle to make sure it was ready. Then at Stanley, peeking over the bunker himself, squinting as if trying to see between the blades of grass.

Should he be doing the same thing?

Again he thought of the VC. This time he visualized one taking a round in the back, sending him forward into a clump of reeds, blood running down his shirt. The next guy took advantage of the clearing, stepping on the dead guy and springing off him like a diving board. It made him think he definitely wouldn't complain about work details again.

Later the sergeant came by and explained the VC had been spotted crossing the river. So the plan was to take two platoons and chase them. But Stanley and he would stay here in a hold-the-fort mode on alert until the operation was completed. Which, of course, could take all day.

"I got all the time in the world," Stanley said.

"Me too."

"Well, don't fall asleep," the sergeant warned.

That was easier said than done. It was early in the morning, the sun was just over the horizon, and he was still tired from the day before. He could've effortlessly dozed off for the rest of the day.

He yawned. Stanley yawned. He wiped his eyes. Stanley wiped his eyes. They went back to staring out at the marsh.

"How come we ain't having fun, man?" Stanley asked.

"Well, we could be riding in a chopper chasing the VC. But then we'd be getting shot at too."

"That's a fact."

"Of course, if all this hadn't happened I'd be sleeping right now."

"Not me, man," Stanley said. "I was on watch when all this shit came down."

Only an hour had gone by when the sergeant came back around, though it seemed about four hours to him. Once again the sergeant warned them to stay awake, no nodding out whatsoever. They couldn't disagree, since both of them had watery bloodshot eyes, and since he yawned right in the sergeant's face.

"You oughta learn how to sleep," the sergeant said.

Yeah, he'd work on it. Soon as he was relieved.

Not too long after the sergeant left, he noticed something different about the reeds. Stanley saw it too, even though he was still wiping his eyes and squinting. Something different was happening out there, like they weren't alone anymore. Like someone across the room who you don't know is watching you. The reed-tops weren't moving. It was quiet as a church. But something was out there, all right. Stanley was pivoting on his toes like he was anxious to get the hell out of here, and he didn't feel all that comfortable either. He checked his rifle, and Stanley did the same. He made sure his slot fit so his head wouldn't stick out over the top of the bunker, and Stanley did the same. Then he looked out again, this time concentrating on one spot instead of scanning the area. He wiped his eyes, squeezing them towards the bridge of his nose. When he opened them again he noticed something: the VC dead were all gone. But had there ever been any out there to see? All he could remember was his own private vision of the lone VC getting it in the back.

Then he heard a whistling sound.

"Holy shit!" Stanley whispered. "There's a million of them."

A mortar exploded about fifty feet away, over by the southwest corner of the base. He watched the dirt and bits of grass settle, then looked back out at the reeds. They had transformed themselves into a picket fence of black-clad men sneaking along, humped over as they jogged from one reed clump to the next, slowly working their way toward the base.

He looked back towards the other bunker for the sergeant, but no one was there. But there were a couple of officers on the tower searching to the south and west. He waved at them and one finally spotted him. He pointed over his head to the swamp. The officers began scanning the area, and then one picked up the radio.

"They know what's going on, man?" Stanley asked.

"I sure hope so."

So he had been fooled. He had thought he wouldn't get a chance to fight today, that it was just going to be another mundane day being Mr. Janitor. But things were shifting fast now. There were quite a few of those mothers out there, with half the base out on a wild goose chase. There was only him, the custodian, and a bunch of sleepy-eyed mama's boys. But what was he talking about? He himself hadn't killed anyone yet.

"What we going to do, man?" Stanley asked.

He tried to think. "I don't know," he said. "I guess we're here."

From somewhere behind them the first mortars were being launched. As soon as they hit the marsh the VC countered with their own, concentrating their fire on the fence and concertina wire they were working their way to through the grass and muck. The coiled wire took the most beating. It was bouncing up and down as if receiving an enormous electrical shock. The wire fence wavered back and forth as if high winds were butting into it. But all of it was holding so far and the VC stayed holding back somewhere near the edge of the vegetation, well hidden again and waiting patiently.

"Should we fire into the grass, man?" Stanley said.

"No," he said. "Let's wait until they're out in the open."

"They'll be on top of us, man."

"That's okay," he said. "They still have to make it through the wire and fence."

As soon as he finished a fence post took a direct hit and exploded into hundreds of splinters as the fence quaked and radiated out in both directions from the center of the blast. Then another mortar sent the concertina wire into a frenzied fit. When most of the dust settled a small hole was visible in the fence. Then another mortar threw a large piece of post boomeranging up in the air, to land like a spear in front of the bunker, like a large punji stick pointed at them. Now a lane had been cut through the barbed wire along with a larger opening in the fence—one a person'd have to squat through, but passable just the same.

Now, too, the VC didn't wait for the dust to clear, but darted out of the grass at full speed. The shock of seeing their advance froze him, his hands started shaking and he felt chilled. This was it. He had to kill now. He had to aim and shoot. No one could or would get through that wire.

He aimed at the hole in the fence and flicked his safety off. His trigger finger felt wet against the cold metal. His eyes started to dry up, and another shiver shot down his spine.

Off to his left another mortar exploded. He ducked but as soon as the debris sailed over the bunker, jumped up and placed his rifle back in the slot. At the fence was a black-clad man bending the wire back. He aimed at the guy's chest and fired a spurt. The man fell back, leaning against what was left of the post until another man darted through the concertina wire and shoved the first man out of the way.

"*Shit!*"

He rose a bit and fired again, this time a little more. The rounds sprayed the ground before the second man then quickly ripped their way up his legs and chest. The second man partly stood up then fell forward on the first.

Another man came. He shot him.

Another man. He shot him.

And another one.

And another.

They were piled in front of the fence like sacks of flour.

"*Goddamn it!*"

He dropped down and switched clips. As he came back up a mortar hit in front of the bunker, sending a shovelful of dirt into his face. He caught some in his eyes and mouth, dropped back down and coughed and gagged, spitting out as much sand as he could. The particles under his lids scraped his eyeballs like sandpaper. But he didn't have time to mess around.

He went back up and fired blindly at first. As his eyes cleared, though, he saw the VC had piled the bodies to protect them as they crawled through the fence. There were four all together, and one was already inside the post getting back up on his feet. At first he didn't know which one to shoot, but then he chose the man on this side of the fence. He hit him in the chest and the man went down flat on his face. The next man was halfway through the hole, but as he went to shoot the other two began firing from behind the cover of the dead bodies and the bags around him started spraying plumes of sand up into the air. He ducked, came back up swearing, went for the man squeezing through the fence first, got him, then laid down the rest of his clip at the other two. The bullets shredded the backs of the dead bodies and with luck he got one of the VC in the head.

"*You fuckers!*"

But more VC came and another mortar landed in front. It gave him time to change his clip and to spit out what dirt remained in his mouth. His throat was so tight and sore, he could barely swallow. One more blast sent more sand through the seams between the bags.

Again he jumped up. There were about a half dozen VC now. One was through the fence again on his way to the bunker. He shot him in the chest and like the other one he went down face first.

Suddenly a head skirted around the backside of the bunker. So he dropped back down, pivoting his body and rifle to the back. As he came around a VC ran out from the back corner, dropped to his knees, and fired. The sandbags next to his head burst into plumes of dust, hindering his vision, and the noise popped his left ear as if someone had slapped it. He fired back and hit the VC's chest and head, sending him back as if he had been hit head-on by a car.

"*Fuck!*" he shouted.

"We got to get out here, man!" Stanley yelled in the midst of reloading. "I got a hole over here now."

He ignored Stanley, went back up and laid down fire at his hole in the fence. But more VC had slipped through. By now some were halfway to the bunker, lying prone, hiding behind the two dead guys he had dropped earlier. They were shooting straight at him, hitting the bunker so often the flying sand was making it hard to see. Blindly he emptied his clip and, as he went down, glanced over at the other hole to his left, where there were about seven or eight guys waiting to squirt through the new hole. At least two were already inside the camp, firing from their prone positions.

"I'll cover!" he yelled. "Head back to the sixty."

Stanley nodded, hesitating. The two of them stared at each other.

"Go!" he ordered.

When he came back up a dark object was flying straight at him. He ducked down, bracing himself against the wall, and heard the grenade thump against the top row of sandbags, then a large blast that knocked him off the wall by a few inches and popped his ears. When he landed back against the wall he jumped up and fired once more, finished his clip, changed it, and scooted to the end of the bunker. When he peeked back around the VC were still concentrating their fire on his defensive parapet. On the other side he didn't know what was happening. But Stanley had made it to the next bunker and its sixty machine gun was firing full bore.

"Three!" he yelled, jumping up and making his dash.

It was hard to run staying hunched over trying to keep your head up. The whole world before him jittered up and down, the ground was alive with little explosions all around his feet. He could hear the bullets whiz by him and it was hard to resist turning around to see the one coming straight for his back, for his head. Only a fool would keep going, but you couldn't stop.

He was completely out of breath when he rolled into the bunker and bumped into a dead guy. The guy was lying face up, arms at his side, bullet hole in the forehead and neck. Blood everywhere, like a Halloween mask.

"Okay!" the thin faced corporal was yelling. "It's time to get out of here. We're going to make a break for the river. They say there's boats there to take us away."

He glanced up at the two other guys firing from the bunker. Then at Stanley, who was still catching his breath too. No thoughts except his heart beating hard, feeling as if its own muscle were torn.

"Let's go," Stanley said, tagging him on the shoulder.

He snapped out of it, rose to his feet and followed. The five of them wove their way over and around the mortar holes, over and around the sprawled bodies, over and around the canvas tent debris until they came to the south side of the base, where most of the company was taking off down the road towards the river. Strangely enough, he started catching his second wind. The running had cleared his head, though his ears were still ringing.

"Cover everyone!" the corporal yelled.

The five of them stopped and took positions to back up the rest of the company. The VC were still coming but not as fast. They were taking their time, scampering between the bunkers and buildings, maybe to catch their breath too, as the five of them kept the bullets flying, saturating the area the VC were trying to get through.

"Okay, let's go!" the corporal called.

They jumped up and made a beeline to the gate. As they passed through he thought of an idea, stopped and turned around.

"Where you going?" the corporal shouted.

He ran to one side of the gate. Stanley and the corporal caught on and went for the other. Together they closed it and as Stanley and the corporal fired at the VC, he wrapped and tied the chain around the frames in a loose knot.

"Okay!" he shouted.

Just as they split from the gate he heard several loud screams. The VC were charging, weapons blaring. The gate and the ground all around it were exploding into a flurry of flying debris.

"Hold up!" the corporal yelled. "Lay down some fire!"

The corporal lined them into a battlehead facing the base and firing at will to match the VC firepower. A few more guys came back and joined them, some standing behind and guiding the ones in the front line as they moved backwards, handing up reloaded weapons, and helping to keep the barrage steady and deadly. The fence was taking it all now, falling apart piece by piece. Only the part of the gate frame with the chain around it survived.

But still the VC kept coming. Several made it to the fence and fired from there. The ground around the battlehead was like a little dust storm that retreated and advanced but somehow no one was getting hit. When a guy at the end of the line fell, everyone in the front line looked, then went back to firing at the fence. The ground was covered by a cloud of dust, as if a low level fog had drifted in, as they kept firing and the VC kept firing, and more VC were coming and the Goddamn road to the river seemed longer than ever.

Another guy fell from the line, first dropping to his knees then trying to stand back up. But as he did the deadly cloud of dust ran headlong into him and knocked him off his knees like a bowling pin. His helmet flew off and was picked up where it landed and pushed along by the enemy fire straight into his legs. When he kicked it away, it stayed upside down in the middle of the lane. With his next step, though, he stepped on something mushy yet hard, and glanced down to see his heel crushing someone's outstretched hand with a large high school ring. Blindly he veered to the side bumping shoulders with Stanley, and losing track of where he was firing. Then he realized he was swinging his rifle muzzle towards his own guys and swung it back around, forcing his eyes wide to concentrate and focus again just on the gate.

"Okay!" the corporal yelled. "Move it to the dock!"

The line peeled off instantly. As soon as they had their backs to the base there was a loud blast. He looked behind in time to see the gate go up in smoke and, seconds later, the VC running through the suspended debris.

The patrol boats were leaving the dock as Stanley, the corporal and he leaped aboard and were squeezed in with the guys packed on the bow. He sat down like everyone else and dangled his feet over the side. As the boat increased its speed and headed down river with the rest of the flotilla, he looked behind him but again his view was blocked by the superstructure of the boat.

It was over now. He was lucky to be alive.

He took a deep breath and began looking around. They all had blank faces like stroke victims, and some had their heads hanging over as if suffering from a good drunk.

Then his own body started to quiver. It shook from head to toe and then back up. His eyes watered, his sore throat reappeared, his ears began to ring with a sound so sharp and loud it caused a secretion inside his mouth that spread to his throat and burned like lemon juice on a cut. His jaw hinge smarted too, like some kind of acid was both eating it and locking it in place.

"Jesus," he coughed, trying to get the mucus out of his throat.

Not much came out. He was choking like a dog with a bone stuck in its mouth. Then a hot flash came on, popping sweat across his forehead and the back of his neck. He couldn't believe all this. It was like he was coming down with malaria or something. No one else seemed to be suffering. Why him?

The sound of the jets made them all raise their heads. The fighters were slicing across the sunny sky overhead, streaking for the base. Just as they went out of view they released their rockets. Short puffs of white smoke underneath were followed up by rumbling explosions. Then two more jets came over and repeated the procedure. This time the sound of the blasts made him think about how the gate exploded. How he could have been killed. How that was what this place was all about.

At the same time, though, he had started to drift out. Finally his head dropped sharply, snapping his neck and waking him back up. He opened his eyes briefly but then began drifting off again just as quickly. This time, though, as he went out he brought his rifle close, bracing his shoulder and neck against the stock, and tilting his head until his cheek came into contact with the muzzle.

"Ah!"

The muzzle, still super hot, had burned his skin like a cigarette.

He looked to either side of him to see who'd noticed. But it didn't look as though anybody had. "Goddamn it," he whispered, and poked his tongue around inside his cheek to check out the damage. But there was no way of knowing how bad it was, or if it would leave a scar. He tried wetting his fingers but couldn't raise much spit, and the river was too far down to reach and muddy anyway. What little wetness he had to pat on the burn quickly dried, doing nothing at all to quell the sting. Then the inside of his cheek began tasting sour.

His eyes were not watering enough to make tears, but he still looked around again before wiping them dry.

They motored up and down the river for probably about an hour, until the sun was up over the trees. It was already hot as hell, especially sandwiched in the way they were. But he wasn't complaining. No, not him. He liked the sun. It made the burn on his cheek feel like acid was eating his face. But who cared? He was just the shit-burning fool.

Besides, heat was not what was on his mind. Piles of bodies stacked next to the fence were, and guys getting shot as they struggled to get through the fence, and guys who took it in the chest and fell face first to the ground, and the one guy he sent rearing backwards at near point blank range. He had killed a lot of people. He'd never expected he could do that. Somehow he'd thought he would slide through this part of his life without having to participate. He wasn't able to perform properly in school, he'd never had a specific skill, so how could he excel here? Unless, of course, all the army needed was another utility man.

"Boat two will dock first," someone said over a loudspeaker.

Their coxswain revved the engine and they crept upstream towards the base dock. The jets had gone, and all was quiet. But there were still enough clouds of smoke billowing over the treetops to give the impression the base was burning down to the ground.

"Okay," said the corporal who'd led the retreat. "Let's get ready. We don't know what to expect."

It figured he had to be on boat two. It was like being on the shit detail.

No one got ready to disembark. Most guys just kept sunning themselves. Even as the boat closed in on the dock they were holding back, waiting for someone else to be the first to land. He could hear guys complaining that their rifles didn't work, that they were jammed.

He didn't blame them, but he wasn't going to lag behind. He wanted off this scow, the sooner the better.

So he ended up leaping off first, with Stanley and the corporal. The three of them ran up to the bank and took a prone position. Up ahead lay a roadway of sprawled bodies, American and Vietnamese. As for the base, it was burning from five fires he could see: the headquarters, the officer's mess and barracks, the supply tent, and the enlisted mess. The tower, still standing, came in and out between the clouds of smoke, like the Vietnamese flag that had replaced the American one. Not exactly a nice welcome home.

"Let's go," the corporal said.

There were many body poses on the way. Some with arms spread out at the sides. Some tucked at their sides. Some with arms folded across chests in variations of one or two. Some bodies with their legs apart, and some crossed over. Two bodies missing one leg. One missing a foot. Some looked like they were restfully sleeping. Some looked terrified. One head with one eye, two heads missing recognizable profiles. But every one with thousands of bugs swarming around them in a frenzy and all that blood.

He stopped at the body of the guy he had stepped on. The hand was partially buried but the ring was still visible. A fly was doing a ring-around-the-rosie number on it.

"You know him?" Stanley asked.

"No," he said and went on.

He soon discovered while walking through the bodies an unusual physical property of the universe. It was the law of opposite attractions. His eyes were the north poles of the magnet and the severed limbs and the stubs left behind were the southern poles, and they couldn't be pulled apart.

At first, the smell of burning wood and fabric made it easier to grasp what was laid out before him. At least it covered the stink of bodies rotting under the late morning sun. But there was still always an occasional whiff of slow cooking guts, just when you least expected it, like a combination of boiling gizzards, burning hair, a rotten egg or two and a little battery acid. Great for cleaning out the sinuses, he thought as he upchucked a ball of phlegm.

"Fuck," Stanley gagged, doing the same.

The corporal tied a handkerchief around his face like a western highwayman. Stanley and he had to use their shirts. Still, they continued to cough and choke and spit out what kept coming up from their stomachs. The rest of the company was still lagging behind, not even halfway to the base yet.

"We'll take this side," the corporal said, pointing to the north and west perimeter where most of the action had occurred, right where Stanley and he had been posted.

Stanley looked at him and shrugged, but he didn't know how to respond. What it came down to was doing his job. He had accepted the conditions by allowing himself to be drafted. There was no backing out.

Except for the heat from all the fires making him feel like a hot dog on a rotisserie, from then on it was routine. It was the same bloody, torn up mess as it had been on the road and at the gate. A leg here. A body there. A tent smoldering here. A bunker blown to bits there. The only difference was a severed head that had rolled down into a hole about three feet away from its owner. It was a Vietnamese.

He had to catch himself before he fainted. His stomach tossed and he vomited all over his shirt and himself. Stanley and the corporal followed suit.

"Come on," the corporal gagged. "Let's get out of here."

After the helicopters came back the company was divided into groups with different tasks. He and Stanley were assigned to the body detail and when that group was subdivided into those who would piece and bag the bodies, those who would carry the bags, those who would load the bags, and those who would do the paper work, Stanley and he managed to be of that lucky few who pieced and bagged.

"I'm Jake the Snake Harmon. I'm from Atlanta, Georgia, and I was raised to sing gospel music."

"I'm Stanley Long," Stanley said, with an offer of a handshake which Harmon ignored.

Yeah, well he was Dave the Slave Thorne. He was from Syracuse, New York, and you could shove your gospel music up your ass. He looked straight at the hulking black with the huge white-toothed grin and bald shiny head. "Thorne's the name."

"I know," Harmon said, tipping his head. "Shall we?"

He looked down at the body Harmon was pointing to. It was a chest wound, not too bad, not too bloody. The next guy down the line wasn't so lucky. He was a blast victim and he was missing some parts.

But one thing at a time. He knelt down and started to strip the first guy of his gear, ammo and rifle. When Harmon lifted the body for him so he could pull the guy's ammo belt off, he noticed how huge and fat Harmon's hands were. He also noticed, with the dead guy's head tilted back, how all his molars had fillings.

"Blessed are we who rebuild the earth from ashes," Harmon said as he knelt across from him. "Blessed are they who are cleansed with blood."

Stanley and he looked at each other. Stanley frowned and rolled his eyes, as if to say Harmon was one strange dude.

"How fitting it is," Harmon was saying, "for we who have been blessed with the duty of assembling mankind into plastic bags, to stand here now before an assemblage of material waste and ask forgiveness from the Lord."

"Do you always quote something from the Bible?" Stanley asked.

Harmon looked up. "No," he said. "It's from the heart."

Like anything, after a while it became a routine. If their eyes were open, he closed them. If their guts needed jamming back in, he did it. It felt like playing with finger paints and silly putty, and sometimes his hand scraped the rib cage. But nothing could be damaged anymore, no matter how hard he pushed or stuffed or shoved. And all the evidence would be buried anyway.

When it came to matching severed limbs, fingers, hands or feet to the remaining stubs, though, Stanley, Harmon and he tried to get the right parts with the right body. It took a long time but they were all bloody and sticky and gooey anyway and had already vomited everything they'd eaten. Once a while back now, Stanley had said something about how much the family would appreciate it, though in fact they'd never know. But the three of them did it just the same and in those instances where they couldn't match the parts with the body, just made sure they didn't put a white finger on a black hand.

"Let the Lord be with us," Harmon prayed as he smoothed over the small mound of extra parts.

He looked at Harmon and Stanley. Stanley and Harmon looked at him. What else could they do? They'd been told they were too slow, they were trying to be too perfect. No one wanted that extra junk. Get rid of it and hurry up. So they did.

Next guy had a bullet right through his eye.

"Let the blind lead us."

"Amen," Stanley lamented.

Looking at the dead man's face he realized for the first time that blood stood out as much on dark skin as it did white. Maybe even more so. That was something he wouldn't forget.

By the afternoon his shirt and pants were covered with particles of dirt and sand clinging to the bloodstains, so the fabric felt more like cardboard than cloth. The front of his shirt scratched his chest and rubbed his nipples burning raw. His lower back hurt, his neck was stiff, his nose, throat and skin were all parched sand, and wiggling his nose was enough to crack his burnt face, dried blood and all.

He held out his hands and looked down at the sticking fingers, the lines and fingerprints highlighted by the blood.

"Hmmm," he said as he lifted and sniffed them. "Chanel Number Five."

By early evening all the American casualties had been dealt with. But before they could eat and rest the Vietnamese bodies had to be rounded up and moved outside the compound. No one was happy with that and when two of the guys began dragging the bodies by their feet nobody objected. Then came hauling the bodies face down. Soon it was a race between teams to see who could drag their bodies quickest to the pile, across a course that included mortar holes, tent debris and wood, and finally a short stint over the metal landing pad.

"It's the devil's work," Harmon said.

Stanley and he agreed as they picked up their body the old-fashion way, by the hands and feet. At this point he could care less. He just wanted to get it all done and go home. This Vietnamese's feet were cold and callused. From wearing sandals he guessed.

"You three," the lieutenant said. "After you drop this one off, go over there and take that one."

"Yes, sir," Stanley said.

He was glad Stanley had the energy to think of an answer, let alone speak. Double shifts back home were looking fairly easy now.

Unfortunately, the body the lieutenant referred to was the headless one. Harmon knelt down by the body, placed his big left hand over his heart, bowed his head and began a silent prayer. Looking down he noticed several divots in Harmon's bald skull, especially towards the back, as if he had been hit there many times. Looking down on Harmon's skull from this angle the surface as a whole looked a lot like the moon.

"Amen," Harmon whispered. "Let us forgive those who separate the minds and hearts of the meek."

He made the mistake of staring down at the body, focusing on the blood and stringy tentacles pouring out of what was left of the neck like a spilled bucket of worms. A bomb of heartburn shot up from his stomach, but for about the twentieth time he caught it in his mouth and swallowed it back down.

By the luck of the draw Stanley and Harmon took the body while he carried the head out in front of him like a bowl of fruit. Everyone else in the camp looked on as if he were the only parade in town, but also stayed a certain distance away as if he were carrying a bomb.

So much for the day's work.

Somehow Harmon convinced Stanley and him to skip dinner and head directly to Harmon's favorite spot. Harmon had some awesome, knock-your-dick-straight stuff. Make your dreams come true. Who cared if it was still a little light out? No one would bother them.

"They'd better not," Stanley said to Harmon. "Or I'll kill you."

For him, it was a different matter. He had pledged before leaving for boot camp to give up dope. He'd never had a good reason to start in the first place, so it seemed right to end it as he began anew. But now all that seemed as much like horse shit as it had after college. There was no way he could make it through his tour without smoking. And today he had good reason to start.

Harmon smiled in his usual Jack-o-Lantern manner, lit the Thai stick, and took in a chest full of smoke. Harmon held the smoke in a while, pondering the joint, then let it out through his flaring nostrils like a dragon cooling its jets. "Smoke this," he said, offering it out, "so your soul will be reborn."

He took it from Harmon. It had an amazing yellowish-purple color. "What's in this anyway?"

"The blood of a thousand hearts."

He knew he shouldn't have asked.

"Blessed are they which do hunger and thirst after righteousness, for they shall be filled," Harmon preached.

"Yeah, right, man," Stanley said. "Blessed are the meek, for they shall inherit the fucking earth."

The instant his lips touched the joint they went numb. Then, when he drew, his brain felt as if it was expanding inside his skull, pushing against the sides and screaming to be let out, at the same time as he realized he was getting a hard-on.

"Are you there?" Harmon asked him.

He handed the joint to Stanley. He thought for a moment he would puke. He let the smoke out through his mouth, and as soon as he inhaled his lungs began acting funny, like worms were burrowing holes in them.

Stanley drew in a larger hit and began coughing and choking before he could finish. "Wooie," Stanley said, letting his head fall back as he caught his breath. Stanley seemed to be ready to say more when his eyes suddenly locked straight ahead as if the glaze on them had frozen. He ended up just sitting there, staring out at the marsh.

When Harmon took the joint from Stanley's hand and held it up for them to ponder, Stanley still seemed oblivious. "Eat it. Snort it. Wipe it on your face. Shove it up your ass. Rub it on your dick. Opium," Harmon said in a deeper, more sensuous voice. Then he licked his huge lips and took another toke.

"Far out," Stanley said.

Far out was right. He was fucking flying. He couldn't even feel himself sitting down anymore.

"Can you speak?" Harmon asked him as he handed the joint back to him.

Suddenly a flash of reality came over him, and he felt perfectly normal, like nothing had happened. "Blessed are the silent, for they hear the breeze as it travels by," he said. Now where the hell did that come from?

"Blessed me," Stanley said. "A poet."

"Blessed are the pure of heart, for they shall see God," Harmon eulogized.

He took his second hit. This time the sensation was not as dramatic as it had been at first. But talking again seemed like a useless thing to do. He handed the joint over to Stanley.

"Blessed are the merciful, for they shall obtain mercy," Harmon prayed.

Harmon was not such a bad guy after all. He was big though. His mother must have screamed when he was born.

"Blessed are the toes and feet, the hands and fingers, the arms and legs and heads of boys shattered into men."

"Okay, Harmon," Stanley said, holding out the joint. "Shut up."

His head was definitely in another time zone. His thoughts traveled like telegrams across his brain but once they made it to his mouth he couldn't remember them. He wanted to rub his face but couldn't get his hands to do it. He might be doomed to sit cross-legged the rest of his life.

"Blessed are we who wish death well."

Stanley tossed an empty can at Harmon. It hit him on his massive shoulder. Harmon paid no attention and handed him the joint. As he reached out for it he noticed the blood on his hand. Harmon saw it too.

"Blessed are we who wash ourselves in blood."

He took the joint but his fingers couldn't feel it.

"Blessed are we who seek salvation from life."

"Harmon," Stanley said in a motherly tone.

Harmon turned his attention to the sky. "Blessed are we who persecute for righteousness' sake, for ours is the Kingdom of Heaven."

He was holding the joint in his hand, but he couldn't do a thing. He couldn't lift his arm, and his head felt like it wanted to tumble off. His chest was caving in. He was dying, ever so slowly, but dying just the same. It was embarrassing. He couldn't hack it. He was a pussy, a no good rotten crybaby.

He started crying. Tears poured out of his eyes. He couldn't think of a thing. Couldn't remember a thing. His heart was stopping. Life was draining from his limbs. He couldn't go on like this. This was all too fucking much. It was killing him.

"You all right, man?" Stanley asked.

The instant Stanley asked he snapped out of it. He felt okay, and had some idea of what was going on. They were smoking. The three of them. Nothing had changed. Nothing was wrong. Everything was all right.

"Blessed are they that mourn, for they shall be comforted," Harmon prayed again.

He looked over at Harmon, who for the first time didn't have his smile on.

Later on, when it began to rain, they didn't have their ponchos, but that didn't bother them. It was good cooling off at the end of a hot and muggy day. As for the mud splattering up on their clothes, well, it helped cover the blood. When it started getting dark, though, the idea of night made him feel a little chilled. When Stanley complained about being cold they decided it was time to head home, get some sleep, be fresh for the new day. So they stood up, slowly and without enthusiasm, but up nonetheless. Didn't hurry, either, to get out of the rain. Just strolled along, not saying hello to anyone, laughing a little to themselves.

At his barracks they said goodbye and split up, after making a date for the next evening: same time, same place, last half of the joint.

# CHAPTER
# FIFTEEN

It started out as just another Thursday. He got up for early morning watch, walked back and forth, counted the stars, stayed awake then went straight to the latrine to relieve himself when he was relieved. But today, untypically, there was a long line which wasn't moving. Stanley was third in line, but didn't see him because he was reading his letters. He thought of going up and talking with Stanley, but he knew everyone would be pissed at his sneaking up. Besides, Stanley never liked being disturbed when he was reading his mail. So he settled for number twelve, which at least was one better than thirteen.

"That guy's been in there for hours!" someone in the line shouted.

The first guy in line had suddenly been shoved into acting. He didn't want that particular role, but now everyone was watching and waiting. So he began pounding on the door. "Hey, hurry up, asshole."

The pounding wasn't working. He felt sorry for the number one guy up there beating on the door, especially with no one lending a hand. "Open the door," he suggested. "Maybe there's nobody in there."

"No," the guy in front said. "There's somebody in there. Why don't you come up and open it?"

It wasn't exactly what he wanted to do. But he had to pee and shit himself, and it wasn't worth sneaking behind a tent to do it. He'd only have to pick it up later the same way he'd been doing with everyone else's. So he stepped up and everyone in line gave him all the room he needed to get by.

Stanley looked up as he went past, and nodded his approval. "Go get 'em, man," he said.

Then he was up at the front of the line looking at the wood door handle, thinking how it was no big deal if he opened it while the guy was squeezing one out. He'd seen people shit before and for sure the guy knew people out here were getting anxious. So what the fuck? It wasn't like anyone was going to get killed or anything.

"One thing," he said. "I get to go next."

Everyone in line looked at one another, nodded and shrugged, as back behind everyone, he noticed Harmon standing with his arms crossed like some Indian chief.

He turned back to the door and tried knocking. "Hey." Then cracked the door gradually open to about the width of his hand. In the dark inside he could see one of the guy's legs, swung to one side as if his legs were spread apart, the knee of that same leg resting against the wall. Maybe the guy was beating off? "Hey." He opened the door wider and brought his head in far enough to see first the guy's rifle leaning against the wall, then the morning light reaching up to the guy's lap, where there was a knife.

He looked up from the blood all over the guy's pants and shirt to his dimly lit face, his forehead drenched in sweat, his eyes wide open as if still seeing a truck about to hit him head on. It was one of the black guys that had come in with him on the helicopter on his first day here.

"What's wrong, man?" he heard Stanley call out behind him.

The noise made him jerk back. "He's dead."

"What?"

"He's dead," he said, closing the door.

"What are we going to do now?" the guy in front of the line asked.

Yes, what was he going to do with him? Bag him no doubt. Send him home wrapped up like a Christmas gift.

All the guys began to leave, except for Stanley and another black guy toward the end of the line, the white guy who had been first in line, and, of course, Harmon. The others headed for the back of the barracks, favorite spot for those who couldn't wait in line.

The black guy peeked in. "Jesus, man. He done himself in good!"

"I'll go get the lieutenant," the white guy said.

"Yeah," he nodded, feeling suddenly tired.

"He slashed both his arms, man!" the black guy exclaimed.

Right, he thought. Thorough son of a bitch, wasn't he? He couldn't wait to wipe up all the blood.

He looked at Harmon who was staring back at him. But he didn't look long. He never could with Harmon. It made him think too much about life and death.

"You can leave," Harmon told the black guy. "We can take care of him. He's our brother."

The black guy shrugged and left. But while he unslung his rifle and got ready to take the guy off the can, ignoring Harmon as much as he could, Stanley stood off to the side clutching his mail in his fist, looking like he hadn't slept well or had been rejected by his girlfriend. He couldn't decide which. But he figured the bags under his own eyes were just as large and dark, so Stanley had to deal with his own problems. He had this body to take care of.

He used the guy's rifle to prop the door open. The guy didn't seem to mind. He was just slumped in the corner staring out ahead of himself, bleeding the length of his forearms. It was a little strange the way the guy sat there as if he really were shitting, shitting so hard blood was coming out. But then again, nothing these days was surprising. The established routine now was one suicide per day, four total, four days since the base had been overrun.

He stepped one foot in and reached out to close the guy's eyes. In these cases it always seemed like the first thing to do.

"Blessed are those who die before their time," Harmon prayed, somewhere behind him and off to the side.

Maybe this was his time, Harmon. But he wasn't going to say that. After all, everyone died before their time if you thought about it. Everyone would. Even Harmon. Even him.

Next was the knife. It was bloody and not just on the blade. It was as if the guy had slit his wrists first and then decided he wasn't bleeding fast enough, so he picked the knife back up and drew it farther up his arm, more so on his left than his right.

When he handed it out to Harmon, the blood was sticky like caramel on his hands. But that was only the beginning. Then, when he stepped in to grab the guy under the arms he felt the rush of warm air rising from the body as if he were over a forced air vent.

But hey, he was used to it now. He had done this many times. It was just a routine.

He looked at the guy's face one more time. It didn't seem all that frightened now. It almost looked as if he had settled in for the journey, maybe even reached his destination already, in the arms of his mother. Maybe everyone was wrong and death wasn't painful. Maybe it was only the wounds.

The floor was slippery from the pooled blood. It made a lapping sound as he shuffled around, and stuck to the soles of his boots like tacky glue. But he ignored it or at least kept pulling the guy out, until he could hand him over to Harmon. There was no time to be distressed about bloodstains or worried about slipping, or concerned if the victim was uncomfortable.

Outside, Harmon laid the kid out on the ground, crossing his arms and hands on his chest, and straightened the head so it looked up like a choir boy.

"Blessed are those who take their lives and leave us to die by the hand of God."

"Harmon, would you fucking shut up for once?" he said.

Harmon looked up. "Blessed are those whose anger relieves them of their pain."

He took a deep breath and looked at Stanley holding the same spot in line even though the line had disappeared. Stanley didn't look up. He folded his letters, placed them in his breast pocket, and left without a word.

He looked at his bloody hands, at Harmon, and then at the body. He couldn't blame Stanley for not wanting to be a part of this mess. He, too, felt suicide was a cheap way to go. But he would never refuse a person the right to use it. You never knew, it might come in handy one day.

# CHAPTER
# SIXTEEN

This was day number twelve. The twelfth day of slogging through the marsh in search of arms caches. The twelfth hot, sweaty day of finding nothing but more bugs, more snakes, more rodents, more will to resist drinking the swamp water down around your knees. Today, however, it was raining. Fortunately the tall reeds protected them from the downpour, but everyone still wore his poncho. Unfortunately the reeds also hid everyone from each other as well. At one moment someone would be at his side and at the next step the guy would disappear. It was like walking through a large hair brush, the bristles a foot or so over your head.

"See anything?" Harmon whispered over to him, as Stanley stepped out from behind Harmon, his breast pocket stuffed with those same letters of his.

He shook his head no to Harmon and looked to his right. They had come to another corridor, their fifth one in this area. Army intelligence thought these corridors were humanly made. That was why they were here. To find out. Simple.

"See anything?" Stanley asked.

He nodded no again. Harmon was grinning. Probably because Stanley had just asked the same question. But with Harmon's strange sense of humor you never knew. Just today Harmon'd said everyone wearing a poncho was no more than a walking talking condom, and in the rain a lubricated one at that. Too bad they all had holes in their tips. But that just meant they were discarded or used up.

"Blessed are we who enter hell together," Harmon prayed.

He tried to mimic Harmon's huge grin, but discovered his mouth wasn't big enough.

The next group of reeds was thicker. He had to cut through them sideways, and the clattering that made soon drowned out all other noise. Even the sky was almost blocked out above him, and the farther he went the more it felt like he was entering a cave. The water, too, was black and oily looking, and no longer showed his shadow or took the pelting of the rain.

He stopped a moment. Listened. Looked to his left. To his right. Nothing. Not a sound. He checked his safety, his clip. Looked down to make sure he still had his knife. Then listened again. Nothing but buzzing and chirps. Shit, where did everybody go? He couldn't have lost them in such a short distance. Could he?

He started again, this time a little slower, a little more carefully, searching for Harmon and Stanley and for any booby traps.

At the next wall of reeds he had to force himself between the blades, like pushing through a crowd for a better view of the parade. It sounded like he was scratching his fingernails on a chalkboard and gave him the impression the razor sharp edges sliding across him were slicing off scraps from his poncho. Though it was stupid he kept his head down and eyes closed.

Then, on breaking through, he found Harmon crouching down in front of him. One of them had gone off course.

"See anything?" Harmon asked.

He nodded no.

Stanley came out on the right as if he too had veered off. "See anything?" Stanley asked.

He nodded no again.

After the next wall of reeds he came upon another corridor, this one much wider than the others. Here the water seemed to have a current. A few broken grass blades and sticks were floating by. He looked to his right but there was no sign of anybody. To his left the same.

He checked his rifle and knife again. How could he have gone off course again in such a short distance? The fucking army was dumb as all get out. He fucking hated it.

He knelt down in the water and concentrated on listening. Nothing but the same old buzzing and chirping, the same bugs flying in erratic spirals. But this time the sound seemed much more hollow and distant, like he was in a huge covered arena all alone.

He looked behind him. Nothing but reeds. To his right, reeds and the winding corridor. To his left, the same. Ahead, more reeds.

Then he noticed the mud swirls drifting through and around his legs, coming from upstream to his right. He searched along both walls of reeds, half expecting to see one of the squad poke through. The bugs were getting more intense, attacking his ears and hands as he stayed squatting. He shook his head and barely kept from swatting as he stayed focused on the corridor.

Then, just twenty feet away, a sandal came out of the reeds and stepped out into the water.

He rose up and leveled his rifle at the black-clad man emerging from the tall grass. A mosquito landed on the tip of his nose just as the man saw him. The VC swung his weapon towards him but he fired first, spraying his burst across the VC's stomach and chest. The man fell backwards into the wall of grass, careening off it as if it were brick, landed in the water and sank. A few seconds later, his face and shoulders popped up like a fishing bobber.

Suddenly, a little farther up the corridor, another rifle shoved out and pointed downstream. He dove into the marsh, water splashing up into his face. The VC fired, spraying the water behind him and shredding the grass. Bits of it floated down on him like confetti as he fired back blurry-eyed. The rifle disappeared before his rounds reached the spot. As soon as he stopped firing the VC jumped out closer to him, firing in a flurry down the corridor. The VC must not have seen him lying prone in the water less than fifteen feet away. He fired a shot back and hit the VC in the chest, so the guy dropped back onto his ass in the water, but otherwise stayed upright. After a brief second he even raised his rifle as if about to fire again, even though the glassy look in his eyes suggested he wasn't all there. Before the VC could do anything, though, he had fired again, hitting him in the chest one more time, sending him down like his buddy, just another face in the water, bobbing up and down.

It was so quiet all he could hear was the ringing in his ears. The smell of gunpowder was still strong. The corridor up ahead was empty, almost serene, tranquil as if birds were about to sing. Even the rain had stopped. But the bodies made him look carefully along the wall of reeds as he felt for his next clip.

"Blessed are they who salvage victory for the victoryless," Harmon said, directly behind him, coming out of the reeds.

He looked back at the bodies floating in the water, blood swirling out of them into the current like so much mud. Their noses stuck up the furthest, then maybe their lips and chins.

For some reason he remembered going back to close the gate during the attack on the base. That had been a stupid thing to do. He could have been killed.

He looked back at the second man he had killed, and flashed on him after he had first shot him, sitting up like a kid playing in a small pool, too young to swim or play with his toys with any real coordination. And he had shot him just the same.

Maybe he wasn't going to die here. Maybe he was here to kill.

That made him shiver. No wonder he had flunked out of school. No wonder it had taken so long to discover the one skill he had an aptitude for.

"You know Stanley?" Harmon asked.

He looked back at Harmon pulling the shit sled like an ox, Harmon's favorite chore aside from being strange. What he didn't understand was why Harmon was asking the question. Harmon knew he knew Stanley. "Yeah, I know him. Not that well though."

"Yeah, he said he knows you. He said you sure could shoot some."

He guessed Harmon was referring to the VC he had killed the other day. It was the talk of the town. It turned out they'd uncovered a large cache of weapons and food.

"You have one hell of a reputation around here."

He ignored Harmon and poured the diesel into the shit barrels.

"Everybody respects you."

"Yeah," he said. He rechecked the barrel to make sure he had the right proportions.

"You put that much in there?" Harmon asked.

"I do. That way you don't have to keep refilling it. Just burn the hell out of it the first time."

"Praise the Lord."

He noticed some shit splotches on Harmon's boots and pant legs. The flies were massing in one huge clump on the heel, cramped as tight as they could, head to head, head to butt. Someday he would have to modify the sled by adding a board in front to stop it from slopping on the puller's legs. But that would be another day. Today, right now, he started pouring diesel in the second barrel instead.

As usual nothing unusual happened. Shit burned. Smoke smoked. Heat. Sweat. Soot. Stink. All in a good afternoon's work. Only today Harmon and he kept talking, and talked about the world. About how the government didn't represent you, how politics was for the rich by the rich, how being who you were was enough for society to justify your not getting a job, not getting a chance to prove yourself, to get decent schooling, to find your dream. It went on and on until they both were totally frustrated. Then all they had to do was wait for the barrels to cool.

Harmon stood up and started wandering along the water's edge, passing the spot where some jerk had dumped the barrels of shit into the river. A fair distance upstream from there Harmon stopped and gazed down at the muddy water for a long time, like a man in a trance. Then he searched around, mostly back towards the base and the guard at the dock. Finally Harmon checked all his pockets, looked around one more time, then jumped and landed, cannon-ball style, in the river. The humongous splash reached as high as the bank.

"Yahoo!" Harmon yelled.

He stood up to get a better look. Harmon had completely disappeared under the muddy water. It took a couple seconds for him to come back up.

"Come on in!"

They could get into a lot of trouble for doing that. It was especially unauthorized, probably because it would be so much fun. He started walking upstream towards Harmon, thinking he might join him, but then maybe he wouldn't. It was getting late and the barrels were almost cool.

"It's refreshing as a gospel revival."

"I bet it is." It was also a good eight foot jump. "How deep is it?"

"I'm on my tippy toes," Harmon said.

"I don't know. I can't swim that well."

"I can't swim at all!" Harmon said.

"Yeah, but you're taller than me."

"I'll hold you."

He laughed.

"Come on!" Harmon said. "Before they come."

He looked up at the base. There was no one around but the watches. The guard at the dock was busy searching upstream and why would he give a fuck anyway? He looked back down at the muddy water. It didn't seem that inviting, but the thought of cooling off did.

"I can't stay in here all day," Harmon pleaded.

He chose cannon-ball fashion, like Harmon, and closed his eyes as soon as his feet touched the water. The water rushed up into his pants and shirt and cooled him off instantly. His hearing was cut off as he sank to the bottom, hitting first on his rear end then with his feet. It was slippery and muddy as he pushed off. On the way up he felt the water streaming past as if his face were the bow of a ship.

"Yahoo!" he shouted as he surfaced. He was on his tippy toes but it didn't matter. He felt clean even in the dirty water. It was his first bath since he'd left the States.

He noticed Harmon was standing still, looking up behind him at the bank. He turned around and there peering down was the Officer of the Day.

"Since you two are having so much fun maybe you wouldn't object to some extra duty for a whole week."

"Yes, sir," Harmon replied.

"Yes, sir," he said with less enthusiasm.

"Report to the Corporal of the Guard as soon as you're finished here."

"Yes, sir," they both answered.

As soon as the officer was out of sight, Harmon splashed him.

"Hey!" He slapped his hand on top of the water but Harmon was running to the bank, so it barely reached his back.

"You son of a bitch. I'll get you someday."

"Many a white man have tried," Harmon called back.

"Yeah, I bet," he laughed.

They had just finished loading the sled when they were visited again. Some guy in a corporal's outfit was strolling along the river as though viewing his property. He wasn't wearing a helmet. He didn't even have his rifle with him. He had blond hair and walked with his hands stuffed in his pockets, handsome in a movie-star way.

"It's Stephens," Harmon said. "His crony Doran shouldn't be far behind."

"Who's he?"

"A dope dealer. Doran's his protection."

How Harmon knew all these things baffled him. He had no inkling who was who, or what was happening on the base. But then Harmon was the one who supplied the dope. It would stand to reason he would need to know this stuff.

The closer Stephens approached the more everything about him looked fit and slender, right down to his thin, sharply contoured nose.

"How you guys doing?"

"The Lord is just," Harmon answered.

"Pleasant day today, isn't it?" Stephens said, as if ignoring Harmon.

"Depends what you're doing," Harmon said.

Stephens looked down at the sled. "Yes. I believe you're right."

"We'd better get going," he told Harmon.

"You two look like you've been swimming," Stephens said. "I've been thinking about that myself. How's the water?"

"Can you swim?" Harmon asked.

But instead of answering Harmon, Stephens looked straight into his eyes. "You're Thorne, aren't you?"

This time he did the ignoring. "We ought to go," he said to Harmon again.

"I've heard about you," Stephens said. "You're quite the soldier."

"So?" he said.

Stephens bent over and picked up a piece of branch, looked at it, and threw it hard towards the river. It landed short. "So, I've been wondering if you two've been doing more than inhaling diesel smoke out here." Stephens looked back at him. "Understand," he began, holding one hand up. "You've been doing this—detail for so long I started to think you were having more fun than just swimming."

"The Lord works in mysterious ways," Harmon said.

"Good point." Stephens bent down and picked up another stick. Again it fell short of the river. "Well, I'm sorry I disturbed you. If you ever do get bored, though, come see me. I might be able to help."

"Thanks," he said.

"See you later then, boys," Stephens said as he wheeled around and headed back towards the base.

He watched Stephens go as Harmon finished preparing the sled, and wondered if Harmon had played it cool. If Stephens was a dealer, did Harmon deal with him? Or was Harmon Stephens' competition? If Stephens was trying to force Harmon out of the market, that would explain Stephens' interest in him.

"Something the matter?" Harmon asked.

"Is that who you get your dope from?" he asked.

But before Harmon could answer he had picked up on someone else standing on the side of the road, maybe fifty yards away, just off the path. "Who's that?"

"Probably Doran," Harmon said, without even turning to look.

He watched as the guy who was probably Doran removed his rifle from his shoulder, released his clip, checked it for ammo and slapped it back in. Then he turned around and started back towards the base.

What the fuck that had been all about he didn't know. But he didn't like standing out here in the open like a sitting duck.

"Well," he said, "we'd better get our asses moving before we end up doing this for the rest of our lives."

On the way back Harmon told him how he had worked at Disneyland once but only for less than a day. He'd been a sweeper sweeping around the Matterhorn and it looked like such great fun that he hopped on. He'd gotten caught, though, then they'd fired him. But the way Harmon looked at it, it had still been one hell of a lot of fun.

Harmon had a point. In fact, by the time they got back to the latrines, Harmon had a lot of points. Like, why didn't the army fix the barracks like they had fixed the officers' places? Why didn't the army get better food, better mail service, better water? Like why did it take them so long to repair the enlisted latrines?

He didn't know. It all seemed easy enough to fix. But then, he was just a utility man, that was all. And he still didn't know where the dope was coming from.

# CHAPTER SEVENTEEN

"Where the hell's he at?" he asked Harmon.

"I'm not sure," Harmon shrugged.

Each time he looked up the rain drops spraying off Harmon's helmet hit him in the face like spit.

"Well, he'd better hurry up. We got to go."

"Here he comes."

He looked across to the mess tent and saw Stanley tiptoeing between the puddles. Stanley didn't like mud and since the monsoon season had started there was nothing but mud.

"Nice morning," Stanley said as he reached them.

They didn't bother to answer.

"So did you hear?" Stanley said.

"Hear what?" he asked.

"Two guys killed themselves last night."

"You're kidding!" he said.

"I heard the black kid was murdered," Harmon said.

"Where did you hear that?" Stanley jumped on Harmon.

"In the mess," Harmon said.

"From who? Some brothers who want nothing more than to cause trouble? Maybe the white guy was killed too. For revenge or something. They say he was found dead later."

It was the first time he had ever seen Stanley pissed. He didn't have the slightest idea what was going on, but he did know several notes had been left around saying blacks were nothing but lazy niggers who should be shot along with the nigger-lovers. But that was too normal to worry about. Just like maybe it was normal for everyone to start killing each other, too.

"It's just what I heard," Harmon said.

"Well, you better keep your mouth shut or someone might close it for you," Stanley said.

"I'm not worried," Harmon said. "The Lord is my shepherd."

"Hey," he interrupted. "We got to go before our asses are in a sling."

Harmon didn't bother to say another word. He took off, brushing by Stanley like he was a telephone pole.

"What's wrong with him, man?" Stanley asked.

He shrugged. "Too much rain. Too much mud. Too much heat. The usual, I guess."

"Well, you'd better tell him to keep his mouth shut, man. There are some people around here that could make problems, big problems."

"So you think the black guy was killed then."

Stanley looked straight into his eyes. "I think I'd be careful. Even if I were you."

The more he thought about it, the more he realized Stanley was right. The whole thing had been getting too weird lately, what with the rain shutting them in and then all those notes left around. It was like someone was watching him all the time, but what did he have to worry about? He hadn't done anything but mind his own business. Still, he couldn't help remembering the Civil Rights workers who had been killed in the South. It had scared him when he was a kid. And he was a little scared now.

"You don't look so good," Stanley said.

"Yeah, well, you don't look beautiful yourself."

Stanley had eyes that looked like they would go blind if the sun ever hit them again, and that was without counting the dark bags under them. But he figured his had to be about the same. The dope was making it hard to get up in the morning, and so was the weather.

"Let's smoke tonight," Stanley suggested.

"That'll be different," he said.

"You don't want to?"

"No, I want to."

This time Stanley didn't look him straight in the eye. "Well, you'd better get going."

"Yeah," he said.

As if walking in ankle-deep mud, as if often falling down on his ass, as if mud flying up in his face wasn't enough, the sergeant found a manmade canal for them to get in, a short cut he said. Never mind the leeches and parasites: the canal was a good six feet down a slick bank, long enough to get up a good head of steam, and the damn water wasn't exactly shallow.

"Looks like a fanny run to me," Harmon said.

That it did and the two guys who had just gone down probably wished they hadn't chosen the belly method. They immediately fell backwards as they entered the water and the sergeant didn't lift a finger to save them from dunking.

The fanny technique worked well. Harmon and he stayed on their feet without any help. Yet he was still not completely happy now. The water was up to the middle of his chest and it seemed impossible for them ever to get out anywhere around here. The banks on either side were just too high and steep and slick.

"We're going upstream a ways and then cut back," the sergeant ordered. "Keep together and keep your eyes open. There's been activity in the area. Thorne, you take the rear, Thompson, the point."

The bottom was so slimy and slippery, it made it hard to turn and look behind, but that wouldn't stop him from doing it. Even though nothing was there, just more mist and rain, he couldn't help imagining a crocodile sneaking up on him. So he kept looking back even though it always looked the same, as if they hadn't moved at all. And in fact, they weren't moving very fast. The sergeant's short cut was proving not to be easy. He could feel his legs straining against the current as he stepped ahead, and when he turned around his poncho bloated out like a pregnant woman. That slowed him down, but also created a cool pocket underneath his rain gear, so it was okay. Then there were the hollow thumps on the balloon-like poncho, that made it sound like he was inside a coffee percolator. He liked them too. But even so, turning around was still a bitch.

He turned back and looked ahead at the squad. They were apart now, in three ragged lines, some in the middle, some on the sides. The canal varied but was somewhere around twelve feet wide. The walls were staying high though, and the fog was lowering too, closing over them like a coffin lid. It was also raining harder, making the water muddier as the banks eroded in a thousand little streams. The drops were closer together and larger, spattering on the water like a shower of automatic fire. And now his poncho wanted to fold between his legs as he went forward, plus there was body heat pouring out from around his neck as if he were a broiler and it was the vent.

Jesus, bitch, bitch, bitch. Just do your job.

He tilted his head back and stuck out his tongue for some refreshment. The drops hurt as they hit, especially around his eyes. But anything was better than being this parched.

Just as he had collected enough rain to swallow, a burst of fire erupted up ahead. The first flash came from the upper right bank, then a second one from the left. The fog lit up like lightning streaks were bolting through it. A group of water splatters like cars splashing through mud puddles swept into the squad and four men in the middle dropped their rifles and went down as if the air had been let out of them. Then, as quickly, another burst of fire came from both sides making two lines of boiling water that crisscrossed the next group, who twisted and fell.

Beside him, Harmon fired to the right. He chose the left, but couldn't see a thing through the fog. He ran closer to Harmon, firing as he went. Someone else was firing up ahead, probably Thompson and the sergeant. Harmon emptied his clip. Just as he started to reload another burst came from high on the bank and Harmon reeled backwards as if beginning the backstroke.

"Harmon!"

Harmon went under fast. The rifle in his grasp, like the mast of a ship, was the last to go down.

"*Fuck!*" he screamed. "Harmon!"

He fired to the right, finished off his clip, heard someone cry out and saw a VC falling down out of the fog, making a head-first dive into the canal. He reversed his double clip, fired again, and another person cried out but this time no one fell. Up ahead there was more firing, answered by fire from the bank up on the left. He was reaching under water for Harmon but finding nothing. Then he swung to the left and fired at the flashing bursts of light radiating from the fog.

The firing stopped. Everything stopped. Again there was just the ringing in his ears.

He reached down again, this time found him, pulled him up by the shoulder with one hand. Harmon's head came out bent back, mouth open, water pouring out of it like an overflowing bowl.

"Harmon," he cried.

Then another burst came from the right. It ran past him but the second came straight for him and hit Harmon again across the chest. As he let Harmon go and started for the nearby wall, a man grew visible up on the bank. They fired at each other simultaneously. Water splashed up into his face and before he could reopen his eyes somebody was on top of him, driving him underwater. He tried to close his mouth but it flooded with muddy water, and the guy on top kept pushing him down. He tried opening his eyes but they burned and the silt in the water scratched his eyeballs as he blinked.

Then they hit bottom, him first on his back. His helmet came off as the VC crushed into him and then seemed to give up. He could sense the VC floating, totally listless in the water. He kept his eyes shut as he pushed the body off, hurrying up for some air, and accidentally stuck his hand into the VC's mouth as he gave him the final shove away. The teeth raked his knuckles, but he hardly felt it. He was on his feet rocketing up towards the surface, bubbles ripping away from his face.

The sound of the rain pelting the water rushed into his ears as he broke the surface, gasping for air. He looked up the canal and saw one of the squad clawing at the bank to pull himself up, then suddenly go limp and slip back down as if lowering himself into a tub. It was the sergeant, blood all over his face and mouth wide open as though letting out a silent cry.

He brought his fist up to his mouth to cover his cough and gag, then spit the silty dirt out of his mouth. Then he heard Vietnamese voices over on the far bank and saw, shrouded by the fog, two VC scanning the canal. He raised his rifle, aimed, and let go several rounds. The VC collapsed and fell into the canal with a huge splash which sent a wave across to him.

Then it was quiet yet again. Nearby Harmon floated, face up, chest high, blood over his poncho. Off to his right a VC drifted slowly by, face down, bullet holes in his back.

He rested against the canal wall, letting his head fall all the way back. Now what? Yell? Scream? Catch his breath? Die?

Jesus Christ. This was way too much.

He opened his eyes and brought his head back down. The whole squad was drifting by in front of him like a group of whales. He suddenly felt so cold his feet and hands stung as if they were frostbit. He was shaking so badly he made the water ripple, the bodies around him jiggle and bob.

He closed his eyes and took a couple more deep breaths. They settled him some. He looked up the canal, then across, then down and then behind him. No one was around. The fog seemed thicker, lower too. It was getting darker for sure. They had to have been out at least four or five hours, maybe more. In a couple of hours it would be dusk.

He rechecked his rifle, counted the number of full clips he had left, then scanned the canal again. He'd have to hurry. He could tie the squad together somehow, with their ponchos, make a raft and drift to the river. Patrol boats'd be there if the weather wasn't too bad. He couldn't leave them here, not here in this coffin, this God forsaken hole.

All he had to do was do it. That was all anything was: just a matter of doing it. That was how he was raised. That was what he would do.

His tears dried up as he waded towards Harmon.

"So long, Harmon. I'll see you in hell."

It wasn't as easy as it sounded. You had to move along and fight the current to get the bodies tied together. Plus the stiffness of his cold hands made it hard to secure the knots. Then the damn raft wanted to rotate clockwise all the time. But he kept working, tying anything anywhere he could. It wasn't coming out a square raft. It didn't have any shape. But it worked.

"This way, Mr. Harmon."

Harmon was next to last, the sergeant last, and like most of the others they weren't easy. Plus now the raft was larger it wanted to go drifting down the canal just that much faster, that much more, and his legs were near exhausted and the bottom even more slippery.

"Come on, Harmon," he gasped.

It was like pulling a barge. Harmon's head and shoulders plowed a good wake and he was much heavier than the others. But they made progress and as he got closer he increased his leg speed and dug his feet in deeper to avoid slipping. Out of breath, he reached with his free arm to grab one of the floating ponchos. But on the next step, inches away from grabbing the raft, he ran into some legs trailing underwater and had to force his way between them and kick them aside. Finally he grabbed a poncho and pulled with both arms, hauling Harmon and the raft closer together. But now the damn raft was rotating again, the guys' legs forcing him out of the way. He decided it was best to go with the flow, and walked backwards with the raft, fighting to stay up as he tried to tie one long piece of Harmon's poncho to somebody else's, some other guy's.

"Fucking piece of shit!"

But finally he did it, even though Harmon didn't look all that comfortable.

"It ain't the best seat, buddy. But it's better than being cramped in the inside." He let Harmon go, stepping out of the way as the raft began to spin like a merry-go-round.

He was looking for the sergeant but found two Vietnamese first and tied them together for the hell of it, though he wasn't sure what to do with them. Then there was still no sergeant. The raft was drifting farther away and the only thing he could think of was the sergeant had somehow gotten hung up somewhere farther back. But he couldn't go back upstream, not now. Then he saw a body floating downstream several feet ahead of the raft and began running to catch up. Even running downstream his poncho still resisted the water, making his legs ache and his lungs short of breath. Fortunately he was able to pass the raft as it slowed down against a slight bend in the canal, then cut a diagonal to run down the body. But as he got closer he realized the body wasn't wearing a poncho. It was just another Vietnamese.

"Fuck!" How the hell would he explain he hadn't found the sergeant? Everyone would think he had left him out here because he hated him.

Some heartburn came up, searing and constricting his throat. He spit out what he could then let the Vietnamese go, shaking his head, thinking he didn't need this at all. Suddenly he was pressed from behind.

"Ah!"

What had scared the shit out of him was only the raft heading down the canal, determined to make it downstream. Instantly he was entangled once again in a mess of legs, this time with no bottom to step off from or for traction, he grabbed some ponchos and tried to pull himself up from being sucked under. But it was slippery, his hands were still cold and stiff, and the ponchos slipped off the backs of the bodies. He was going down, being plowed under by the raft.

"Help!"

He closed his mouth and eyes as he went under, and dropped straight down onto his rear, letting go of the ponchos up above. A couple of knees knocked him in the face, and then he was entangled in a mess of dangling legs, like a little kid lost in a crowd of adults who have ignored his pleas and kept on walking. He fought with his arms to keep the legs spread apart but they kept pushing on, one after the other, and he was losing air, close to bursting his lungs. He flipped over onto his stomach and fought to get his rifle around too, then lay flat as he could while the squad's feet slowly dragged over his back and head like a windmill in a slight breeze. Longer, he kept telling himself, you can hold on longer, no matter how much his lungs and mouth and his whole face felt like exploding. The legs kept coming, nudging him like they wanted him to roll over, be a man and face his peers. But he stayed flat. He fought the urge to stand up, to escape, to breathe. He squeezed his whole body tighter, forcing the air out of his lungs until his ears popped. Bubbles leaked out of his mouth, nose and the corner of his eyes. Finally the last foot dragged across his back, neck and head. He waited only a second then lifted himself up, sort of like beginning a push-up. He got to one knee feeling a bit faint, and then with his hands on his knees made the final push to surface, eyes still closed. On the way up he let go of his breath, blowing out a few bubbles and taking in some water from the lack of pressure inside. His lower back and legs strained, his body screamed, but he broke the surface gasping for air, spitting out the dirty water he had taken in.

He wiped his panting face and held with one hand onto the bank. The raft was still on its way down the canal, still rotating clockwise up ahead of him, still without the sergeant.

When once again something rammed into him from behind, he turned around and found the two Vietnamese he had tied together earlier trying to encircle him. He tried stepping back and dropping down to shoulder level in the water, but the bodies kept coming. The Vietnamese heads bumped his, the tied shirts started to wrap around his head. He back-pedaled a few steps, took a breath, got his arms under the bodies and lifted, then ducked under again and let the bodies pass overhead.

"*Fuck!*" he screamed when he came back up. "You son of a fucking bitches!" He slapped some water at them. "Pieces of shit." He could kill those bastards.

Yeah, right. You could kill them. You did fucking kill them. So what else could go fucking wrong?

He wiped his face off and started jogging through the water to catch up with the raft. That was all he could do now. He was totally exhausted, and his stomach was burning. But he was going to make it and get most of the squad back.

He caught up with them much quicker than he'd thought he would. But what was he going to do now? He was too tired to keep running. He could ride them, he guessed. He could rest that way. He would need all his strength when they reached the river. Besides, who was to know?

He began humping and pulling his way up onto the backs of the guys of the squad, this time grabbing onto the ponchos up around their necks. It made their heads lift up and look like they were being choked, but at least the ponchos didn't slip like before.

Once he was all the way up it only took one full turn to realize hanging on to the outside of the raft would make him too dizzy. So he started sliding his way towards the center. The bodies were closer together here, and also he would stay further up out of the water, not sink down so much. But it wasn't easy moving. The way the bodies bobbed up and down, every effort was answered with a countermotion, bodies either dunking or drifting apart. Spreading his legs out to distribute his weight helped some, but made his own legs become useless for scooting him across the raft any more. He had to use only his arms, grabbing ponchos by their necks.

Finally he made it, not quite to the center but close enough, and where the bodies felt as if they could hold him. Spread across three of them like this, his shoulders and head were out of the water and the rest of him didn't matter. Soon they would be home. Soon he could rest.

After a while it seemed like the day was getting lighter and the fog was lifting, like they were coming out to a more open area. Then as the raft revolved he could see the confluence of the river and canal. At first it didn't seem too turbulent even though his speed was clearly picking up. Then the raft began bobbing and spinning like a saucer ride at the carnival.

He grabbed on tighter and spread his legs further apart.

"Yahoo!" he whooped. "Ride 'em, cowboys!"

It was great to be out in the open, even though he couldn't see the other bank and it was raining as hard here as anywhere. And then, when the raft next came around to face downstream, there before him was a tree-snag leaning out into the river. All he had to do was pull himself across the bodies and get to the edge in time to grab it and pull them all in. Only trouble was, this time the bodies weren't as cooperative as before. The more he tried to move the more they spread apart, leaving gaps for him to span, until he was spanning a gap that stretched from his feet and chest.

He tried stiffening his legs to keep his body from slumping but all that did was make the body his toes were on sink still further, dunking him into the water up to his waist.

"Shit!"

He was also sliding off the body he had his chest on. Plus he couldn't reach the body in front of him. All he could grab was the end of the guy's poncho and that immediately began to slip. Then his feet slid off the back body. He held on to the body he was still part way on with all his strength, but it rolled over like a log and down he went all the way.

He came back up, grabbing the same body as best as he could and kicking his feet to stay afloat. Then, quicker than he'd estimated, the tree loomed overhead like a giant bony hand. The front of the raft compressed against it so that the bodies began compacting together and all the gaps swiftly closed. He was pinned between two guys, his face pushed into the side of the one in front. He tried rearing and struggling to get at least high enough on the body in front to keep from being suffocated, or being trapped underneath again. Then the raft began rotating counterclockwise, drifting back out into the river. He kicked and reared up to catch a small branch that bent down like a fishing pole when he caught it. He grabbed it with his other hand and, as the raft slowly turned away from the tree, lurched for a larger one. Holding on like that with one hand, he felt the raft move away without him, his stomach and rear sliding between the bodies like a cigarette pulled from a pack. The branch bent down more and he grabbed on with the other hand, twisting as his legs cleared the raft.

As the raft drifted out from under him and he swung free from it the branch broke. Blindly he plummeted into the tree's underwater net of branches, but his head stayed just above the water. The current kept pressure on him, keeping him entangled and pressed against the tree. But finally he rolled to his side, freed his arms, then reached for a branch and pulled himself up.

Time after time, his feet still continued to slip and catch on the underwater branches. Then, when he started to climb onto the trunk his rifle caught under a branch.

"Fucking piece of shit."

He yanked on it and came close to hitting himself in his face as it pulled free.

"You fucker!"

He looked down the river but didn't have to look far. Not twenty yards away the raft had fallen prey to another part of the huge leafless tree.

He was steaming mad by the time he made it to the bank, thanks to getting tripped up constantly in all the tiny branches. Everyone could fucking die as far as he was concerned, he didn't give a fuck if the whole world blew itself up. But what pissed him off the most was that the raft was a mess, not to mention the branches poking guys in the heads and faces and everywhere else. But fuck it, he couldn't do anything. No way was he going back out in the water. Not for all the tea in China. As for the guys trailing out into the river like the tail of a kite, well, they were dead anyway. And they could go to hell, too.

He shook his head. There was no need to get upset. He had done his duty, the best he could. He should feel lucky he got them this far.

He stared at the raft for a moment. Then he felt like he had to pee. That was great. All he needed now was to get shot while he was holding his dick.

Where the fuck was he anyway? He looked around. Nothing but fog, rain and more rain. But what did he care?

He peed and then sat down for the duration, letting his head take the brunt of the rain.

Being alone is scary. Everything heard or seen is the enemy. Everything not heard or seen is the enemy. The only noises are inside the head, along with the little twitches and pains inside the body. Not having someone around makes a whole lot of difference, even if that presence doesn't make a whole lot of difference. In other words, dead bodies help. For one, they don't bring up the negatives of the situation. Like that you could die out here all alone.

It was maybe an hour, maybe two, time enough to count the bodies about twenty times, enough to worry he hadn't found the sergeant, that he didn't know where he was, that he wished he'd taken more time to look for the squad radio, that he'd been closer to the squad when he was bringing up the rear. The fact was, he fucking daydreamed too much. Still, after maybe an hour, maybe two, they found him. It turned out he had somehow ended up near the rendezvous.

"You're the only one?" the Navy chief asked again.

"Yeah."

"No one else?"

"No." Suddenly he didn't have the urge to get back so soon after all, especially if everyone was going to question him about what had happened. But what could they say? He'd killed a bunch of VC.

Maybe he had killed them all. He hadn't run away. He had stayed to the last man.

Now he realized this whole fucking place, this whole fucking war, any fucking war, was nothing more than fucking suicide. Why he hadn't thought of that when he was in college was beyond him here and now.

"What?" the chief asked, as if he had actually said something.

"Nothing," he said, looking back down at the sailors trying to untie his knots.

# CHAPTER
# EIGHTEEN

"Not bad shit," he said as he passed the joint to Stanley.

"Yeah," Stanley sighed.

The monsoon rains were at their peak, yet somehow Stanley and he remained undaunted, though terribly, terribly stoned. Life was almost at a standstill for the whole base, even for Operations, but he and Stanley just couldn't sit still. They wanted more out of life. So they had built themselves a lean-to out at the end of the landing pad. The area no one ever went to, over near the latrines. He and Stanley didn't mind as long as no one bothered them. And no one did.

So every night they donned their ponchos and trekked out to the Little Home Away From Home, also known as Harmon's Place. It wasn't all that much, just some scrap wood for the sides, corrugated tin for the roof, a board for their asses, torn sandbags full of discarded cans for the part of the back wall above the existing hole in the ground, plus a few real sandbags to hold everything together. Like Harmon would have said, real Southern living.

"I wish Harmon was here, man," Stanley sighed.

So what were they going to do? Sit in the lean-to all night and watch the rain and moan over Harmon's death? He'd done that all week, thank you. He didn't feel like doing it anymore. His strategy had changed to blocking out that part of his life. Now his sole purpose in meeting out here, braving the weather and the night, was getting high.

"Harmon would have some stories," Stanley sighed again.

"Yeah, like I'm in the mood to laugh," he replied.

"Man, you are so cynical at times. You know that, man?"

Stanley meant it. He was angry. But what the fuck had he done?

"And stop trying to make this fucking place so neat and tidy all the time," Stanley scorned. "I'm tired of it. It ain't nothing but a trash heap anyway. It don't need to be beautiful."

All right, already. He wouldn't touch a fucking thing. Let the fucking thing leak like a sieve, what the fuck did he care?

Stanley set his forehead on his knees, rubbed it some and yawned. Then it seemed like for a while he didn't breathe. "I hate this fucking place," Stanley said finally. "I hate it so Goddamn much I'd shoot my leg off to get out of here."

Stanley wasn't telling him nothing.

"I want to get fucking out of here. *Now.* Pronto. Forever. Understand, man?"

He couldn't let this shit get to him like it was getting to Stanley. Think of sex or something. Anything.

"You know what I heard, man?" Stanley said.

"What?" He was surprised by the sudden change of subject.

"I heard this guy named Doran bumped off a few guys."

"Doran?"

"Stephens' crony."

"Oh, yeah." The guy he had spotted down by the river. "So he's killing people?"

"Fuck, man. You honkies are all alike. You stick together no matter what."

"Hey, fuck you and eat shit. I don't even know what you're talking about."

"Oh yeah?" Stanley went to slap him on the shoulder but he pushed Stanley's arm away. "Fuck you, asshole," Stanley said. "Go be with your white brothers. You're not wanted here."

"Fuck you, asshole," he said. For this grief he could have gone back to his bunk and gotten wet in peace.

But it ended as soon as it had begun. Stanley rested his head back down on his folded arms and knees, leaving only the rain plunking on the tin roof, and the sound of his voice in his own head telling him to keep cool, forget it, don't get hung up on being fucking mad. He and Stanley weren't about to shoot it out. Which reminded him of the note he had found floating in the water near his bunk this morning. He would've thought nothing of it, except for all the other notes people had been finding around camp. So he picked it up and read it but all it said was: Y.A.D.M.

"Hey, you know what the letters Y.A.D.M. mean?"

Stanley didn't bother raising his head. "Your ass is dead meat."

That was quick. "You didn't happen to leave a note by my bunk, did you?"

"Nope."

That was too bad. But what the fuck? He wasn't even sure it was meant for him. Besides, it didn't have to mean what Stanley said. It could mean a lot of things. It wasn't for him anyway. It wasn't that close to his bunk. Someone could have dropped it. It could have floated down from anywhere.

"It could also mean you're a dirty motherfucker," Stanley said. "Or a dumb motherfucker."

"It couldn't mean anything nice, could it?" he joked.

"Not in the English language."

He chuckled. "Well, do I detect a little humor there?"

"No."

Sorry! He hadn't meant to upset Stanley's bad mood. He couldn't wait to go home and let this place and everybody else's problems rot in hell.

"Every time I think of Harmon," Stanley said, "I think of what my mother always told me." Stanley paused. "She told me there were hundreds of dangerous things out there in the world and everyone needed to make sure they didn't fall into any traps. Me especially. She kept a tight rein on me. Didn't want me to get into any trouble. I had to work around the house with her all the time. I especially hated hanging the laundry because all the neighborhood kids would call me a sissy."

Stanley raised his head from where it had been hanging. "Anyway, my mother liked telling me stories to keep me occupied and off the streets. That's why I think of her when Harmon comes to mind. You know how Harmon liked to tell tales."

"Yeah," he nodded, thinking how he'd liked the one about Disneyland.

"Anyway, I wish I had more dope," Stanley lamented. "And I wish Harmon was here."

The sudden thought of dope sent a wave of numbness throughout his body. Their asses were dead meat if they let that problem get out of hand. And Harmon's stash was definitely getting low.

He wiped his forehead and pressed against it hard to spread his headache over a wider area. It had been a long dreary day, with many more to come. That was how Stephens came to mind, Mr. High Society Dope Pusher. Who cared if Doran was killing people? It seemed normal for this place.

Stanley raised his head and pulled out his letters. He had three or four of them, some of them pretty wrinkled and chewed up. One day he'd have to ask Stanley more about his mother. She sure did seem like one hell of a letter writer, that was for sure.

This July fifteenth, his birthday was turning out to be one hell of a day. First he woke up to find a guy pissing several feet from his bunk through the unfixed hole from the base attack five months ago. First the guy was swirling it around, and then he shook it for a long time, jiggling off the last few drops and then some. Finally the guy let go of his cock, pulling his pants out so it fell back in place all by itself, untouched by human hands. Now that was something to write home about.

But birthdays were supposed to be fun, and he needed to forget about Harmon anyway. So he decided to sweep out all the caked dirt from his bunk. He would find some soap and take a sponge bath. He would wash his pants and shirts and even polish his boots, though he knew the moment he stepped outside it would all be a waste.

So maybe he should just forget it. Maybe instead he should just think about a new name for the crap out there waiting for him and everyone else. Slick, soupy and mud were old tired names. Pig slop was okay, but he wasn't a farmer. Shit was better, but he wanted to reserve it for other things. Diarrhea was better yet. It described his condition this fine day, this past week in fact. Better known as the shits.

The next thing making July fifteenth such a lovely day was lunch. His ration box was virtually empty, except for a note explaining it all. It said: Hi! How's the weather where you are? It's raining cats and dogs here. Hope you are having fun. Have a nice lunch. Good luck.

What he was missing was: one can of spaghetti and meatballs; one can of applesauce; one package of crackers and one chocolate bar. Contents present were: napkin, fork, knife, spoon, can opener, salt and pepper, and one small can of Vienna sausage, partly opened.

So Happy Birthday, sucker. You deserve it.

However, he did receive a birthday card, first communication from his parents since he'd gone away. That didn't bother him. He hadn't written either, and his family never had communicated well or much long distance. In fact, far as that goes they didn't do all that well in close proximity, either. But it was his birthday and there was no need to start blaming people. His parents had taken the time to wish him a happy birthday. They even sent him a check for ten bucks. He guessed they didn't know there was no place to cash it here. But then, maybe he could sign it over to Stephens for at least one joint.

# CHAPTER
# NINETEEN

August 31st was the last day. It had to not rain today for August not to be one long rainy day.

It was cloudy.

In a way he had lost the bet. Although it didn't rain, the sun didn't come out either. The bet was strictly rain or shine. Yet he hadn't shaken on it so it didn't really count. Besides, he had made it with himself. And besides that, nothing counted out here in the marsh, except maybe the number of leeches on his legs and groin. But what was a patrol without a little inconvenience?

Oh boy, he was in another great mood today. Five in a row, to go along with five days of patrols in the marsh. Never dries when it rains was his motto. In other words, go tell someone who gives a shit. Of course, talking to himself didn't help. Just the same, if he had to break through one more wall of tall grass he would shoot himself. For Christsake, an elephant could walk by and he'd never know. That was why they called it elephant grass, stupid.

Oh, yeah. He forgot. Sorry.

He stopped when he heard the voices coming from his left. Three of them, or maybe four. A girl screamed. There was a sound like a slap. The girl whimpered. Some guy was mad. They couldn't be more than twenty yards away. But what the fuck was happening?

The girl let out another cry, more subdued than before. Now he knew what was happening. Yet he still couldn't move. His feet were planted like trees. What the fuck was he supposed to do?

"Yahoo!"

Someone was having fun at someone else's expense. He should stop it. Just walk out there and stop it. They wouldn't shoot him. Would they?

"Ahhh!"

Holy fucking shit, some guy was coming. The thought of it made him shake from head to toe. He swallowed, forcing himself not to choke or gag out loud.

The girl screamed again. Then there was a slap but no cry.

"Hey, man. Don't fucking knock her out. I haven't had my turn."

Do something. Move. Anything. Get the fuck out of here.

He started to move but his first step made him stop and think. The least he could do was take care of the girl afterwards, help her back to her hamlet, anything but run. Oh yeah, right. Be the big hero. The truth was maybe he wanted some too, or at least a look at her without her clothes on. It had been a long time since Greta, the blonde bombshell.

He started towards the reeds separating him from them and strangely enough felt less scared and more excited. But still he didn't want to be caught. So he hunkered down, waddling like a duck until he got close enough to see. There were three of them as he had guessed. Two white guys and one black. The black was on her now. But she was a lot younger than he had imagined. She wasn't just a girl. She was a small girl.

Jesus, he was a sick son of a bitch.

"Come on," the tall white guy complained. "We don't have all day."

The black guy didn't respond. He was humping wildly, bouncing above her wide open legs with all his weight and engulfing her completely.

"Come on!" the tall white guy yelled again.

The other white guy was just standing there, watching as if he had nothing better to do. Then he realized who it was. It was Doran, Stephens' crony, the guy he had spotted down by the river. He was surprised at what a shrimpy kind of guy Doran was now that he got a good look at him. A skinny, hollow-chested guy with a black heavy beard.

"Yeah," the black guy bellowed now as he backed away and put it in his pants. The girl had blood and ooze running out from between her legs. They had ripped her clothing apart.

"My turn," the tall white guy with them said as he dropped his pants and knelt down in front of her, his erection pointing to the sky. He spread her legs back open and grabbed her tiny breasts like he was trying to rip them off. When she grimaced and began to cry again he reached up and slapped her. "Keep quiet, or I'll kill you."

Just as the tall white guy entered her a helicopter came within sight overhead. Doran stepped forward and knocked the tall white guy on his side.

"Hey!" the white guy yelped.

"Move it, sucker," Doran barked. "We got to get out of here."

"Fuck, man—"

"You'll get more later, you slob. *Move it!*"

Checking the perimeter for his own escape route, he also kept an eye on the tall white guy jumping up and pulling on his pants. As he watched the guy try to stuff his erection in his pants, he was startled by a blast that almost made him lose his balance. Then a second shot went off and he turned in time to see the girl's body shudder.

"What the fuck you doing, man?" the black guy was saying in a panicky voice.

"Shut up and get out of here," Doran ordered, lowering his rifle.

The tall white guy was frozen looking down at the body, his pants still unbuttoned.

"Move it!" Doran yelled, shoving the guy along.

He looked back at the body as the three of them left. She was shot in the chest and head. She lay still with one leg extended, one foot turned out to the side. The other leg was bent and leaning out from her too. But her legs truly weren't much of anything. Her whole body, in fact, was mostly bones. Small bones. Very small bones.

His legs could hardly stand when he tried to rise up. His feet were stuck in the mud. He should have stopped them. He should have walked out and stopped them. He couldn't have saved her. She would have been raped, but she'd be alive. Fuck, he had fucked up.

Goddamn it. You are such a fucking dumbshit.

He struggled out of the marsh and up onto the mound of land where it had happened. The choppers were still roaring around in the distance, now out of sight. Doran and the other two were completely gone. He looked back at the girl, first at her vagina and the blood and ooze surrounding it, then at her chest to the left of her tiny right breast where the bullet hole was. Then to the slight wound an inch or so above her right eye near the temple.

Jesus fucking Christ.

Bits of her torn clothes were hanging in the reeds as if a tornado had blown them around. The least he could do was cover her up, keep the flies and bugs off her. Then he would report what he had found, and she would get picked up.

He went over to her and covered what he could with the strips of clothing. First her vagina, her sunken belly, then up to her chest. Her skin was so smooth looking. Her legs so sleek and slender. She had pretty black hair too. A nice face, a young face. Maybe twelve or thirteen. No more than that.

He stared at the cut on her lower lip. It had swelled some. Blood had streamed down her chin onto her neck. The fucking bugs were having a feast, no matter how many times he swatted. Then he noticed something almost imperceptible. Her lips were quivering. Her eyes were not completely shut.

It was like she was playing possum. But it had to be reflexes. She couldn't be alive.

He leaned over placing his ear near her nose, but as he listened a firefight began somewhere off to his left, some helicopter gunships firing their cannons. He checked for her pulse but couldn't find one. Yet he had a feeling she was watching him. He didn't like that, didn't want to be the last one she saw. Besides, he'd better get out of here.

Then he saw something that wasn't there before. A tear. He was sure when he had first looked it hadn't been there.

Suddenly a chopper scared the crap out of him by zooming overhead. He jumped up and dashed for the reeds. The chopper had been banking to the left so he was sure they hadn't seen him. He hoped they hadn't seen him. He'd be in a world of shit if they had.

He looked back at the girl. Fuck! When he'd jumped away he must have pulled some of her clothes off. God fucking damn it. He couldn't leave her naked. He shook his head, looked up at the sky, listened. The chopper was going away. He jumped up and ran over to her, throwing the clothing scraps over her, not worrying about how it looked.

But now there was another tear starting from the other eye.

What the fuck was he going to do? If he carried her she'd be dead in no time. If he left her she would die slowly, rotting in the heat with bugs all over her, remembering what had happened.

He stood up. He unslung his rifle, raised it to his shoulder, aimed it at her forehead. Maybe she would thank him. Maybe she would hate him. It didn't matter though. Head shots were the quickest. It was the only thing to do.

Tears filled his eyes without spilling over onto his cheeks. When he fired the shot jerked her head back and twisted it to the side.

An electrical jolt bolted through both his arms as the rifle dropped away, out of his hands. A sudden pain attacked his chest and he wanted to reach for it but his arms tingled useless at his sides.

"Goddamn it," he gasped, reeling in pain. For a moment he thought he would die.

Then he bent over to retrieve his rifle. His right hand had regained most of its control so he tried grabbing the strap. But to do that he had to bend over more and as he did he felt his helmet starting to slip. His legs still felt rubbery as he leaned over and reached as far as he could, so far his helmet fell off, hit his hand and rifle, bounced on the ground, and started rolling towards the girl's extended leg.

"Fuck."

He hobbled over, regaining some strength, but still managed to stumble as he reached the helmet and kicked it still closer to the girl. Then he heard the chopper coming back around, left the helmet behind, and ducked into the reeds near the body.

The chopper came over within a few seconds, this time making a wider sweep above the mound. He could see the pilot and co-pilot but not if they'd seen him. The chopper came around one more time, then zoomed off firing its cannons.

He felt better now. His composure was back. He stood up and checked behind him to make sure no more choppers were coming. Then, in one motion, he ran past her, bending down to scoop the helmet up as he went by. But he only managed to grab the lip, and then, as he brought the helmet up, the damn thing slipped out of his fingers. He tried trapping it against his side but the helmet bobbled away from his hand, and landed out in front of him and before he could stop running he kicked it again, so it shot out from him, bouncing like a ball right to the edge of the mound, then down into the water, where it landed like an upside-down turtle.

"You son of a bitch!" he yelled, and fired two rounds from the hip. The first one missed but the second one grazed it, rotating it a quarter turn.

This was fucking stupid. But the helicopter was making another round. He could see it coming now. He dashed into the reeds grabbing the helmet firmly this time, holding it so hard against his chest the rim dug into his skin.

"Fucking piece of shit."

The chopper roared over again and banked sharply to head back. As soon as it straightened out and vanished from sight he started sprinting down the narrow embankment, without bothering to look back or put his helmet on. He just ran, until he came upon a huge pond at the end of the bank. Then, as he stopped he slipped in the mud and fell down on one knee. His helmet popped out from under his arm, landed in the water, and sank out of sight.

"*Fucking Goddamn it! You son of a fucking bitch!*" He looked up and raised his rifle at the sky. "*God* fucking damn you! *Kill me,* you son of a bitch! Get it over with, you worthless piece of *shit!* Cocksucker!"

He looked back down at the pond where the helmet had sunk. "You ain't fucking shit, man. You ain't fucking shit."

"Where were you?" Stanley asked.

"I got lost," he muttered, flopping himself down inside the chopper bay and looking out to avoid Stanley's stare. In the other chopper he saw Doran, sitting like him, staring blankly out as if nothing had ever happened.

Doran's chopper lifted off. Then his did.

He looked off in the distance but no way would he be able to spot her lying in the reeds. Still, he could picture her there, strips of clothing strewn over her, blood dribbling down her forehead. But he still didn't seem to care, no matter what he thought. It was really just another day.

# CHAPTER TWENTY

Well, what do you know? Here comes Mr. Stephens. Mr. Cool. Mr. Neat and Clean. Mr. Dope Entrepreneur. What the hell would Stephens want with him? He guessed he'd soon find out. Maybe Stephens hid his dope supplies out here in the lean-to without anyone knowing it. He could have been sitting out here all this time on a gold mine while doing everything short of eating his fingers to get the last scrap of dope into his starving body. Yeah, that would be about his fucking luck. If Stanley was here, he'd agree. He wasn't in any better shape.

"Enjoying the evening?" Stephens asked, kneeling down in front of the lean-to, but making sure his knees didn't touch the ground.

"I was," he said.

Stephens smiled. "Once a tough guy, always a tough guy?"

"Maybe."

He couldn't wait for the show to begin. He hadn't seen it himself but he had heard from Harmon that this guy had his shit together, and it was smooth. He could palm a joint or two to you and take your money as he let go of the handshake. He could do it right in front of anybody and they wouldn't know. Plus Stephens had any other dream you might like. All packaged. All expensive. All risks to be borne by the consumer. Sweet dreams.

"Not too bad around here when it's not raining." Stephens looked up at the evening sky. "I hear come November all this sky-is-falling stuff will cease."

"It's only September," he said.

"Well, I could make the time go by faster for you. If you want."

He gave Stephens his mean-eyed look. Why suddenly was Stephens so interested in him? It had been months since Stephens had even said boo! Was business getting bad? Did Stephens feel the need to expand his horizons?

Stephens chuckled. "I like you, Thorne. You don't let anybody get by with any shit. I respect that. There isn't a guy here that doesn't. And that's damn good in this hole. There's no one here that respects anyone. So you're sort of the unsung hero here."

This guy was full of shit.

"You might think I'm jiving you," Stephens said. "But I'm not. You're too much of a loner maybe to realize it. But it's true. Everyone respects a hard worker."

So give him an award then.

"So I can make you a deal."

All right.

Stephens pulled a Thai stick from his sleeve and held it straight up by one end. "You can have this for nothing. It's a present. An award, you might say. But when you want more you'll have to pay the price like everyone else. We can't have the best liked guy on the base getting too many deals. Then he wouldn't be liked any more, would he?"

"Probably not," he said.

"But be assured my prices are competitive and probably lower than what you're paying now. And the quality goes without saying."

"I could take this and never see you again."

"And I could kill you," Stephens answered quickly and evenly. "But just let me check some items here."

"Don't bother," he said as Stephens pulled a little black notebook from his breast pocket. He wanted this asshole out of here before Stanley showed up.

"Yes. According to my figures you can have this void of any obligation. Do with it what you want. You don't even have to see my pretty face again. But I have a feeling you will, and on your own recognizance."

As Stephens held out the Thai stick, he noticed Stephens' notebook had the same lined paper as the 'Y.A.D.M.' note he had found by his bunk weeks ago. But there were a lot of those notebooks around.

"A deal?"

He kept his eyes on Stephens' as he took the Thai stick. To his surprise they looked slightly glassy.

"Good," Stephens grinned. "I'm glad you trust me."

"I don't."

"I was wondering," Stephens began, ignoring his last comment, "whatever happened to that friend of yours when we first met out on the river?"

Fucking asshole. Stephens knew what had happened. "He's dead."

"That's too bad. He seemed like a nice fellow."

"I'll tell his folks you said that."

"Thank you. I'd appreciate that." Stephens stood up and looked around. He noticed how polished Stephens' belt buckle was.

"Well, I'm glad we could do business," Stephens said as he looked back down. "We white people must stick together. It's a mean world out there."

He held up the Thai stick. "Then here's to our friendship."

Stephens smiled.

When Stephens left he noticed Doran standing no more than ten yards away, his rifle slung over his shoulder, and what looked like a semi-automatic tucked in the front of his pants. Doran was smiling, laughing to himself, as if he'd just seen something funny, or thought of a joke he liked.

He didn't know what was going on but Stanley didn't show up. So he waited and waited but Stanley still didn't show. Which made him mad. Which made him think about Stephens, then Doran, then the raped girl. So he decided to go back to his bunk, at least get some sleep. He could wait another day to smoke the Thai stick. In the meantime maybe try facing reality on its own terms for once. He didn't want this girl thing to haunt him the rest of his life.

When he entered the barracks he found some of the guys were playing cards at a table they had made up by the door, in the light of a lantern they had hung from the ceiling loops using someone's belt. It was ingenious, but he hoped they didn't want to play all night.

"Hey, Thorne. Want to join us?"

"No thanks. I got a watch."

"Don't we all."

"Hey," another guy said. "Did you hear about why God gave women legs?"

"No, I haven't," he said, stopping briefly.

"So they could get off their backs to do the housework."

Everyone laughed so he laughed a little too, even though it wasn't all that funny, plus he wasn't in the mood. It reminded him of the girl again, like so many things did. So the guys went back to playing cards without him and as usual he leaped over the hole in the floor and looked up at the rip in the canvas, thanking the Lord once again for a non-rainy day. Someday he'd have to fix that. Maybe after monsoon season, when the bugs would get in.

He knelt down by his bunk and completed the homecoming routine by running his hand along the bottom rail to see how much the rats had chewed away. Some sucker had started another bowl-shaped dip a few inches from his head. They seemed to like it by his head no matter which way he slept, so he had given up on trying to fool them.

He rolled into the bunk slowly, stretching out his legs, keeping his heels an inch or so off the mattress. He held them up until his lower back and groin began to burn, and then counted to ten before slowly lowering them. With his arms at his sides he was safely home again. Who cared if it was damp and stunk?

He turned his head to the side and closed his eyes. But his cheek touched something cold and wet on his makeshift pillow, as if someone had spit there. He pulled back, opened his eyes, and found a dark object setting on his bundled shirt. At first it looked like the collar of the shirt but then it seemed to move. He rose up on one elbow and swatted it away with the other hand. But he hit more of his shirt than the bug and the bug didn't go far. It landed on his bunk right next to his groin. He twisted away from it but the bug didn't move at all, and now it didn't look like a bug, didn't have the shape of one, unless it was mushed.

Fuck.

He pulled out his matches, lit one, and made out some pale curves and folds and some red smudges. As he brought the match closer and bent over it became evident it was an ear that had been cut off with a sharp knife, so its severed edge was razor smooth.

The match burned his fingertips.

"Goddamn it," he swore. "Jesus fucking Christ." He dropped the match on the bed, where it went out by itself. He sucked and blew his fingers, but the skin wasn't burnt bad. How in hell did an ear end up on his bunk? A rat maybe. But more likely another message, one that wouldn't accidentally float away, one he'd know for sure was meant for him. But who from? Stephens? Funny he had shown up suddenly. Or maybe Doran. He had been seeing a lot of him lately too. Maybe Doran knew he knew about the raped girl. Maybe Doran was telling him that this could be him. In any case, he didn't need this shit.

A rat suddenly poked its head over the back corner of his bunk. Its nose was up in the air, twitching in search of a scent. Then it saw him, stopped sniffing, and looked straight back. It was a big mother, but they all were here. And no matter how cute their long snout and whiskers were, they all needed to be blown away.

As soon as he took hold of his rifle the rat began crawling onto the bunk. Then it scurried down the rail until the ear was midway between them, a foot or so away.

The rat twitched some more and then froze, as if it were part of the bed rail. Maybe it thought it was hiding. Maybe it was waiting for him to make his move. It had a slight advantage but he had a rifle. Though shooting it would scare the hell out of the boys playing cards.

"I know what you want, fucker. You don't kid me."

Sure enough, as he reached for the ear the rat's nose twitched again, and its eyes looked even deeper, darker, with a shine to them.

He laughed. "Go ahead, fucker. Go for it."

As his hand got closer the rat took a cautious step onto the bunk. The fucker was big, about the size of a half-grown kitten, and with one hell of a long tail. It placed the other foot on the bunk, and he jerked his hand back a bit.

"You fucker. You scared me." This was fun. "Go ahead. Go for it."

The rat moved one of its back legs down.

"Beat it," he said in a deep voice.

It brought its last leg down, its nose still twitching. Then, it stretched its neck towards the ear.

"Get out of here, you son of a bitch."

The rat went for it. He jumped back but also raised his rifle up and swung it. The rifle stock hit the rat broadside as it snatched at the ear, so it let go and scurried off and over the end of the bunk.

"Yahoo!" he yelled.

"What's going on back there?" someone shouted from the card game. "You beating off again?"

Oh, fuck off. He was having fun for once. In fact, he couldn't believe how excited he was. He was laughing. Jesus Christ.

"Come on back," he whispered. "We'll have a rematch."

But when he looked back down at the bed, the ear was still there. He still had to do something with it. He wasn't about to keep the Goddamn thing.

Shit.

He reached over and picked it up by the top fold. Like pulling on a kid's ear to make him come along. Between his thumb and index finger it felt callous and dense. Some heartburn came up. His hand tingled like it was falling asleep. But now that he had it, it felt like a permanently attached piece of flesh.

"Goddamn it."

He moved to the end of his bunk, looking for the rip in the side wall. It was hard to see in the dark, but after several seconds his eyes adjusted. He flipped the ear like a Frisbee and to his surprise it went where he'd aimed it, through the widest part of the tear.

He looked at his hand but it was too much to go wash. So he wiped it on the post first and then on his pants. It didn't matter that much anyway. As it was he was filthy beyond belief. But he did turn over his pillow, so as not to have that shit anywhere near his face.

He stretched out again, keeping his heels up until the count of ten.

"Hey, Thorne. Do you know why God gave women a pussy?"

"No," he said. Suddenly the ear came back to mind. He could feel it on the tips of his fingers, the deadness making them feel cold.

"So men will talk to them."

Everyone thought that was funny too. But all he could think of was that damn ear. Outside, when the laughter died down, he could hear the rats fighting over it. It sounded like a cat fight. He closed his eyes and saw the raped girl with rats all over her, chewing off her nipples and ears.

He opened his eyes. Looked like he wasn't going to get to sleep tonight either. And now he had to think hard about Stephens and Doran.

# CHAPTER
# TWENTY-ONE

"Where did you get all this scrap lumber, man?" asked Stanley, looking down from the edge of the hole.

"I found it," he said. "I'm the King of the Scrounges. It's a great family tradition."

He went back to slicing the walls of the old mortar hole to make them more plumb. He had designed his new hovel in a T-shape so the leg was the entrance ramp and the crossbar was the long and narrow all-in-one kitchen, living room and bedroom. It was just big enough for him to stretch out his legs and lean back, like a guy in a chaise-lounge. He had also dug channels around the outer perimeter so the rainwater would drain away from it, a trick he had seen Boy Scouts do.

"What's the board for?"

"The floor," he said, tossing out a shovelful of mud.

"The tin's the roof?"

"Yeah," he grunted.

"You won't be able to stand up in it?"

"Nope."

"Water won't fill the bottom?"

"I'm going to have the floor raised a bit just in case."

"Where you going to store your stuff?"

"I don't have much stuff," he said.

"Seems cramped to me," Stanley said.

He growled under his breath and went back to digging. Stanley knelt down and looked closer at the hole. If Stanley didn't like it that was fine with him. It was his place, not Stanley's. "It ain't supposed to be a palace," he told Stanley.

"That's for sure."

"Hey! It's better than that damn tent I'm in. At least it'll be quiet."

"You might be able to move in my place. I can talk to the brothers about it."

"No, this is fine," he said. "I don't want to get into any more trouble than I'm in already."

"The brothers won't kill you, man," Stanley said.

"I'm not worried about them."

"Yeah," Stanley said. "I heard you, man."

He went back to his shoveling. He had to get this done by dark and before it started raining again.

"It's going to be damp."

"Hey," he said rising up. "Go sleep in my bunk if you want to feel damp."

"I can't see how you're going to keep the rain out."

"Jesus Christ, get off my case for Godsake. It ain't perfect. But I ain't living in that fucking tent anymore. It fucking stinks. It's fucking wet. Fucking rats all over the place. Okay?"

"Well, fuck you, man," Stanley said as he stood back up. "Just don't drown in your sleep."

"Thanks. I won't." He went back to digging and ignored Stanley standing over him just like a boss. Sometimes Stanley fucking bugged the hell out of him.

"We going to smoke tonight?" Stanley asked.

"Yes," he said, still pissed.

"Just asking, man."

"I got to get this done, all right?"

Stanley held up his hands. "Don't shoot, man."

He shook his head and jammed his shovel into one of the walls, so a larger section of it than he'd wanted came tumbling down. When he looked up again, Stanley was gone. Stanley must have known he was about ready to pulverize the whole thing with his shovel. This whole project was quickly becoming a pure pain in the ass. He just knew he couldn't live in that barracks anymore. The thought of it sent shivers up and down his spine. More and more he couldn't stand being near people at all. Even his own little dark corner of the barracks was too close.

And yes, he wished fucking Harmon was here. Harmon would know what to do.

He looked down at the pile of fallen dirt. Maybe he could make a shelf or something, anything. It didn't matter. Not now or later.

A couple large raindrops plunked down on the sheet of tin he had for the roof. It sounded like pebbles were hitting it. They even made the tin tremble some. Then more fell. He looked up at the sky beginning to pack tight with gray clouds again, like tuna in a can. A drop hit him on his right cheek, and some of it sprayed into his eye.

"You fucking piece of shit."

When he lowered his eyes he noticed someone standing by the lean-to, twenty yards away. At first he thought it was Stanley again, but it wasn't. It was Stephens, his hands stuffed in his pockets. Off to the left a few yards was Doran, in a mountain-man pose, his rifle cradled across his arms.

He had figured Stephens might make trouble for him since he was striking out on his own. He was sure all this was against army regulations. But Stephens abruptly left as soon as he made eye contact with him.

So he grabbed his rifle and placed it within arm's reach between him and Doran, then went back to digging. If he had to he'd drop down in his little foxhole for cover.

More drops of rain pinged on the tin. Then some pelted him on the head and back.

Anything else you got in store for me, God?

As he started back in digging, his mind flashed on the girl in the reeds. What he'd done was the Christian thing to do, period. He had ended her suffering. Never mind he'd never told anyone. God knew, didn't he? Maybe that was why she kept coming back, that is, whenever he thought about God. So maybe he should forget about God altogether. He had never believed in Him anyway, especially since coming here.

When he looked up, Doran was gone.

✧✧✧

Since it was Friday. Since he had completed his hootch for the most part. Since it was raining. Since they didn't have anything else to do, he invited Stanley over for a housewarming party.

"Make sure the door's shut tight," he said.

"Tight? How could this thing be tight?" Stanley struggled with the corrugated tin sheet, banging it into the roof and gutter and slicing dirt from the sides.

"Not so fucking hard! You're going to bring the fuckin' place down, for Christsake."

"Well, how do you close this fucking thing then? I can't see a fucking thing. Why don't you light that candle?"

"I can't until the door is closed. The lieutenant got on my ass already about the light shining out."

"Oh, fuck him," Stanley said. "There ain't a soul within a hundred miles of here."

"Just fucking set it on the board, please," he said.

"Easy for you to say," Stanley grunted.

Probably easier for him to do, too.

"I've been in this poncho for so long," Stanley said as he adjusted the door, "I know what my dick feels like in a rubber. You know what I mean, man?"

Yeah, he knew. Still, he was worried about the door.

"Is that good enough?" Stanley asked.

"I guess so."

"Don't worry about it," Stanley said. "There ain't a soul out there except the guards, and they ain't doing nothing but nothing."

He lit the candle as Stanley crunched up in the corner, knees against his chest. The wavering light made it seem like they were sitting by a campfire.

"Well, let's get the party going," Stanley said.

He lit the Thai stick Stephens had given him and the hootch quickly filled with the aromatic smoke, the kind that would get them high just smelling it, just thinking about it. That was one advantage of having such a small place.

Stanley breathed in a huge hit and held it as though he were underwater. "Good shit," Stanley finally said, handing the Thai back.

He took another hit off the Thai stick and handed it back, but Stanley held up his hands and shook his head. Okay, he'd take another one then. What the hell? It was his party. But by the time he raised it to his lips it seemed like a lifetime had passed. Like this was a different day, a different night, a shorter candle.

"What's wrong?" Stanley asked, letting out the smoke through his nostrils.

"Nothin'." Though the smoke blowing out of Stanley's nose made him remember Harmon.

"So what do you think?"

"About what?"

"About life," Stanley said.

"Yeah."

"Yeah?" Stanley frowned.

"Yeah, it's nuts."

"That's what I think too," Stanley said.

Better put the Thai stick out before he wasted any of it. He pinched it with his wet fingers and then crushed it on the floor board.

"Do you know any smart guys in the army?" Stanley asked.

"Not that I know of," he said.

"That a fact?" Stanley said.

"That's a fact."

"I guess they don't want us to get any ideas," Stanley said.

"I don't have any ideas," he said.

"Me neither."

He looked at the Thai stick still in his hands. Yeah, right. Have some more!

"I wish you'd make this coffin bigger. It ain't big enough for two people."

"It wasn't built for two people," he said. He was tired of Stanley always putting his place down.

"If I was a woman you wouldn't be saying that."

"You ain't a woman," he said.

"Well, I'll leave then," Stanley said.

"Go ahead, asshole. And don't bother coming back."

"I won't."

Stanley snuffed the candle by pinching the flame. Then he reared up and busted his way out of the hootch like a raging bull, knocking the door completely out of the entrance way.

"Hey, fucknut! Watch it," he said as he followed Stanley out.

"Take this Goddamn hole of yours and shove it up your ass, honky!"

"Yeah? Well, eat shit, motherfucker!"

Stanley didn't bother looking back. He made a beeline towards the latrines and when he got to one went straight in. But fuck him. Stanley could die and eat shit. He was tired of this fighting all the time. If Stanley had a chip on his shoulder, well, he could lay it on someone else. The fact was he didn't even like Stanley. He only knew him because of Harmon. Harmon had soul, but all Stanley had was a big mouth. Stanley was more the everyday complainer type. Christ, if Stanley didn't want to be here than why'd he let himself get drafted? Harmon never complained. Harmon did his work and didn't try to escape from it. Plus he would give the shirt off his back to help. Plus he also managed to be his own person. The best Stanley could do was bitch. Shit, he was glad he didn't spend much time with Stanley. He'd go crazy.

He picked up the door and tried to straighten the part Stanley had bent. It wasn't all that bad, but it wasn't perfect. Still, standing out in the pouring rain wasn't his idea of fun. He'd have to fix it later. He rushed back inside setting the door in its usual position. The bend let a few drops in but it wasn't as bad as he'd thought. At least it only dripped in the entrance way.

He leaned back and stretched out his legs. Water dripped from his hair down his face and the back of his neck. He should have put his helmet on before he stormed out, but it was too late now. And it was too late to light the candle. And too late to apologize. He hadn't meant all that shit about Stanley. Stanley had to put up with him too, and lately he'd hardly been a gem of a friend. Anyway, it was better to sleep and enjoy being high. That was what he was, wasn't he? High?

Fuck, he had to stop losing his temper so quickly. Or quit smoking. God knows he couldn't do both.

On his way back to his hootch a few days later, he found Stanley in the lean-to, staring out at the rain with his legs tucked up against his chest and his letters clutched in his hand. They had hardly said a word to each other since the housewarming party. Harmon would have tried to coax them back together, but Harmon was gone. All they had was each other. Which might not be all that much.

"Been out here long?" he asked.

"No."

"Nice day, huh?" He thought he might entice Stanley to bitch a little, sort of bring things back to normal. But Stanley just kept staring out at the rain. "So you going to shoot every honky on the base?"

Stanley finally looked up at him. "I could start with you."

"Don't do me any favors."

That made Stanley chuckle, and broke the ice a little. "Where you headed to?" Stanley asked.

"I was going to go back to my place to try and write a letter."

"Who to?"

"Home."

Stanley sighed. "I should do that too."

He should do it for the first time. It had been over eleven months since he had left home for boot camp, and he hadn't even thanked them for the birthday card. As far as his parents knew he was dead. But what could he tell them? That he killed people? That he'd shot a girl almost point-blank in the face? At least it would take their minds off being disappointed he'd dropped out of college. Jesus Christ, what was he going to write about? What was he thinking?

"You really going to write?" Stanley asked.

"No," he sighed.

"Want to smoke?"

He chuckled. "Sure. My place or yours?"

"Yours," Stanley said. "I've been waiting for you."

As Stanley got up out of the lean-to, he noticed Stanley still had his letters in his hand. For a second, as Stanley held his hand out and the rain began to spatter over them, he thought Stanley was handing them over to him. But instead Stanley dropped them, then buried them in the mud with his foot, twisting them back and forth until they were so smeared and ripped no one would be able to read them again.

"Let's go," Stanley said.

# CHAPTER
# TWENTY-TWO

He found Stephens standing in the rain by his hootch, and immediately scanned the area for Doran. There Doran was, over by the latrines this time, semi-automatic in hand. Meanwhile, here beside the hootch, the clanging sound of the rain on the roof was as loud as if a dozen metal workers were beating the tin.

"Oh!" Stephens exclaimed. "You scared me. I didn't hear you coming."

"Kind of loud around here," he said, noticing Stephens was still clean in spite of all the mud.

"So does this float?"

"Only on dry land."

Stephens laughed, but he didn't. He just wanted to get home, get out of the rain, and not have to deal with anyone. That was his official mood these lovely days.

"Well, I see I shouldn't waste your valuable time, so let me get on with business. I had a thought that since your main man, Mr. Harmon, is gone, you might need something to get you through all this messy rain. Soon we'll be in the dry season and maybe life will brighten up, but for now it's certainly dismal. Wouldn't you say?"

"Little wet." If nothing else, he didn't want to seem desperate, even though Stanley and he had been milking what little dope they had for about three weeks. It didn't surprise him that Mr. Business had waited this long to make his pitch. It was shrewd, very, very shrewd.

"Yes?" Stephens asked when he didn't say more.

"Hmmm." He cocked his head to make it look like he was thinking hard about it. "Maybe."

"Maybe usually means yes."

"Maybe one stick. Maybe."

"Well, the man of stone has an Achilles heel."

"Well, I hate to see a man of your stature go out of business."

"Thank you. I didn't think you cared."

"Oh, I care," he said, smiling like a goon.

"Yes," Stephens said. "I bet you do."

"Should we go inside?" he offered by holding one hand out.

Stephens made that polite, sneering snicker of his. "No," he said, "I think I'll stay out here and enjoy the rain."

"Yes, it is lovely. I'm thinking of starting a swim club. Would you like to join? It's free."

"Sounds wonderful. But I'm used to pools. Swamps aren't my cup of tea."

"Too bad. We could've used another rat."

They both chuckled. He had to admit Stephens sure brought out the best in him. He'd still have to kill Stephens though. That is, if Stephens didn't kill him first.

"Well," he said, "I don't see the goods."

"Very good, Mr. Thorne. You are a shrewd buyer. That's commendable." Stephens pulled out a plastic baggie with one Thai stick in it. "This one is also free of charge, just to renew our friendship. But in line with our new beginning I could use some help."

"I don't do laundry."

This time Stephens didn't laugh. Instead he smiled in a way that signaled he didn't think this was funny anymore. "Information," he said.

"Information?"

"Yes, information. I need to know if you know the whereabouts of a certain weapon. A certain type of weapon. A forty-five semi-automatic."

"How would I know that?"

"It was your friend's. Harmon's. It was known that he had one. Illegally, of course. But they didn't find it on him or in his gear after he was killed. So, one could assume he hid it. And possibly someone close to him would know where it was."

"Possibly," he agreed. "But why would it be such a big deal for you? Might I ask?"

"I'm the corporal in charge of weapons accountability."

"Ha! What the fuck's that? I never heard of it."

"Certainly you know all the weapons in the army are accounted for. Your rifle had a serial number, right? And it's registered in your name. Right? So it's my responsibility to find this weapon and turn it in to the command for proper filing."

He believed Stephens like he believed in Santa Claus. So he still didn't say anything.

"You can ask the captain if you like," Stephens said.

"Maybe I will." But he knew full well the captain had left the base.

"He'd be happy to meet you," Stephens said, smiling like he was having fun again. "He's heard a lot about you. He's quite impressed."

"Well, I can't help you. Harmon never mentioned any semi-automatic and I never saw one. He must have kept it secret so his friends wouldn't get into trouble. He was that kind of considerate guy. But then you wouldn't know that, would you?"

"I heard he was a generous guy. And I always respected him for that. There's not many people like that in the world."

Shut up, will you?

"Well, I'll let you have this anyway," Stephens said. "You've been more than helpful and gracious. I've narrowed it down now. The captain will be glad to hear that."

"Say hello for me, will you?" he said, smiling back the same way. "Tell him I'll have him over for dinner one night and we can talk about being unsung heroes. He'd like that, don't you think?"

"Yes," Stephens said. "I think he would."

"Don't get muddy on the way back," he said as Stephens walked off.

"I never do. And don't you smoke that all at once. It could be fatal."

After Stephens and Doran left he went into his hootch. Inside he found a piece of small note pad paper like the one he'd found months ago in the barracks. The writing was smeared as if it'd been written in the rain, but the capitalized letters Y,A,D,M were easy to read. This time they were underlined and the words were spelled out. They said: Your A Dead Man. Which must have meant: You're a dead man.

He looked around outside once more and began digging in one corner of his hootch. About a foot down he found what he had been looking for. He pulled out the bundle and unwrapped it. It was still there. Still as shiny as when he'd got it from Harmon. The extra forty-five clips too.

It was about time to start carrying it.

# CHAPTER
# TWENTY-THREE

On Wednesday he shot a man running to escape on his small boat. The man hit his head against the stern of the boat and fell into the water. The canoe-like craft went skimming out of the reeds into the main part of the river, as the man lay face down in the water among the reeds. The tiny shoots of grass rising all around him made it look like he had been impaled on a bed of daggers. The boat, on the other hand, drifted quietly away.

On Friday he shot a man standing atop a bank near the river. They fired simultaneously, but the man was the one who was hit. The man slid down the bank toboggan style, and ended up in the water like the guy on Wednesday. But not all the way in, just his head.

The following Tuesday he shot two men on the river in a small boat. They shouldn't have fired at him. He would have given them a break if they hadn't, or at least would have let them make it to the shore for more of a challenge. But no, they had to shoot at him. So he knocked them off like tin cans on a fence post. Again the boat continued down river. It made him wonder where they were ending up.

On Thursday two more. He was starting to wonder if it would be three someday. Then four. And so on.

On the following Monday he finally broke the three mark. Thursday was Thanksgiving. He didn't get anybody. Friday he got one.

He wasn't sure why he was so intent on fighting, unless it was because he couldn't sleep again. In sleep he kept dreaming of the girl rotting in the swamp, and awake he kept thinking about Harmon taking a few in the chest. In either case, in both cases, he knew he had done wrong. He could have saved them both if he had just stopped thinking about himself.

Next day he came upon a body alongside the river, face down in the muck, rifle about five feet away in the reeds. He was American.

It had to be one of the guys who'd been posted to watch the river. But supposedly they had pulled out when the sweep began. So how did this guy get left behind? Why weren't they out looking for him? It didn't make sense.

He looked around again but there was no one in sight. Better hurry up or he'd be left behind too. He knelt down and grabbed the back of the guy's shirt, and the stiffness of the collar, combined with the blond hair neatly combed under the helmet, made him realize who it was.

Stephens.

He pulled him out of the muck and flipped him over. Stephens' whole front side was soaked with mud, very uncharacteristic of him. His muddy face looked like cream had been rubbed on to prevent wrinkles, and his nose was stuffed full of it. It looked like someone might have deliberately jammed it in.

Stephens' chest had a huge hole over his heart, powder burns on the shirt and the skin around the wound. It was evident the weapon involved was not a rifle but a high caliber semi-automatic. Very likely a forty-five.

Not good.

He reached in his shirt, took out Harmon's semi-automatic, looked at it for a moment. He knew he had to get rid of it. It would be too easy to nail him for the murder. And he was sure it was murder. That was why Stephens had been left behind without being noticed.

He stood up, looked around, then threw the semi-automatic out into the river as far as he could. As soon as he let it go he wished he'd tossed it somewhere it wouldn't have been so obvious to look. Damn it, he'd fucked up again. He guessed he wouldn't make a good murderer.

But now what? Leave Stephens here? Move him? What if they did find the semi-automatic? Would it still have his finger prints on it? He didn't think so. The water would wash them off.

He sighed. Why did this happen to him? He was just on fucking patrol. He hadn't asked to be here.

Then he stopped and thought. Doran. It had to be Doran. But fuck, this was all stupid. He didn't know who had killed Stephens. It could just as easily have been the VC, and the army could be out looking for Stephens right now. They could have missed him the first time around. He was back in the reeds some. That was all it was. Nothing out of the ordinary.

Yeah. Nothing out of the ordinary. Just ask all the people he had killed over the last week or so.

He knelt back down, pulled Stephens' dog tag out from under his shirt. His full name was Michael Harold Stephens. He was Catholic and had O-positive blood. The first two digits of Stephens' service number were the same as his. Thirteen.

"A little bad luck," he said.

He shoved the tags back under Stephens' shirt. Then he looked at Stephens' breast pockets. They were buttoned, but it looked like there was something in them. His body started tingling, like at the start of a good smoke.

Why the fuck not? Stephens wouldn't miss it. No one would know.

He unbuttoned the pockets and sure enough: two Thai sticks in one, and a bag full of opium in the other. He stashed the bounty in his own pockets, then searched Stephens' pants. In one there was money, U.S. dollars he hadn't seen in months. And, to his surprise, his birthday check from his parents. Shit, it'd been ages since he bartered that away. Now it seemed Stephens had only traded to get him hooked, since the check was worthless. But that was history now.

The other back pocket had military bucks and some Vietnamese money. The front pockets had nothing but packets of gum and a foreign coin from Singapore. He left the gum and all the money, but ripped up the check and put it in his breast pocket along with the dope. That was all he wanted.

"See ya in hell," he said, with one last look at Stephens' muddy face.

He carried Stephens about a mile until he came upon a drop zone where a helicopter was picking up some of the platoon. He didn't bother asking anyone what he should do with the body. They all watched him walk straight up to the chopper and flop Stephens in.

"What happened?" the lieutenant asked.

He looked up into the bay at the lieutenant's face. "He's dead," he said, and turned around and walked away, passing the group of guys gathering by the chopper to see who it was. Doran was at the end of the line. He stopped in front of him, made eye contact and waited until Doran looked away. Then he left.

# CHAPTER
# TWENTY-FOUR

As the monsoons subsided and patrols along the river were upped, he got to know a lanky black guy named Crawford. Crawford had huge ears like butterfly wings and his face was a mass of scars as if someone had beat him with brass knuckles. But that didn't bother Crawford. If someone dared to ask him what the hell had happened he would nonchalantly say his father worked in strange ways, like with a baseball bat. That always shut everybody up and Crawford would resume what he was doing, which was usually relaxing. Crawford was known as the one and only Mr. Leisure. Whenever he got a chance, Crawford would stretch out on the ground like a guy in a hammock, whether it was raining or not.

He and Crawford became a good team out on patrol. They went into every hole, dark spot, swampy area, every tight spot, every everything to find those shifty VC. Then, when they were far enough in where no one could see them, good old Crawford would pull out one of his homemade joints and they would take a hit or two—Crawford usually three. It seemed a totally crazy thing to do but that didn't stop them. They even started volunteering to do more dirty work so they could get high, or get higher. They never found the slightest sign of the VC, but that didn't stop Crawford or him. In fact, it made it easier to keep volunteering.

Eventually, though, the search effort moved from the swamp area to the villages farther down the river. So now their team specialty was searching the tall grass and brush on the perimeter of the villages, again out of sight.

"Smoke this. It'll help you forget your problems," Crawford said.

"Me? Problems? Never heard of them." He took the joint and drew in. His forehead tingled immediately, like it always did when he was on his third or fourth round. Even after weeks of doing this it still blew his mind that here he was in the middle of Vietnam, sitting in the tall grass. Supposedly fighting a war, supposedly looking for a fight, supposedly defending his country. And all he was doing was getting high. Weird.

"Now this is the life," Crawford said.

That it was.

"So," Crawford said, "what do you think of Mr. Stanley?"

"Stanley?" he said. Why was Crawford asking him about Stanley? "Oh, I don't know. He's okay I guess."

"Just okay, man?"

"I don't know," he shrugged. He still wasn't sure what Crawford wanted. "He seems like a regular guy to me. Nothing overly unique about him." He remembered back when Harmon was still alive, all three of them standing in line at the latrine. When they discovered the suicide. He remembered Stanley standing back as Harmon and he took care of the body.

"You don't think Stanley's unique?" Crawford asked.

He shrugged his shoulders. "Not particularly. Not like Harmon anyway."

"Yeah, I heard Harmon was one different dude."

"He was. That's what I liked about him."

"Stanley talks about him a lot."

He wondered if Stanley felt the same as him. That Harmon was the one who had kept them together. Now it was just dope, and now he was spending more time with Crawford just like he had with Harmon. It wouldn't be surprising if Stanley didn't like him anymore.

"I still think Stanley is a pretty sharp dude," Crawford said. "He's got a lot of dreams and I think he'll make it big someday. He's the type of dude you want to stick by. Things are going to come to him."

That surprised him. Stanley never mentioned any of his dreams to him. They rarely said much to each other, matter of fact. Just got together and smoked up.

"I can't believe you don't see Stanley's qualities," Crawford was saying. "He certainly thinks you have your shit together. He wonders what you're doing here."

Stanley wasn't the only one. But then why should anybody be here? That was what he wanted to know. Or maybe he didn't.

"So you can't think of anything special about Stanley?" Crawford asked again.

God, he should if Stanley thought he was something unique. "Well," he sighed. "He can certainly hold his breath a long time when he inhales." And held up the dope to make sure Crawford knew what he meant.

Crawford laughed. "That he can. That he can."

Unfortunately that was an asshole thing to say. Maybe he'd better start paying attention and stop thinking just about his own ass.

As usual Crawford and he found nothing. But when they came out on the other side of the village the rest of the squad was gone.

"Holy shit, man," Crawford said.

"They couldn't have left us here," he said, wide-eyed, looking around again. "They must be in the village somewhere."

"I sure hope so, man. I don't like being out here alone. Even if there ain't no VC around."

"Come on," he said, looking around again, making sure no one was about to jump out of the brush at them. "Let's walk down this way." He was amazed how much he was shaking in his boots. For Christsake, they had spent all their time going into the thick brush looking for the enemy, a job no one else wanted, and it didn't faze them a bit. But now that they were out here in the open it was like everyone was watching them, waiting for them to turn their backs, and boom, you're dead.

"I don't like this, man," Crawford said as they started down a path between the rows of thatched huts. "I don't like this at all."

Well, this wasn't exactly a favorite time in his life either. But he hadn't heard any choppers and it was too far from the river for a boat to have picked them up. The squad had to be around here somewhere.

They walked down the path like total strangers lost in the big city. He didn't appreciate everyone staring like he was some freak, especially the older ones whose eyes seemed as glazed as his. But the worst of it was the young men gawking at them, sizing them up, waiting for the most vulnerable time to do them in. They could easily be relatives looking for sweet revenge, anxious to shoot him in the head or back.

"I don't like this," Crawford said as he stepped around some kids playing. "I think they left us, man."

"No. They're here somewhere."

"I sure hope so, man. These people look ready to slit our throats."

"You're just stoned, man."

"You're not?" Crawford said.

Yeah, he was stoned and he definitely was concerned that as they walked along the villagers were closing in so that eventually they'd have to stop. But no one truly was. They were keeping their distance, except the kids playing in the lane. The villagers were as scared of Crawford and him as they were of them. That was the one thing he and Crawford had in their favor.

"I don't see anybody, man."

Then he heard it. Crawford did too. Choppers coming in. A wave of relief slid down his body. A slight smile sprouted on his lips. Crawford was smiling too. What geeks they'd been!

They both turned around. Off to the east several choppers in formation, one after another, seemed aimed exactly where Crawford and he were standing. Right in the middle of the lane between the huts, about halfway down from the start. But something was funny. For one, there were too many of them.

"Gunships," Crawford said.

"Cobras," he muttered.

He no sooner said it than the villagers began to shout and scatter as if they understood that these choppers were about to attack. People grabbed what they could, mostly crying children and the older folks, and scampered off into the reeds. It was like Crawford and he were 'it' while everyone else was running away to play hide-n-seek. And like they were 'it', Crawford and he stood watching the mantis-like ships come closer and closer, spreading out to cover the whole village.

"I think we'd better make a move too, man. I don't like the look of this."

"Yeah," he said.

As soon as he said that the choppers were firing their Gatling guns. The ground at the head of the village became an advancing dust storm, shredding baskets, stools and kid's toys as it entered the row of huts. It spit out everything it had gobbled up, like a giant lawn mower. A few chickens became instant pillows. The huts turned into confetti. Bits of grass whirled around as if in a small hurricane. Then the crackling sound grew louder as more choppers began to fire.

"Shit," he said.

Crawford and he turned and started running down the lane. Just as they split apart two small boys and a dog ran out from the back of a hut, stopped in the middle of the lane and looked up at them, the two kids with tears running down their cheeks.

"*Get them!*" Crawford yelled.

They each grabbed one on the run. Crawford took the older boy and he snagged the younger one by the wrist, pulling it away from the kid's face as he wiped at his tears. The kid fell down as he dashed for the protection of the hut but he kept on going, dragging the kid along like a sack of leaves. Suddenly the roar of rounds racing down the path and the rush of air that came with it struck him on his backside like a gust of wind from a storm. He felt a jerk and a sharp pain in the arm pulling the kid as the rounds zoomed past, and the weight of the kid dragging behind abruptly diminished, as if he had been pulling a small wagon when the handle broke. He looked behind him as he reached the hut and several feet away in the settling dust the young boy lay on his back, his clothes ripped to tatters, looking as though he had been bathed in blood.

He looked down at his hand. Blood was streaming down the back of his arm, over his wrist, into his palm and fingers that still held on to what was left of the kid's arm. The arm had been torn off from the shoulder and was dribbling blood like drips from a melting icicle. He dropped it and flinched at the sudden roar of the first chopper zooming overhead and veering off to the left.

"*You fucking bastards!*" he screamed as the second chopper flew overhead, as he raised his rifle and fired a burst of rounds at its belly. Some he could see hit the tail section, but the chopper went on.

"*Thorne, you crazy fucking bastard.* They'll hang you for that!"

He looked across the way at Crawford lying on the ground, with his shoulders and head leaning against the wall of the hut and the kid on the other side of him, peeking over his arm and chest. Crawford was right. He had fucked up royally now. Trying to shoot down your own chopper was treason. He shook his head and wiped the water from his eyes. He had totally lost it. What the fuck was he going to do now?

He looked down at his bleeding arm. His palm had filled with blood and it was running out between his fingers. When he looked closer at the back of his arm he realized he'd only been grazed. But still it hurt like hell, especially flexing his hand.

"*Thorne!* I'm hit in the foot."

He looked across again and as he spotted Crawford's red-stained boot another wave of rounds came screaming down the lane, this time predominantly on his side. The hut he was hiding behind began disintegrating into fine pieces of straw and wood chips. He ducked and threw himself farther away from the lane. As he hit the ground the chopper roared overhead, this time veering off to the right.

"Hurry up, man," Crawford yelled. "Get over here."

He rose off his stomach, jumped to his feet, went to the edge of the caved-in hut and peeked up the row. The coast was clear so he dashed over to the other side.

"Holy fuck, man," Crawford said. "I can't believe this shit. They blew my fucking foot off."

"You're all right," he said, looking up from the bleeding foot. The sole of Crawford's boot had been completely blown off. The bottom of his foot was mangled. Some bones were still there but they didn't resemble anything like a foot. "We're going to have to wrap this up to stop the bleeding. Hold tight here."

"Whatever, man."

He looked over at the kid still clutching Crawford's arm like nothing in the world could make him let go. The kid was staring back at him like he was a monster. His eyes were wet with tears.

"The kid's all right, isn't he?" Crawford asked.

"Seems to be. A little shocked, maybe."

"Yeah, right, man. Fancy that."

"Just be quiet, man. Let me wrap this."

"Be my guest."

He started by stripping off his shirt and wrapping it around as tightly as he could.

"You shouldn't have fired at that chopper, man. They'll kill you for that."

"Yeah. Well, that's my problem." He did the last wrap. "That too tight?"

"I can't feel a thing, man. It's like nothing's there."

He took out his handkerchief to tie the wrap off.

"Well?" Crawford asked.

"Well what?"

"Is it still there?"

"Is what still there?"

"My foot, dumbshit."

He looked Crawford straight in the eye. "Yeah, it's still there." It wasn't.

Another chopper zoomed by overhead. Crawford flipped it the middle finger. He pretended to look up at it too, to hide his tears.

"Fuck them," Crawford swore.

"Yeah," he murmured.

He glanced at the back of his arm again. Blood was still trickling out but most of it had dried up. His hand felt like it had been dipped in paint then baked. But what was bothering him most was that he was feeling faint. This was no time to lose it. He had to at least pretend he was cool, calm and collected. He couldn't quit now. He just couldn't. He had to see something completely through once in his life, no matter what.

One more chopper roared overhead, but it seemed like most of the firing had stopped.

# CHAPTER
# TWENTY-FIVE

"How many days?" Doran asked.

"Seventeen," he replied neutrally.

"Going back home right away?"

Why did Doran want to know that? And why was Doran suddenly talking with him? Was there a setup planned within the next seventeen days?

"You know," Doran began after he didn't answer, "I always thought the dead ones were the luckiest. They don't have to live this shit over and over again in their head. You know what I mean?" Doran didn't wait for his response. "They also don't have to explain anything to anybody. That would be the worst part. Telling people you killed someone. In your case, a lot of someones, huh?"

"I didn't rape anybody." He made sure he was looking straight into Doran's eyes when he said that. Doran looked a little surprised. He must not have known that anyone had seen him rape and murder the girl. And maybe there were plenty more to remember.

"Well," Doran said, "it'll be interesting to see if you're one of the lucky ones. A dead one, that is."

"I'm all for it," he said.

"I think you should be on point today," said Doran. "Maybe it'll help you think about how ironic the world can be."

He wanted to tell Doran how impressed he was by Doran's use of such big words, but he'd better keep his mouth shut. No sense getting in deeper than he already was. Besides, Doran was in charge of the patrol. What else could he do?

Each step on the muddy floor of the canal sucked in muck through the rips in his boots. The gritty silt rubbed between his toes. It was rare to be wet this time of year, but even the sunny blue skies were cloudy today, and it was starting to rain. Nothing like a monsoon but still enough to soak him, since he didn't have his poncho, but then nobody did. Besides, walking through water up to his chest was just like old times.

As they went up the canal the sky became more opaque, the clouds made a roof over them, the raindrops grew larger and more plentiful. The wind came up, swayed the towering reeds along the banks and rippled the dark surface of the water. It reminded him of when their patrol was ambushed and Harmon was killed. Ever since then everything seemed to get lost in all the dope he'd taken in. Everything except for the raped girl. That was etched in his thoughts like a circuit board. And the little boy's arm hanging from his hand. And Crawford's missing foot. And the water spilling out of Harmon's mouth when he pulled him up out of the canal.

In any case, he had definitely broken his earlier pledge to abstain from dope. But otherwise he had at least managed so far not to quit what he was obligated to do. Next time he would definitely stick with an F in English, and take it through from there.

He glanced back at the squad trailing behind in a long dispersed line. He didn't know anybody personally, not even Doran. But he got along with most everybody. If that made a difference. But what did it matter? It was pointless to make friends now that he was leaving. What he ought to be worrying about was home. Doran was right. What would he tell his family? That he killed people? He smoked opium? He managed not to have a friend in this whole fucking place?

Up ahead he spotted two large rats skirmishing over a small piece of something, maybe an ear. One had it in its mouth, the other one kept snapping at it, darting back and forth. The first one snarled like a dog, standing its ground. Then they both dashed into the wall of reeds as though they had heard something. He looked to his left, thinking he had seen something move out of the corner of his eye. But nothing was there. Nothing but more impenetrable tall grass and rain. It sure had scared the shit out of him, though. His heart had damn near stopped.

Getting short, huh? Don't want to be one of the lucky ones, now do we?

He looked back at the squad. They were still coming along, searching to the left then right or vice versa, holding their weapons high out of the water, most of all wishing they were somewhere else, struggling to keep moving and letting the rain pelt them in the face.

He kept on and when he looked ahead saw something drifting down towards him, a black hump which looked like a shark heading his way. But there were no sharks.

He stepped aside, readied his rifle, waved for the squad to hold up. Close-up, the hump looked more like the back of a turtle. In the next second he knew it was an inflated shirt and someone was in it. Now he could see the back of the head.

"What is it?" Doran whispered loudly, behind him and off to his right.

He lowered his rifle. "A body."

He dipped his hand into the bubbling water and grabbed the Vietnamese's shirt collar as the body drifted by. He raised the head far enough out to see the bullet hole behind the man's ear, all puffy and wrinkly and washed out as though it had been bandaged too long. He didn't bother to lift it any more to see the face. He knew what that would look like well enough.

He let the body go. "Watch out for snags," he called back.

The rest of the squad backed away as the body went past them on its journey to the river. Then they fell back in line and Doran waved to begin again. So they started upstream looking to the left then right or vice versa. He looked ahead but nothing was there except raindrops splashing in dark water, like in any mud puddle in the world.

# CHAPTER
# TWENTY-SIX

"I can see the headlines now." Stanley spread his hands apart like an artist envisioning a country scene. "Local hero returns home, gets married to his high school sweetheart, goes back to his good job, buys a home and a fast car. What do you think?"

"I think I still have nine days left."

"What's the matter? You don't like my prediction? It's not enough?"

"No, it's enough," he assured Stanley. "Doesn't have nothing to do with me, though."

"Your high school sweetheart leave you or something?"

"Never had one."

Stanley chuckled. "Me neither, come to think about it. But what the hell, man. You'll have a good job when you get back. Right?"

"That's one thing I can say for sure I'm not going back to."

"Why not?"

"It sucked."

"Well, at least you had one, man," Stanley said. "I didn't have shit. That's why I'm in the fucking army."

Stanley let his head rest back against the dirt wall of the lean-to. But it didn't seem like he was bummed out. By the look on Stanley's face it seemed just the opposite. Stanley was thinking, looking ahead, planning a strategy.

"You got to change your attitude. That's the key," Stanley said. "You got to get involved in the system. You got to keep moving. No looking behind. No feeling sorry for yourself. You can't sit on your ass for one second, otherwise you're as good as dead."

"You been sleeping at night or something?" he said.

"College," Stanley said, as if he hadn't heard the question.

"I tried that."

"And?"

"I'm here, aren't I?"

"Bad attitude. That's your problem."

"So what can I do, counselor?"

"Stick with me, brother." Stanley held out his hand to be slapped. "Electronics is the wave of the future."

"Electronics? You must be dreaming," he said, but slapped the hand anyway.

"Think about it, man. Think about it. That's the key. Get yourself ready. Be ready. It's coming soon. Real soon." Stanley nodded and started to stand up.

"Where you going?"

"I got to take a shit, man. I'll be right back. Then maybe we'll smoke some. All right?"

"Sure," he said. "Take one for me."

"What?"

"Never mind." It was a bad joke anyway.

"Start thinking, man," Stanley yelled back. "There's not much time left."

Yeah, yeah, yeah. There was never enough time left. "Hey," he hollered. "How many days you got left?"

"Fifteen!"

Six more than him. Time was getting short. Still, he didn't want to think about it. He knew one thing though. He wasn't going home right away. He would check out California first.

Electronics, he thought. Christ, the seventies were just around the corner. What the hell were they going to be like?

His second to last day he walked through more tall grass and marsh than he had the whole first month of his tour. At least it felt that way. This time, though, he found a body. A rather ripe one. Or as it was said: It was history now. So it didn't matter if he left the guy behind to be eaten by rats and bugs. He had already let a little girl rot. So why give a fuck about an old man?

God, would that girl ever leave him alone? It made his chest feel heavy all over again. But there were only two more hours left on this patrol, then he could go to sleep and hopefully forget everything. And there was no sense being judgmental at this stage. Plenty of time for that when he got home.

When he returned to the base, he ate his rations and packed his duffel. By then it was dark so he settled in for the night. But as he began to fall asleep someone knocked on his door. It was Stanley, Mr. Long himself. And he had dope.

"So where'd you disappear to these last few days?" he asked. "I've been looking all over for you."

Stanley crawled into the hootch and crammed himself in his usual spot. It seemed like he hadn't heard the question until he got comfortable and looked over at him. "What?"

"I said where have you been?"

Stanley shrugged. "Here."

"I looked for you at your place. Everybody said they didn't know where you were."

"Been in a funny mood lately. You know. Thinking about home and shit. What to do. Other things."

"Yeah," he sighed. "I know what you mean."

"Got a light, man?"

"Yeah."

The smell of the dope flooding the hootch felt so relaxing he was high before Stanley handed over the joint. This was what he needed. And it had been almost three days.

"So tomorrow is it, huh man?"

"Yeah," he sighed, looking at the new bunch of letters stashed in Stanley's breast pocket. "Day one." He took another small hit before he handed it back.

"Seven for me, man. I be one happy dude."

Tell me about it.

"Guess what, man?"

"What?"

"Doran gave me this dope."

It'd been what he was just going to ask. "Doran?" he said. So maybe Harmon had been getting his dope from Stephens.

"Yeah," Stanley said, frowning, then took another toke. "It's weird being with that motherfucker. He's dangerous."

"It's just an act. You ought to know that about white folk."

"Yeah? Well, I ain't turning my back on him. He don't like blacks at all."

Stanley handed back the joint but he was already fucked-up beyond a reasonable doubt. Still, he started thinking about what Crawford had said about Stanley. Stanley was an all-right dude. Maybe electronics was the future.

"What you thinking?"

"Not much," he sighed. "Same old shit." He took another hit and handed the joint back to Stanley.

"Too bad about Crawford," Stanley uttered. "He was a good man."

"He was."

"He is," Stanley quickly added.

"Yeah," he muttered. He guessed he wasn't in a thinking mood. And if he was he could only think about himself right now.

Soon after they had finished the Thai stick, Stanley left. That was fine with him since all he wanted to do was dream and go to sleep. So he leaned back and stretched out his legs and started imagining Greta, the blond bombshell, coming home from work. He was in the kitchen making dinner and she comes right up to him and kisses him on the cheek, telling him what a good wife he would make and then she pinches him on the ass and winks at him and tells him to turn off the stove and come here in this bedroom and...

The knocking on his corrugated door woke him up but he wasn't sure if he was dreaming or not. Then the knocking continued and someone whispered outside.

"Thorne?"

He couldn't tell who it was. He felt in the dark for his rifle and aimed it at the door.

"Thorne?" the voice hissed a little louder. "It's me. Doran."

Doran? What the fuck did he want?

"Thorne. I got some good dope, man. Thought you might like to smoke it."

"I don't know, man. I'm kind of tired," he said, trying to make his voice sound that way.

"This will help. It's good stuff."

He had to make a quick decision whether it would be easier to have him come in or just say no. But if he said no Doran could take offense, maybe do something he'd regret. If he was alive to regret it. "Come on in."

"You won't regret this," Doran assured him as he crawled in. "This is some quality shit."

He readjusted the door so it fit tight and then lit the candle. The light made his eyes squint. When he looked at Doran, he was holding up the joint for admiration. It looked exactly like the one Stanley had.

"Got a light?" Doran asked.

"Sure." He offered the candle, but instead of taking it Doran leaned over with the Thai stick in his mouth. As Doran bent over he could see the bulge on the left side of Doran's shirt, a shirt unbuttoned enough to see a very small part of a dark object, the handle of a semi-automatic forty-five.

Doran sucked in hard and got the Thai stick lit. Then, leaning back, Doran himself noticed the semi-automatic sticking out. "Oh, this," he said. "This is my new baby." He pulled the gun out. "I just found this not too long ago. Down along the river. I think someone must have dropped it or something." Doran waved it around like he was shooting a machine gun. It didn't seem to bother Doran to be pointing it at him.

"Don't worry, man. It's not loaded." Doran released the clip and looked at it. "Oh, shit. I guess it is. I guess I forgot to unload after the patrol." Doran looked up at him and shrugged. "Sorry, man."

"No problem," he said, staring back at Doran. If there was one thing he didn't want to show, it was discomfort.

"This is pretty good stuff," Doran said, passing him over the joint. "I think you'll like it."

"I'm sure I will."

Doran stuffed the semi-automatic back into his shirt and looked at him. "How do you like it?"

"It's good stuff," he said, though he had hardly inhaled.

Doran's scruffy unshaven face in the dim light gave him a gangster look, like a guy down on his luck, a guy that killed people after playing with them. Maybe Doran was the one who had killed Stephens. For what reason, who would know? Who would even give a shit?

"You know," Doran was saying, "a lot of strange things go on. You got to keep your back covered. You got to have eyes on all sides of your head. I mean everyone is after everyone. I can't believe it, can you? This place is bad. Everybody's killing each other. You know what I mean?"

He handed the joint to Doran. "It's war."

"You bet it is. On more than one front, too."

That it was.

"Take for example, Stephens. He was an asshole." Doran took a quick hit and handed the joint back. "Everybody thought he and I were in business together. But we weren't. I couldn't stand the guy. He fucking asked too much for the dope he sold. I don't mean just cash, but favors. Too many fucking favors. I fucking took his patrols for him to the point I thought I was him. I was fucking scared shitless. My nerves are gone. I can't sleep at night."

Doran waved him off when he offered the joint back. He actually seemed on the verge of crying now.

"You know what the asshole made me do? He made me stay away from you because he wanted to keep you off balance. He was afraid of you. He felt you were smarter than him and he thought you would turn him over to the authorities or take over the business. It was strange, man. Stephens had everyone else under his thumb. Shit, he was relentless about it. He swore he'd cut me off if I didn't obey him. And, man, I needed the dope. I was doing too many fucking patrols, too many fucking watches, too much of fucking everything."

A hundred questions racing through his mind and not one of them readable. Maybe, though, it didn't matter anymore. Tomorrow he was history, gone forever, regardless of whether he was dead or alive.

"I'm glad you killed him. Believe me, everyone is."

He looked straight at Doran. This had to be some sort of set-up. It had to be. They were trying to get him before he left. Get him charged with murder then put him away for good.

"There isn't anybody on this base doesn't owe you their lives, man. You've kicked ass. Taken all the chances, all the shit. Everyone knows it, man. You're one hard motherfucker. I respect that. I respect it totally. You don't have to explain a thing."

Doran did think he had killed Stephens. Either that or he was putting on a good act. But how could Doran have come to that? Just because he was the one who'd found Stephens, who carried the body through the swamp and dumped him off in the chopper? God, if he had killed him he would have left him. Wouldn't he? Just like the guy who had killed him.

"So where's Mister Stanley Long?" Doran asked.

He looked back at Doran. "On watch, I guess." He looked down at the joint in his hand. It had gone out.

"You can keep that."

"Thanks," he said.

"You and Stanley splitting up?"

What made Doran think Stanley and he were not friends anymore? Maybe they weren't, but it was none of Doran's business anyway.

"Looks like it," he said.

"Too bad." Doran's face looked blank now. All evidence of his crying was gone. "Well, I'd better get going before I fall asleep. I got a watch tonight."

He moved out of the way as Doran crawled out.

"The next time you ought to build this bigger so you don't have to crawl all the time," Doran complained.

"I will," he said. But there would never be a next time.

He didn't even get a chance to stretch out before someone else knocked on the door. What was it with this sudden popularity his last night here?

"Who is it?" he shouted, aiming his rifle at the door.

"Stanley."

Stanley? What the hell did he want again? "What do you want?" He, himself, wanted some sleep.

"You okay?" Stanley asked.

"Yeah, I'm okay," he shouted back. Why wouldn't he be?

"I saw Doran come by after I left. So I hung around in case anything happened."

He suddenly remembered what Crawford had said: Stanley was an all-right decent dude. Stanley cared about people. He gave as well as just received. Stanley was the one who had scrounged food for Harmon in return for the dope. He, himself, on the other hand, had never lifted a finger to do anything for Harmon or anyone else. He'd never even said thank you. And here Stanley was now, risking his life watching out for his friend.

"Can I come in?" Stanley asked.

"Sure."

Stanley crawled in and sat in his usual corner, looking wide awake, like he could stay up all night talking. And he guessed he owed Stanley at least that.

"So what's up?" he asked.

"Doran give you a bunch of shit, man?"

"Not really. It was mostly a white man's act."

Stanley shook his head. It was obvious Stanley wasn't taking Doran's visit as lightly. But he himself wasn't going to take it seriously. After all, it was history now, too, same as him.

"I thought maybe Doran was seeking revenge for Stephens' murder," Stanley said. "I heard he was looking for the guy who did it."

The way Stanley was staring he got the impression Stanley thought he had killed Stephens too. That was great. Everyone thought he was a murderer now. What did he do to deserve that? Be a good soldier? Christ. It went with the job, and he accepted it and did it. It was called responsibility, for Christsake. But who the hell could understand that?

"He just wanted to smoke dope," he said.

"What did he say?"

"Not much. He got pretty wasted."

He knew Stanley didn't exactly believe him, and that more details wouldn't help. On the other hand, he realized silence was one of his major faults. He always let people think what they wanted about him. It wasn't surprising so many misperceptions occurred.

"He must not know then," Stanley said.

"Must not," he said.

"Harmon told me he gave you the semi-automatic to hide."

He nodded his head yes.

"Did you get rid of it?"

"Yeah, I did."

Stanley nodded in approval, looking well stoned. He felt high too, but not as much as he figured he should after smoking twice. It was as if the second Thai stick had countered the first and mellowed him out.

"I hate this place," Stanley said out of nowhere. "You know what I mean, man?"

He didn't bother answering. He was thinking again about that girl he had shot. She was still out there and he was still here. Maybe he was a murderer, maybe that was why people thought he had killed Stephens. His guilt was plain as day.

"This fucking place is crazy. All the killing and hatred is too much, man. I mean when people commit suicide just to get out of here, you got to wonder, you know?"

Stanley was looking up and over at him but he still didn't feel like answering. But then he remembered Stanley's reaction to the black kid in the latrine and it all started to make sense.

"But you know," Stanley was saying now, "slitting your wrists isn't the only way you can get out of here. You can do dope, man. You can have the best and worst of both worlds. All you got to do is plunge yourself into drugs. After that, who gives a fuck? I mean that's what I feared most about this place. Not that I'd want to get killed, though at times I felt that's what I needed the most." Stanley paused. "What scared me was I would walk out of here only pretending I was alive. And I've done exactly that, man. I'm hooked, and I pledged to myself it would never happen. But I let it. I let you get more dope when we used up Harmon's stash. I let you risk your life dealing with Stephens and I felt like shit for it. I should've said no, we don't need this shit anymore. We can face life. We can get out of here and start over."

Stanley looked up at him. Tears were running down his cheeks. "I'm sorry, man. I was wrong for letting it all happen."

He was so fucking stoned now. Doran's dope was finally slamming his head against the wall just when he should be listening, should be counseling and holding his friend. But fucking Goddamn it, all he could think of was that damn girl and how, for Christsake, he still couldn't even cry.

"The fucking army wasn't part of my dream," Stanley was saying. "It never was. I mean all we're doing here is killing people. Is that what I'm going to be, man? A killer. I mean this has nothing to do with freedom. I'm not even free in my own country. What the fuck am I doing here?"

Stanley's ranting was settling him down now. The juices were flowing again, his mind seemed able to concentrate. It made him remember his shooting the helicopter when Crawford lost his foot. Crawford thought he was crazy but he knew exactly what he was doing. It was hard to admit how much he hated this job. After all, he was the one who allowed himself to be here, and so he did have an obligation. But that was all shit now. It didn't even matter if someone thought he was a quitter. He was never going back to work again. They could take their jobs and shove them up their asses. He would never bow down.

When he let his breath out the tension in his chest came with it. Stanley too seemed relieved, almost sober even, though he still had his eyes closed, his head leaned back against the wall. Maybe they'd come to the same conclusion at the same time. The fact was, the world was a lot bigger than he and Stanley. Their only problem was their attitude, their reluctance to submit. All they had to do was toe the line, but which line? Not college. Not the factory. Not the army. So what would it be next?

# CHAPTER
# TWENTY-SEVEN

It was a beautiful day to leave. The sun was out but it was not even humid. It almost felt like he was on the beach.

The pilot signaled him to load up so he slung his rifle over his shoulder and picked up his bag. There wasn't much in his duffel, just an extra change of clothes and his poncho, and he wondered why he was even taking that.

As he settled in, the chopper lifted off. A blustery cloud of dust obstructed the base like a white-out on the snow. As they rose it thinned out and once again he could see everything. Not that there was much to see. There never had been. Just a fenced-in tent camp with bunkers and a tower in the middle. Nothing to write home about, not that he ever had. Yet somehow he thought he would miss the place, miss being in his hole, miss getting high. But that would wear off. Soon, deliberately or not, he would forget this place. Forget it like it'd never happened. In fact, rumor was the army were going to do the same, that they'd decided to abandon the base as a monument to the swamp.

The chopper unexpectedly banked back, as if the pilots were granting him one last look. He wasn't all that interested but it did give him a view of his hootch and the lean-to. They were still there, still intact, now empty forever, hopefully. Stanley had been right. They'd only chosen a different kind of suicide. But that was all in the past now. The future was ahead. Stanley was ready to regain his dream, and it seemed like there was room for him as well. But this time he had to hold up his end. He owed that to Stanley. He owed lots of people, especially his parents. So no matter what, from now on he would never run away, never quit or bitch, never feel sorry for himself. He would take what life offered and give back a whole lot more.

Finally the chopper headed east, over the wide flat expanse that ran eventually to the ocean. For a minute there he'd been smiling, but not for long. Something was wrong. Somehow he had managed to fuck it up. He couldn't even feel good about leaving, about being free, about finally going home.

He set his rifle up on its muzzle and leaned his head against it, staring out the bay. Soon he'd have to give the rifle up. Then he'd be defenseless. Then he'd have to face life for real, on its own terms. He only hoped Stanley would forgive him for being so selfish. Matter of fact, he'd have to start things off by telling Stanley thank you for being his friend.

# PART III

# CHAPTER TWENTY-EIGHT

"The City of Angels," Stanley said, grinning as he got off the bus.

"That it is," he said. Though the Los Angeles he'd been in, hanging out at the bus station day and night for the past two weeks waiting for Stanley to show up, might better be described as the 'City of No Place to Sleep'.

"Got any money?" Stanley asked.

He noticed Stanley wasn't carrying any bags. In fact, he didn't even have the coat the army handed out when you were discharged. All he had on was a short-sleeved shirt and slacks. Poor Stanley was about to learn just how cold it got in L.A. in March, something he himself had found out the hard way. But what worried him more was Stanley's bloodshot eyes, runny nose and generally rundown look, like he'd been drinking or not sleeping, or both.

"You got any money?" Stanley asked again.

"Oh," he said. "Not much."

"What the hell'd you spend it on? You didn't go back home, did you?"

He wanted to ask Stanley where the hell his discharge money was. After all, Stanley'd just gotten out, practically, whereas he'd been living out here for the past two weeks.

"No, I haven't gone home," he said. "I spent it to live. And believe me, on nothing fancy, except maybe these shoes. The ones the army gave me were a piece of shit."

"Look at mine," Stanley said, holding one foot out. "Fifty bucks."

Fifty bucks and a rip-off job.

"So how much you got?" Stanley asked.

Jesus Christ, he couldn't believe this. Okay, he had spent a couple of nights at some dogshit hotel. So what the fuck?

"Hundred bucks?" Stanley asked.

"More like six bucks," he said.

"*Six bucks!*"

People in the bus station looked at them standing near the coin lockers. Now he wished he'd waited outside.

"How the hell can you only have six bucks?"

"Things cost money," he said. "The fucking bus down here was thirty bucks for Christsake."

"Hey, man," Stanley said. "We can't be blowing money away."

He raised his hands. "Sorry." He was sorry he hadn't just gone back home. In fact, he was thinking now he wouldn't say anything about going to that disco place he'd walked by in East L.A. to celebrate a little, possibly make a few new friends.

"Well, we got to use our heads now," Stanley said.

"I think we're in trouble then," he said.

"Don't be so negative all the time, man."

He raised his hands again. "Sorry." He was only trying to be funny.

"Let's get out of here," Stanley said, wiping his nose on his arm. "We got some serious thinking to do."

He took Stanley through downtown by the glossy stores and financial offices, then into the industrial area where they crossed the railroad tracks and canal into East L.A. Then there was another warehouse district, then a bunch of smaller, shabbier storefronts and finally into a rundown residential area where he'd staked a few claims, mostly apartment dumpster areas, to live and sleep in.

"This is it?" Stanley asked.

"It don't get any better than this," he said. "Not on six bucks."

"Don't worry about the money," Stanley said. "I got it all figured out. The seventies are the key. We just need to be prepared."

That gave them approximately nine more months. But before he could ask about the details, Stanley started off down the street, racing as if he were late for an appointment.

"Where're you going in such a hurry?" he shouted.

"Let's go to a store," Stanley called back. "I'm hungry."

Stanley didn't bother to wait up, so he had to jog a bit. But when he caught up, Stanley kept his eyes glued to the ground. He assumed Stanley was busy with the plan. Fine with him. He was here just for the ride.

Then suddenly Stanley stopped. "We have to reaffirm our oath," Stanley said.

He didn't know they had one.

Stanley's eyes were still lowered, his head and body turned away. "We can't get hooked on dope again."

He wasn't so sure he was over that hump or not. Though he hadn't smoked a thing since leaving the base, drinking was another thing.

Stanley turned towards him slightly but kept his head down. "Sorry I jumped on you back there. I just got a lot on my mind."

"No problem," he said.

Before he could say anything more Stanley was off again and again he had to jog to catch up. Back by Stanley's side he thought about asking more about the oath. Like should they have a ceremony or something, like blood brothers. But Stanley still had his eyes hard on the ground.

After they had passed a couple small neighborhood stores and were heading into downtown East L.A., surprisingly close to that disco, he figured he'd better say something.

"Is it still electronics?" he asked.

"Yes, it is," Stanley said, slowing down and looking over at him.

"We still going to go to school on the GI Bill?"

"Yes, we are."

"Are we still going to stop at a store?"

Stanley stopped walking. "What's with all the questions?"

"Nothing," he shrugged. "There's a store just over there. I thought you said you were hungry."

He watched Stanley look across the street and through the large windows, to where the cashier was pulling out money from the cash register and counting off the change into the customer's hand.

"You're not thinking of robbing the place, are you?" he asked.

Stanley quickly dropped his eyes again. "No," he said.

"That's good." Though now he was sorry he'd said anything.

"Give me some of the money," Stanley said. "I'll go get some snacks."

"Can't I go?"

"You'd better stay here. You look like shit. They might think you're trying to steal something."

"Thanks," he said, though he had to admit it wouldn't be long before he did start stealing anything and everything he could get his hands on. "How much you want?"

"Three bucks."

He gave it to Stanley but it wasn't easy. "Get me a candy bar and a Coke, okay?"

"Sure, man."

Stanley entered the store and went to the cashier. He couldn't tell what Stanley was doing. It looked like money was changing hands without anything being bought. Then Stanley disappeared in the back of the store—headed for the coolers, hopefully.

A car pulled up to the restaurant next to the store. The restaurant looked closed, but the guy went right in. He'd left the car running and it seemed like someone inside the car was smoking a cigarette on the passenger's side.

Looking back at the store he still couldn't see Stanley. He could only hope Stanley was getting something good. But he was beginning to worry that Stanley's plan was stuck in Stanley's head, just like the plan to meet in L.A. that had never quite firmed up. The question was, what was he going to do about it?

The guy came out of the restaurant carrying a pizza box and followed by two giggling women dressed in fur coats. The passenger door of the car opened and another man stepped out and held the back door for the women, both of whom thanked him with a kiss. Then, as they got in, this second well-dressed guy patted each of them on the butt, slammed the door shut and jumped in himself. On the other side the driver was already back in with the pizza, and the car screeched as it lurched off.

Now Stanley was finally back at the cash register. But it didn't look like he had much. Maybe the cashier had already put it in the bag, though the bag he was handing over sure was small.

"What's the matter?" Stanley asked as he came back across the street and over to him.

"Nothing," he said, staring at the bag.

"Here."

He took the bag and peeked inside it. It only held a bag of chips, a small one at that. He looked again, pulling the chips out, just to make sure there wasn't anything else.

"What's the matter?" Stanley asked again, right at his shoulder now.

"Is this all? No drinks?"

"I didn't know what you wanted," Stanley said, getting huffy.

"I gave you three bucks, and I specifically asked for a candy bar and a Coke."

Stanley looked back across the street shaking his head. "You know, man? You're nothing but a bum. You dress like a bum. You look like a bum. You think like a bum. You are a bum."

Wrong question, he guessed. But again, he wasn't going to say anything. He was sure Stanley had a good reason for doing what he did, whatever it was. So fuck it. He still had three bucks.

"Where you going?" Stanley asked as he stepped off the curb.

"I'm going to get a Coke and a candy bar."

"I called my mother, man. Okay?"

He turned around and Stanley was looking straight at him.

"That's what I spent the money on. All of it."

"Fine," he said, looking back at Stanley and thinking. He knew he should do the same, but now he didn't have enough money. It was better to eat and stay alive and call another day. Besides, it was probably too late now, with the time difference and all. "You want anything?"

"Something good to eat," Stanley shrugged. "A Coke too."

He nodded then headed for the store. Dirty or not.

# CHAPTER
# TWENTY-NINE

Downtown Los Angeles looked impressive with its tall buildings and mirrored windows. But the canal separating the city from East Los Angeles was the opposite of that. There wasn't even any water in it, just small islands of dirt and weeds in a field of litter specializing in broken glass. But even so, the canal was the largest storm drain he'd ever seen. The walls were nearly twelve feet tall, and yet the concrete was so bleached from the sun it seemed like there had never been a drop of water in it, let alone a raging river. Maybe somebody knew something he didn't.

"Pretty bleak, huh?" he said to Stanley.

Stanley stood holding onto the bridge rail, staring down at the canal. He'd warned Stanley beforehand that this place wouldn't quite fit Stanley's dream. And this was just an upscale dry wash with businesses lining both sides. It would be like living in an alley with delivery trucks and loading docks on either side, and him and Stanley down below in a giant concrete rut. Plus the funky chain-linked fence running along the top of the canal walls made the whole place seem like a chute for cattle or a prison yard. But beggars couldn't be choosers. And it would be better than the dumpster areas. That was for sure.

"Well?" Stanley asked. "Can we get down there?"

"I don't know," he said. "I'll have to look around."

As they headed over to the south side of the bridge, a car came from the east on its way to L.A. proper, with two black guys inside it drinking from quart bottles of beer. They looked intently at Stanley and him as they passed on by, then came to a stop two car-lengths or so further along. The guy on the passenger side rolled the window down a couple of inches and stuck out his beer bottle. The radio was blaring so loudly it was a wonder they still had eardrums. Then the guy let some beer pour out on the car and pavement, which spilled even more when they took off, laying a little rubber and swerving down the rest of the bridge like it was an obstacle course.

"What was that all about?" he asked.

Stanley just shrugged and kept on moving. "Some lost brothers, I suppose."

They crossed over to the other side of the bridge and looked back down at the canal, dry wash, river, whatever it was supposed to be. Then something over here on the east end of the bridge caught his attention; a place where the fence pole butted up to the bridge was bent so someone could squeeze through. On closer inspection he could see a path leading down to the abutment that formed the bridge foundation. There might be a landing underneath, a perfect spot to be out of the weather, and completely out of sight.

"Got it figured out yet?" Stanley called from behind him.

"Maybe."

He went down to the end of the bridge and inspected the narrow opening. It was definitely made for skinny guys, which was perfect for Stanley and him. And the beauty of it was, unless you wanted to risk jumping the fence, it seemed to be the only way down.

"Why don't you check it out?" Stanley called over the bridge rail to him.

He squeezed through the narrow opening, holding onto the fence pole until his feet dropped to the bridge foundation. It was a scary moment, since the ledge was about two feet below the bottom of the fence and no more than three feet wide. One slip and his head would be spaghetti on the concrete floor. But it looked like people had done it before. A skull and crossbones was spray-painted on the bridge's concrete girder, with the initials D.M. below it. For a second he thought of Dead Meat. But old D.M., whoever he was, would not be waiting around down here now.

"What's the verdict?" Stanley asked.

"I'm not sure yet," he said, holding his body flat against the concrete foundation. "You got to get used to doing this, though."

Next he sat on his rear, dangling his feet over the concrete sill to shorten up the jump to the dirt path. Once on the path he could see that under the bridge the abutment jutted out about ten feet from the canal wall and was full of dirt. He crouched down to get under the girder and found a man with blond hair flowing down to the middle of his back and a long blond beard, sitting on the abutment ledge, dangling his legs over the side.

A buzz of panic jolted through him. D.M.? he thought.

The man—an older man, deeply tanned, wearing a Hawaiian shirt with shorts—was holding an envelope several inches from his face, peeking at it as if trying to read its contents without opening it up.

"Howdy," he said, as soft and friendly as he could, staying squatted down.

The man was startled. He stuffed the envelope inside his shirt and swiveled on his butt, bringing his sandaled feet up from the side. The man crossed his legs Indian style and faced him directly, like a guru. "Aloha, brother. My name is Hawaiian Dan."

He nodded without answering and looked around at the bridge's underside. A slope of concrete blocks led up into the far reaches of the bridge sill. At the top of the incline, where the girders rested on the foundation, there were little dark cubbyholes where you could keep cool and hide.

"Aloha, brother," the man said again as, behind where he was squatted, Stanley slid down the path and ducked down. "Hawaiian Dan's the name."

"Who's this guy?" Stanley asked.

"Hawaiian Dan, I guess."

"What can I do for you, men?" Dan held out his arms as if he were some official host. "There's plenty of room here. The ground's soft and there's even a hard slope for those with bad backs."

"You live here, man?" Stanley asked.

"Sure do, brother."

"Aren't you kind of old for this shit?" Stanley asked.

"Middle-aged," Dan said, as if that answered the question either way. "You boys thinking of living here?"

"Sort of," he said.

"Depends on if the genius here thinks he can fix it up," Stanley added.

"I see," Dan said, grasping his chin. "Well, let me show you around." When Dan stood up they saw he was skinny too, with scrawny legs, and short enough to stand erect under here with a good foot to spare. "Come on in, it's nice here. No one bothers you, not even the cops."

Stanley and he waddled in from under the main girders then stood up. They could stand erect too, though there wasn't much more than a thick Sunday newspaper between them and the bridge.

"Ah, you see," Dan bellowed. "The place was made for you. And it has lots of potential too. I've always thought about remodeling it myself. But time just seems to fly, doesn't it?"

"Yeah, man," Stanley said, frowning and rolling his eyes in disgust.

Dan offered to show them some things and started off with the dirt. He explained how the shade kept it moist and cool so there wasn't much dust. Also you could germinate mushrooms in it for money. Then Dan showed how the abutment ledge could be used for preparing food and how one could knock everything over the side when finished.

"Modern," he joked.

"Very!" Dan added.

Stanley shook his head.

"Don't worry, my brother," Dan tried consoling Stanley. "I won't be here to bother you. I'm leaving. Going back to Hawaii to relax and forget the world."

He and Stanley looked at each other. Stanley lifted his brows and raised his eyes at the same time.

"You see, boys," Hawaiian Dan said, "I was born in Los Angeles. I grew up here and worked hard. But after many years as a used car salesman I finally got tired of it all. I divorced my wife, sold everything I had and became a free spirit like yourselves. So now when I'm not in Hawaii I'm here, living a life free from bills and whatever else the great big cruel world doles out. And I have no regrets."

He and Stanley looked at each other again.

"By the way, gentlemen. Do you have anything to smoke?"

"You mean dope?" he asked.

"Dope, grass, weed, Mexican, Colombian, anything, brother." Dan pulled out a fat joint from his breast pocket. It had long stringy leaves sticking out from the ends. "This stuff."

He looked at Stanley, but Stanley was eyeing the joint in Dan's hand, touching his fingertips to his mouth. They had managed to stay clean for about two weeks, but as the moment of truth reared up in their faces, the aroma was making him lightheaded and his eyes watery. Besides, what was wrong with a little home grown? Christ, compared with what Stanley and he were used to, it'd be like smoking a cigarette. But what about the oath? If there ever had been one.

"Let's do it," Stanley said.

"Well, then," Dan beamed. "Let's go up to the den and give it hell."

Squeezed into the small cubbyhole it didn't take long to get stoned. And Stanley especially was enjoying it a lot. After the joint had done the circuit twice, Stanley started taking two hits before passing it on. By that point he wanted to swat it out of Stanley's hand, but he was trapped in the argument between minding his own business and looking out for each other. Everyone had a right to choose whatever he or she wanted to do, regardless of the consequences. Even so, he wished Dan would complain about Stanley's hoarding, instead of just running off at the mouth. Dan was going on and on, especially about the way American homegrown would some day be better than any other bud in the world, simply because the States had a better climate and soil, and the business know-how. Then in mid-sentence Dan seemed to have switched from the long story he was telling now, to about how he convinced two would-be robbers he had syphilis and since they'd already touched him he would tell them the cure if they would let him be. They agreed and Dan told them they had to jump in the ocean, clothes and all, and stay there at least two hours to make sure the salt water dissolved the disease.

"Don't you have a plane or boat to catch?" Stanley asked when Dan finally stopped to take a hit.

"Yes, gentlemen, I guess I should be on my way. So let me make a deal with you. I'll sell you the place."

"Sell us the place?" Stanley roared. "You don't own this place, man."

"You're right," Dan said, holding up his hands. "But"—Dan started and then stopped to think—"but under the law if a person squats in an area for three years and no one protests, it's his, fair and square."

"But you went to Hawaii, didn't you?" Stanley said, squinting over at him.

"Good point." Dan stroked his beard, glassy-eyed, obviously having a hard time concentrating.

"I'll tell you what," Dan began. "You can have the last of my homegrown stash. I won't need it in Hawaii."

Dan handed a baggie full of dope to him and gave Stanley the rolling papers. "Adios, my friends."

They watched Dan slide down the block incline and stand up at the bottom, performing a sloppy about-face. In another moment like a British officer he was saluting the two of them. "Good-bye, Hollywood. I will miss you dearly. And remember boys, turn off the lights when you leave."

They watched him scamper away, just missing his head on the girder when he started up the dirt path.

"I sure hope I never see that guy again," Stanley said, toking on the burnt-out roach. "I was about ready to kill him he talked so much."

"Yeah," he muttered, handing Stanley the matches.

He looked at the bag of pot in his hand and tried to think about the future. So did Stanley, smiling to himself.

# CHAPTER THIRTY

Stanley was asleep in his favorite spot, on the south side of the local paint store, the same place where Stanley met the local drug dealer he'd befriended, this guy named Prince. But first and foremost, and although the black asphalt sometimes got a little too stinky and gooey even for Stanley, it was mostly a great place to sit out in the sun. And most of the time Stanley didn't mind, let alone realize his butt was sinking into the parking lot. He guessed that was why he was here, to make sure Stanley didn't sink all the way to hell. Besides, it was a good place to study all the details of automobile grills, like right in your face. And it was fun to watch the green coolant drip out of the overflow tube. And listen to the engine groan and moan inside like at the same time things were settling and snapping apart.

But all that seemed to interest Stanley these days was his job as a dope courier, an afternoon siesta, and a tan that would send every chick in L.A. to an early grave. The tan bit seemed kind of strange to him, but Stanley swore black people could get tans too, that white people didn't know that because white people didn't care to know much about black people to begin with. A fact, Stanley said, Prince reminded everyone of every chance he got.

But whatever the case, Stanley was now convinced a good tan was easily worth ten chicks. And also that they had to stay slender. That was no problem because they didn't have any money, and what money they did get they spent mostly on booze and dope anyway. But the slimness and the tan both fit in with Stanley's plan of two chicks coming out of nowhere some day soon—chicks that would be tan and slender and beautiful and rich and horny, though not necessarily in that order—and taking them home.

Fine. Dandy. But did he have to sit out here too? Couldn't the chicks meet him inside the store? Couldn't he just be a little tan instead of burnt to a crisp? Couldn't he just have a little muscle on his ribs, a little more padding on his butt so his ass wouldn't get so sore?

But not to complain. Life was grand. They had no appointments, no pressures, no bills, and no one to answer to. It was the American dream come true, even if they didn't have a red cent.

Jesus, he had lost his train of thought again. Oh, well.

Stanley moved his head to the side.

"You're blacker than black now."

"Mmmm, what?" Stanley mumbled.

"I've been thinking about what you said."

"What's that?"

"I forgot," he shrugged.

"What?" Stanley moaned.

"Good morning. Or good afternoon, whatever it is."

Stanley blinked slowly and frowned. "What's your problem, man?"

"Let's not ask what our country can do for us, but what we can do for it."

"What?" Stanley opened his eyes this time.

"J.F.K. You remember that, don't you? Back when we were young and ready to fight?"

"In one of your moods again, huh?"

"Too much wine and dope last night I guess," he said. "Not enough jam on my toast."

Stanley shook his head and started to get up, using the cinder block wall for support. Even so, Stanley's knees were shaking as if he were standing for the first time.

"You got any roaches left?" he asked.

Stanley shook his head. "I was thinking we should go into the city today."

"Oh, boy! You mean we can actually do something together today?"

"Cool it, will you, man? I don't need any grief this morning, all right?"

All right—even though for the record, it was afternoon. But he'd keep his mouth shut. He didn't want to be known as a Mister Know-it-All. He'd been accused of that too much already. Besides, he knew this going-into-the-city bit was all a crock of shit anyway. Prince would be coming soon, and before Prince showed up he had to make himself scarce. Stanley didn't want him to get into any trouble, the plan being that if Stanley ever did, he'd bail Stanley out. Of course, no mention of where in hell he would get the money from. He'd have to increase his shoplifting from two to three stores a day to six or more. Maybe rob a bank. For sure, Prince wouldn't give him a dime. He never gave Stanley anything but promises, like a car and a place to live, like a steady income and a business of his own. Like some decent dope for Christsake.

"I see you two're enjoying all this heat."

When he looked up a fat man in a white shirt, blazer and tie was setting down two gallons of paint next to his car. The man reached in his pocket and pulled out his keys.

"Never know when it's going to rain," he said to the man.

The man chuckled, though it was obvious he was just being cautiously polite. "I guess so," he said. Then he opened up his door, reached down for the paint and set it back behind his seat. When he was done he looked back at the two of them and smiled. "Looks like your friend has been in the sun all his life."

He looked over at Stanley beside him, asleep on his feet. "Yeah," he said. "He used to be white."

The man didn't know how to react so he kept on smiling and started to get into his car.

"You have air conditioning in that thing?" he asked.

"You bet," the man said. "Won't leave home without it."

"That's nice."

"Yes, it is. Thank you."

"You better get home now before you start sweating. Your wife'd kill you for that now, huh?"

The man's face lost its expression. He put on his sunglasses and started the car. The radiator fan stirred up the dust and debris for a second, but did nothing to cool him and Stanley off.

"Stanley," he called as the car pulled away.

"Yeah?" Stanley moaned.

"We had company."

"I heard."

"He thinks you sit out in the sun too much."

"Fuck him."

The way Stanley was against the wall with his eyes closed it looked like he had been plastered there. But Stanley didn't look totally dead. For one thing, he was holding his arms a little out from his sides and dancing his fingers like spiders along on the cinder block wall. Still, it looked like Mister Sun King was in for another siesta, after which he'd probably read his letters again. So there wasn't much sense sticking around, especially since he'd only have to leave when the time rolled around for Prince to show up.

"Well," he said, "one more day in paradise comes to an end."

Stanley kept his eyes closed.

"I think I'll go shopping," he said. "You know, look at the mannequins dressed in lacy underwear and all that kind of stuff. Maybe even get the saleswoman to show me some bras."

Still no sign of life from Stanley, the Sun King. Even the dancing spiders had stopped.

"I might even get a job. Who knows? Maybe even get married, have some kids that will support me in my old age."

Not even a nibble from Stanley.

"I'm going," he grunted as he stood up. His tail bone was tingling from being numb. "I'm gone."

Stanley still didn't move.

"If those chicks come by, tell them I'll be right back. I just went to check on the stock market."

He left Stanley standing alone against the wall. That was okay since no one was going anywhere, really. Even Prince was a dead-end street as far as he was concerned. After all, Prince wasn't making any promises to white guys like him. Except maybe for promising, though not in words, that he was going to lose a friend.

But now he had to make a decision. Which way was the best nowhere to go? To the left, more fashion stores. To the right, restaurants.

He chose the left, for today.

# CHAPTER
# THIRTY-ONE

He wasn't sure what woke him. It could have been the early morning buses gliding across the bridge, but more likely it was the heat. His whole backside was sweaty from sleeping on the block slope. Plus his lower back and spine hurt like hell. But it always did after lying on concrete. Why should today be any different?

But today was different. It was the four-month anniversary of their first day together in Los Angeles. It was amazing they hadn't either killed each other, or, for that matter, died of malnutrition, since their daily meal consisted of a few slugs of burgundy, however many tokes of dope, and whatever stale French bread or pumpernickel they could scrounge out of the bakery dumpster. Not quite the diet for the seventies. Not quite the life.

In any case, Stanley was still asleep at his side, as close as if the night had been a cold one. Which it hadn't; it was just that after baking all day long, at night The Sun King froze to death.

"God," Stanley yawned. "I had a dream about my aunt hugging me and I got a hard-on. She was rubbing my crotch with her leg, man. I was so embarrassed. I didn't know what to do."

"Did that really happen to you?"

Stanley shrugged. "Not that I remember."

"You're just horny then," he said.

"I must be if my aunt turns me on."

"Maybe it's a premonition."

Stanley's eyes widened. "That we'll get laid today?"

"That we'll get laid at all."

"Very funny, man." Stanley rose to sit with him, rubbing against his side.

"We're still going to the beach today, aren't we?" he asked.

"Why not?" Stanley said.

"No reason," he said. "I was just making sure."

"It's Monday, isn't it?"

"That it is."

"So what's wrong then?" Stanley asked.

"Nothing," he shrugged.

"Something's wrong, man."

"I just had a dream, that's all."

"What was it about?"

"I can't remember." But actually he could. It had to do with Doran visiting him at his hootch. The raped girl at his side was sitting on the lap of an unidentified black man, someone not in a uniform.

"Something...about something," he shrugged, though he thought the black man might've been Prince. "All I remember is I was uncomfortable. But that might have been because I was so hot."

"Sounds like you need a shrink, man."

"Thanks," he said. "Thanks a lot."

Stanley squeezed his forehead as if he had an headache. Then he lay back down.

"Anyway," Stanley said. "We're supposed to have fun today, remember? It's our day off."

"Yeah, I remember." But it was Stanley's day off, not his. He still had to do the household routine. "And I also remember we're not going to argue today. It's our four-month anniversary."

"Who's arguing?"

He shrugged. "Nobody."

"So when do we have to catch the bus?"

He pulled out the bus schedule from his back pocket, all damp and wrinkled from sleeping on it. Some of the print was blurred. He shook his head in advance at the thought of how great it would be if the time table were smudged right where he needed to read it. But fortunately it was okay. "It says here we have to leave at ten thirty to make all the connections."

"Wake me up at ten then."

"Come on, man. How in the hell am I suppose to know when it's ten?"

"Go hang out at a bar or something and come back ten minutes early."

"Yeah, right," he said.

"Okay, man," Stanley groaned. "I'll get up, but only if you shave that funky mustache of yours. You know if you shave it every day it'll come in faster."

"Yeah, you've told me. Like every day."

"Well, I don't want you to go around looking like a fool. Especially today. There'll be lots of chicks out on the beach and you don't want them to think you have a dirty lip, do you?"

"I'll manage, thank you."

"Whatever," Stanley shrugged. "We going to take the sport coat?"

"Yeah. Why not?"

"I don't know."

"We're going to share it, remember? You owe me."

Stanley frowned. "I know, man."

"We're bringing food too and we're going to take turns carrying it, right?"

"Yes," Stanley sighed. "It's covered."

They looked at each other and chuckled. They knew they'd be going back and forth all day long about who would wear the sport coat and who would carry the food and drink. But what was new?

"Happy Anniversary, darling," he said, like Zsa Zsa Gabor.

Stanley blew him a kiss and closed his eyes.

Of course, he had stolen more wine than they planned to take so they had to have at least one bottle before they left and they couldn't drink red wine without smoking a joint and once they smoked a joint they had to have another bottle of wine and since he was so good at stealing wine they might as well drink the big jug because it would be a bitch to carry it all over to the beach and they wouldn't let them have too much stuff on the bus anyway and they'd better smoke more dope because they couldn't do that on the beach and fuck, it was their anniversary and they could do what they wanted to do. So by noon, since they had missed the bus anyway, they decided to take a nap.

Somehow this bothered him. But he wasn't about to let it make him mad or cynical or upset. For one thing, he was too fucked up and for another, what would they have done on the beach anyway? Look at all the pretty girls they couldn't touch or even get near? Why go out of their way to frustrate themselves, right?

Right, he thought. So what was bothering him? Was it because he felt restless at the moment? He was restless all the time. That was why he smoked and drank so much. Obliterate anxiety was his motto. Of course, if he had something to do it might be different. But he had no talent, no skill, nothing to offer but his body for a stupid fucking factory job like the one he'd had back home a hundred years ago, a kind of job he never wanted again, no more than he wanted to become a big-wig, or responsible or respectable for any length of time. But he never used to feel that way. So what the fuck had happened?

Beside him Stanley's eyes slid slowly open and wavered half-focused. "What's wrong?"

"Nothing," he mumbled back. Nothing that mattered.

He leaned back on the concrete slope, resting his skull on his crossed arms. He didn't need this crap. But would it be any different if he'd gone back home, got his job back or attended school again? He'd still be all screwed up. That was one thing he knew for sure. But if it wasn't any different from this place, why didn't he go back? Why didn't he just toe the line like everyone else? What had made him stay here? Why couldn't he move on, trudge along? Everyone else did. What made him so special? Did he see something rotten no one else saw in the great American dream? Not really. He wasn't enlightened. He was the furthest thing from enlightenment, actually.

"What?" Stanley muttered again.

Great. He was mumbling out loud now, talking to himself no less. "Nothing," he said. "My mind is just zooming at full speed at the moment."

"Mine too, man. That pot sure is some kick-ass shit."

"It sure is."

He took one last look at the underside of the bridge and slowly closed his eyes. As his lids squeezed out the last bit of light the world began to spin so fast and dizzily he couldn't keep his eyes shut.

So much for a nap.

He heard the familiar throaty sound of a bus accelerating as it crossed over them, probably on its way west towards the sunny beaches. Then he remembered his dream. The sun brought it back, by reminding him how it had been the only day he had ever made a bet with himself about the weather, the day he'd shot the girl in the head. Now he knew he hadn't done it to end her suffering. He'd only done it to make it easy for himself, the way he was still doing now.

# CHAPTER
# THIRTY-TWO

Stanley liked the old dish towel that was their makeshift tablecloth as long as the frayed edges were tucked under. Stanley wasn't into frills.

Stanley liked the day-old French bread for dinner too, as long as a bottle of dry red wine was there to go with it. If dinner was going to be the only meal of the day Stanley wanted it to be as continental as possible.

Stanley didn't like shopping for food or preparing it, or setting the table—in this case the ground—or cleaning up afterwards.

Stanley did like, in fact loved, the addition of the manila rope he had found and tied to one of the girders so they could drop straight down it into the canal, where he, Stanley, could lie undisturbed under the sun.

He, on the other hand, liked to rotate every hour or so from sun to shade, until it was time to climb the rope and get dinner. Or to check the finances and go shopping, like today.

"Hey, man, I'm home!" Stanley yelled up from the bottom of the canal.

Stanley was drunk again. Drunk, stoned and sun-drained as usual, ever since Stanley had become bummed out about how they weren't going anywhere, mainly because of him, Mr. Lazy Butt Thorne, and his lack of ideas and motivation. Of course, he knew what was really pulling Stanley's chain was Prince himself, promising everything under the sun, but delivering on nothing, except some dogshit dope. Stanley knew it himself, but wouldn't admit it.

"Is dinner ready yet, darling?" Stanley guffawed.

He loved how the rope vibrated like a plucked string when Stanley started climbing. He liked watching Stanley struggling as he ascended hand over hand, holding on for dear life, resting at the knots they had tied to aid weaklings. It had always been fun to watch the other guy grapple with the task of climbing back up. It was a lot higher than it looked. Much higher if you only lived on French bread and wine. Much harder if you were drunk and stoned.

"It's a long ways down there," Stanley gasped as his head popped over the top of the abutment. "Shit, man. It's fucking harder than shit to get up here."

Stanley always said that when he reached the top. When he was drunk and stoned anyway. And Stanley was drunk and stoned so often these days he was thinking of cutting the rope down, with Stanley hanging on it.

"Hey, man. Can you get this bottle, man? I don't want to break it." Stanley reached out with the bottle trying to set it on top of the ledge, but it was like trying to place a peg in a hole that kept moving around. "Help me, man. I'm going to fall."

"You're not going to fall," he said. He did get up to help, though, because it looked a little more serious than usual. All he needed was Stanley smashing his head to smithereens on the concrete.

Suddenly, even though he wasn't all the way up, Stanley leaped for the wall, and landed mid-chest on top of the ledge. His free hand dug into the dirt like a rake. The other one stabbed the bottle into the ground like a knife.

"Grab the bottle, man!"

"Grab the bottle?" he said as he ran over to help. "The fucking thing's empty, dumbshit."

He grabbed Stanley by the back of the pants and pulled as hard as he could, leaning back with all his weight as Stanley came up.

"Try getting one of your knees over, for Christsake," he groaned.

"I can't, man!" Stanley sounded worried. His legs were like the broken wings of a bird trying to fly. But with another pull Stanley was up past his thighs.

"You're all right now," he said, letting go of Stanley's belt. "What were you trying to do? Kill yourself?"

Stanley was busy searching inside the bottle. "It is empty, man. I must have spilled it."

"Yeah, down your throat."

"I'll go get some more. For dinner."

"Who's going to lift you over the curb?"

"I ain't that drunk, man," Stanley scolded.

Yeah, and he was Santa Claus. Nothing like eating dry French bread without anything to drink.

"Are you mad at me because you didn't get any wine, man?"

He sighed. "I'll go get another one. Just don't roll off this thing, all right?"

"I'll just lie right here," Stanley promised, rolling over on his back. "Just tell me one thing."

"What's that?"

Stanley let his head drop back to the ground, then turned to look at the bottle.

"What you want to know?" he asked Stanley again.

Stanley grabbed his arm and pulled him closer. "We were high, remember?"

"You mean this morning?"

Stanley let go of his arm and chuckled to himself.

"What's so funny?" he asked.

Stanley looked up at him. "Nothin', man. Not a thing."

Stanley turned his head away, grabbed onto the bottle and took a swig, tossing it away when he realized it was empty. He didn't know what the fuck was bothering Stanley, but didn't want to be around here much longer to find out.

"If I don't come back," he said, "you can have my share of nothing."

As he stood up Stanley rolled to his side, coughing a bit. He kept going, though, stepping over the tablecloth and heading for the path. He wasn't sure, but it seemed like he could feel Stanley watching his every step.

Of course, this was not the time to get down on one's fellow man. This was the time to help one's fellow man. This was the time to rise above one's own feelings and help one's fellow man. So he stole three bottles of wine. One for his fellow man. Two for him.

# CHAPTER
# THIRTY-THREE

Max was short for Maximum. He was a black dude as broad as a washing machine and almost as short, with telephone-pole-sized legs that pressed tightly against each other from the knees on up, and arms just as gargantuan. Max's favorite story was how he wanted to be a gas station attendant so he could sell dope on the side. The idea was when someone asked him to check the transmission fluid, that would be the code to stash the dope near the battery. Then the customer would pay the bill as usual but, of course, it would be padded to cover the extra service. It was a good idea and everyone thought Max should do it, but Max just wasn't interested in pumping gas all his life. What he really wanted to do was lie on his back with a green wine bottle resting over his eyes. He said the green light was a cosmic source of knowledge, but usually Max fell asleep when he set the bottle on his head, so it looked more like Max was guessing the contents of the bottle than receiving knowledge from the universe.

Larry was another black dude they met with Max. Larry's big thing was to horde the wine and dope while he got involved with his stories. Larry always said alcohol enlarged his memory which increased his ability to tell tall tales. He also said dope expanded his insight so his stories could be of a profound nature. It sounded like bullshit to everyone else, but that didn't hinder Larry. He kept on gabbing, especially about women with long slender legs. Larry had long legs and arms too. He said he was the only kid in his school who could wrap himself around a mailbox. He said he could mount any bicycle with his feet flat on the ground. Finally, Larry said he'd been the only kid in his neighborhood with a bushy Afro, which among them here and now was also true.

Clarence was the site manager and lone worker of a small county landfill that had one of the last old-time incinerators. The dump was nestled in a group of rolling hills north of Los Angeles, west of the interstate and above the train yards. It wasn't used much anymore because the suburbs had sprawled up too close. But Clarence said he was as busy as ever now that he had to make sure the dump didn't offend anyone.

Clarence was a short pudgy guy and white as a sheet. He liked to say he wasn't a high school dropout because he had left school when he was in junior high. Then he came out to California around six years ago, got this job and worked and lived here ever since.

Clarence had a face that seemed to have been struck by a solid oak plank swung by Superman. He showed them how level his forehead, nose, lips and chin were with one another by lying flat on the ground with a board on top of his face. In fact he showed them that every chance he got.

Larry liked to call Clarence 'Clearance'. Larry swore anyone could see light coming through Clarence's ears. Clarence thought that was funny. Clarence also thought the nickname 'Clearance' was the best he'd ever had.

"It's not much of a place," Clarence shrugged, "but it's all Glenwood can offer."

"It's all Glenwood can offer," Max said holding up a crushed can from the ground.

He liked Max. Max was always coming up with funny things. And the more wine and dope they had, the funnier Max got. Today, since it was hot again and the sun was out in all its blazing glory, they'd been taking it in steady. At this point, in fact, he was glad he'd chosen the chain-link fence to lean against, the same way Stanley'd done.

"Don't give this guy any dope," Larry warned them about Clarence. "He could really become dangerous."

"I don't smoke," Clarence assured Larry, obviously missing Larry's point.

"Well, don't give him any wine then," Larry said.

"I don't drink either."

"Jesus, man. What do you do?"

"Don't get him started," Max warned.

"I pile those cars over there and take care of the refuse that comes in."

"This guy's too much," Larry said. Larry took a hit off his dube and then gulped some wine. "He's going to drive me to drinking."

"You are drinking," Stanley said.

It surprised him Stanley'd said anything. The two of them were both practically in a trance, tired from the long hot walk, drunk and stoned, and overwhelmed by the Larry, Max and Clarence Show. It was usual for them to remain quiet, especially now that Stanley was hardly ever around anymore. Prince was keeping him busy day and night, moving dope here to there and back again. It seemed like he and Stanley hadn't held a conversation in the whole of last month. Now that he thought about it, matter of fact, the only time he and Stanley'd been together in the last month was when they were here with Max and Larry. Lucky they'd met these guys, or they might never have talked or seen each other again.

"You guys coming next week too?" Clarence asked.

"Not if we can help it," Larry said.

"Sunday is my day off. So if you come on Sunday I can join you."

"Thanks for the warning," Larry said.

"Larry," Max complained. "Be nice."

"If you don't work on Sundays then you're working today, right?" Larry went on.

He could tell by the tone and the look on Larry's face he was about to trap Clarence.

"Yes," Clarence said.

"So what are you doing here with us? You think we're garbage or something?"

"Larry," Max warned, and lobbed one of his empty wine bottles over towards him.

"I have to clean the tractor today," Clarence said, undaunted.

"It looks pretty clean to me, man," Larry said, still smirking.

"I clean it once a week."

"Well, don't let us stop you, man. It's getting dirty right this minute."

Clarence nodded in agreement but didn't stand up. Instead he settled further down onto his butt, as Larry took another hit of dope followed by more wine.

"You're going to kill yourself doing that sort of thing," Stanley warned Larry.

"Hey," Larry coughed. "Don't give away my secret."

Max lay back down, placing the bottle over his eyes. Stanley took another drink. So did Larry. He followed suit, though it was quite an effort to lift the lip of the bottle to his mouth. Of course he spilled some. He ought to sit up straight like his mother had always told him to do. But no! Not him. Be a slob instead.

But what the fuck, look at Clarence, sitting without a care in the world waiting for Larry to bust on him some more. Christ, this was turning out to be quite the reunion. He couldn't wait for the next one so he could sit and not have a care in the world.

"You wouldn't believe the broad I saw yesterday," Larry said. "She had bazookas the size of watermelons." Larry held his arms out like two watermelons were in his lap. "God, I just wanted to go up and pick them and spit out the seeds."

Stanley handed him the joint. It was out. Not unusual these days. Everything Mr. Stanley Long gave him had something wrong with it. Most of the time it wasn't for him anyway. Stanley just wanted him to fix it, or scrounge a new one, or come up with a new idea.

"She was so shiny in her clothes I had to put my sunglasses on to stop from going blind. I mean she had threads that were brighter than the silvery moon."

"Wow!" Clarence said.

"She had legs that could wrap around your face three times."

Oh, Clarence was loving this, though he didn't quite get that one. Still, he was a good guy. It was just that the world was fucked. In fact at this moment he'd do anything to be Clarence. Except really it was more like he wanted Clarence's job. He didn't need to be Clarence.

On second thought, he didn't need Clarence's job either. He looked at the joint in his hand. Ought to re-light the sucker.

"She could melt your pecker," Larry said.

That widened Clarence's eyes, and when Larry shot his eyebrows up and down, Clarence grinned, exposing his teeth and gums.

"Have you ever seen slanted pussy, man?" Larry asked Clarence.

"No."

"It was everywhere over in Nam, man."

"Yeah," Clarence said. "You know, I wanted to go there."

Larry started laughing so hard that soon he was choking. "*Jesus Christ!* He wanted to go. Did you hear that? *He* wanted to go."

He watched Larry guzzling his wine, letting streams of it drip from his mouth. Stanley was drinking, too, less sloppily, but with the same drive to get as much down as possible. Max, on the other hand, wasn't moving any more. But of course, his bottle was empty.

When he looked back at Clarence, he was sitting there like a Boy Scout around a campfire waiting for the next tall tale. What a dumbfuck he was!

"Shit, man," Larry said. "Clearance here could've taken all our places. He could have saved the whole world for Christsake! Goddamn it, why didn't I meet you before? You could have been a hero, man. You could have taken my place. You know what I mean, man?"

"I wanted to go but they said I had flat feet," Clarence said, untying the laces on his boots.

"Come here," Larry whispered. Clarence leaned over. "Let me tell you something. I got flat feet from going."

Clarence straightened up and looked over at him, stupid and puzzled, asking for help. If he was any sort of friend he would help Clarence. He was his fellow white-man. But fuck Clarence. Fuck all white people. What'd they ever done for him? Not a fucking thing.

"You should let Max here tell you all about flat feet, my man," Larry continued. "He'll tell you all about flat feet. His old man had flat feet. Didn't he, Max?" Max didn't move. "He used them all the time on poor Max. *Max knows all about flat feet!* He's the flat feet king. He's had flat feet in his stomach, on his head and in his ear, man. Just ask him. He won't bite ya, man."

Clarence looked back at him, then down at his lap, wiping his eyes with the back of his hand. Larry and Stanley were back to drinking as before. Max still lay quiet.

When he looked back at Clarence, he was reaching over to tap Max on the foot.

"Don't do it, Clarence," he said. "Just be cool."

"Ah," Larry cried. "You should've let him."

"Yeah, you should've let him," Stanley said, tipping his bottle to Larry.

Maybe he should have, but it was too late now. On the other hand, being able to say anything at all made him feel pretty good. He was tired of talking to the underside of the bridge day in and day out. In fact it was starting to look like Nam had been the easiest time in his life. It was easier than working at the factory back in Syracuse. And now, after six months on the streets, another tour of duty in Nam would be a piece of cake. At this stage of the game he'd be one dangerous motherfucker if they gave him back his rifle. Or if he felt like it, all he'd have to do was shove the muzzle in his mouth and pull the trigger. Then again, maybe it'd be better to go back to the factory and get numb again that way. At least then he'd grow older and have that much more time to suffer. That was what he was into, right?

Yeah, Nam was a cinch.

# CHAPTER
# THIRTY-FOUR

It was the third straight day Stanley had chosen simply to sit on the ledge and peer down at the dry wash. His shoulders were slouched. His spine was curved. His head was down. His hands were at his sides folded over the lip of the ledge, and his feet dangled over the edge. At times it looked like Stanley was bouncing his heels off the wall. Sometimes he thought he heard Stanley mumbling, but most times Stanley sat staring quietly—thinking about Prince's most recent broken promise, was his guess. So what was it this time? Maybe those new shoes, the platforms Stanley'd talked about all yesterday and the day before that?

"Not enough sun today?" he asked, just for a word, a reaction from Mister Catatonic.

Nothing.

"Pretty nice day for November."

Zero.

Yes, Mister Stanley Long was mad, pissed, outraged. And he had every right to be. He took all the risks for Prince and Prince only gave him some coke or smack or a tiny bit of pot. Never any cash. Never making good on any of those bigger promises.

But wait a minute here. What was Stanley so mad about? Unlike Mr. Stanley Long, he didn't get to go to Prince's palace. He never got invited to the parties. He had to go home and sweep the dirt off the concrete. He never had any hot women sitting in his lap and licking his ear. He had to pick up all the trash and haul it to a dumpster. He didn't get a chance to smoke or do any good dope, drink any fine wine or beer. He had to go out for the day old French bread. He had to steal what he could from the supermarket. He didn't have the luxury of sleeping on a couch two or three nights a week. He had to sleep on the dirt and concrete.

"So what's your fucking problem?" he muttered behind Stanley's back.

He never got a kitchen to eat in, a living room to sit in, a toilet to shit in. He had to piss and crap in the bushes or at a gas station. He had to climb up and down the fucking rope. For what? Just to roam around some fucking canal that was no more than a big catch-all for every piece of junk in L.A.

Stanley slid forward, lowering his legs over the edge so only about half of his rear rested on the ledge. It looked like he was moments away from taking the plunge. But it wasn't worth it. He had already thought about it a hundred times. It wasn't high enough. The best you could do was break a leg and end up in the Vet's hospital, a fate worse than death. His advice was to go to the top of the bridge and jump head first. Then even if you didn't kill yourself you'd be a vegetable the rest of your life. And wasn't that what they were working on anyway? The hard way, of course.

Stanley slid back and resumed his original downtrodden posture.

Maybe he ought to strike up a little enthusiasm here. It was Veterans Day, after all. Maybe they could get with the program and meet a couple of babes, being the hot-shit veterans they were. Or better yet, maybe find the boys and get drunk. They hadn't done that since yesterday.

Oh, God. He was losing it again. The world was such a tough place to live. Nobody liked him. Nobody cared. No one even knew he existed. Makes you want to cry, don't it?

He stood up and stretched. "Well," he yawned. "Think I'll go get a bottle. I'm getting hungry. You want anything?"

Stanley didn't flinch.

"See you later then." But actually he had just decided he would never come back. He'd had enough of this fucking hole. It could fucking sink to the bottom of the earth for all he cared. He was gone. Vanished like the great buffaloes. See ya later.

When he came back about an hour later with two bottles of wine Stanley was gone. So for the hell of it he opened both bottles and pretended Stanley was there. He made toast after toast, clinking the bottles together, drinking from them in turn, cheering the forces of evil on to victory. Anything to make the time go by. And when he finished both bottles he thought about getting one more, a big one he could hide under the front of his shirt so he would look pregnant. That ought to work just fine. Maybe then they would catch him and throw him in jail, and maybe then Stanley would be home by the time he got out. Wouldn't that be mind-boggling?

He figured it was somewhere around three in the morning when Stanley came stumbling and mumbling back. When Stanley collapsed next to him, he pretended to be asleep. As usual, Stanley nestled up so at least some part of their bodies, usually an arm or lower leg, was touching. This night he was on his side, though, so Stanley cuddled right up to his back as if they were out in the cold trying to stay warm. His immediate reaction was to move away, but he was a little cold and he didn't feel like talking so he didn't want to take a chance of letting Stanley know he was awake.

"Good night," Stanley mumbled.

He couldn't tell if Stanley had meant that or if it was just habit. Then he smelled Stanley's breath, tainted with whiskey, beer and dope, Prince's favorite trio. And wasn't there just possibly a little coke or smack mixed in too?

When he closed his eyes, what squeezed out was no more than half a tear.

# CHAPTER
# THIRTY-FIVE

It was just him and Max at the cremation. Stanley had to work. Stanley'd also been at work when Max came back to the bridge to tell them he'd found Larry dead in an alley between two garbage cans. And Stanley hadn't been there either when the ambulance came to pick Larry up. And Stanley hadn't been there either when he and Max helped the paramedic place Larry in the body bag. It was just like old times, old times without Stanley. In fact it reminded him of the time in Nam when Stanley stood back while he and Harmon dealt with the guy in the latrine.

But what the fuck? It was over now, except for the crying. It could have been worse. Larry could have used a gun, messed up his face, gotten blood all over everything. But Larry didn't have a gun. He didn't have any money to buy a gun, and guns were too hard to steal.

Larry could have used a knife. But Larry didn't have a knife. Larry had no money to buy a knife. Knives are easier to steal but Larry never thought of stealing one. So Larry didn't use a knife.

Larry used drugs and alcohol. Larry didn't have any money to buy drugs or alcohol but Larry could steal alcohol, drink some of it, trade some of it for drugs, or Larry could do some favors for drugs, or Larry could steal drugs.

There were many options. One option was to OD.

But it was over now, except for the crying. And cremation seemed like a good way to go. After you're dead, that is. He wouldn't want to torch himself like those Buddhist monks. He'd OD himself before doing anything like that.

❖ ❖ ❖

Stanley was at the bridge when he got back but he didn't feel like talking. He hadn't known Larry that well anyway. He wanted to take a little nap and forget about all the funeral crap. So he didn't even bother to say hello. And why should he? Stanley wasn't exactly being talkative. Besides, he didn't know Stanley that well either, remember? He didn't know anybody, not even himself. All he knew heading for the blanket was that he wanted to sleep.

"How was it?" Stanley finally asked from the abutment ledge, dressed real sharp in his new sport coat, shirt, and pants. It looked funny for such a high-caliber guy to be sitting under a bridge, dangling his feet over the side of a wall. But he couldn't tell from where he was standing; maybe Stanley still didn't have his brand new shoes.

"All right," he said, lying down.

"No family there, huh?"

"No," he muttered.

"Where's he from? I forgot."

"New Jersey."

"That's right. Newark, wasn't it?"

"Yeah," he said placing his hands behind his head.

There was a long silence after that and that was just fine with him. All he wanted now was to be alone. Be alone and not have to think. Thinking was dangerous. Thinking should be outlawed. No one should be made to think. Thinking hurt too much. They should all just sleep. Sleep until the whole show was all over.

"I got another late delivery tonight," Stanley said. "I'll probably end up staying at Prince's."

He turned over to his side, away from Stanley. He had a blanket now to keep him warm. He didn't need anything else.

"I got a request," Stanley said softly.

He didn't want to answer, so he closed his eyes pretending to be asleep. Maybe Stanley would give up. If not, he could always say he hadn't heard him.

"I want to be cremated."

He opened his eyes.

"I don't want any part of me left to rot on this fucking planet."

He raised up on his elbow to look over his shoulder at Stanley, still gazing out over the canal. But after a bus glided over the bridge, Stanley turned around to look back at him too.

"How about you?" Stanley asked.

He shrugged. "Sure, why not?"

Stanley sneered. "How come you're so closed-mouthed all the time?"

"What do you mean me?" he said, raising his voice.

"I mean you, you son of a bitch."

"Hey, fuck you," he said.

Stanley turned back to the canal. "Fuck you, man. You're the one who has never given a Goddamn thing about anything. You just sit there and think all to yourself. You don't give a damn about anything but your own ass."

He threw the blanket off and stood up. "Well, tell me this, asshole. Name me the times you opened up, huh? Are we talking double digits? I think not. We're not even talking single digits except for one time, my last fucking day in Nam. And you expect me to bow down and praise the fucking Lord because Stanley fucking Long graced me with a heartfelt confession? What the fuck was I supposed to do?"

Stanley lowered his head.

"You know," he continued, "we always talk about how I ain't doing anything to make it happen. But it's you who fucking destroyed our future because you broke the Goddamn vow."

Stanley raised his head and shook it slightly, back and forth.

"You're fucked up, man!" he said. "You're killing yourself with those fucking drugs. The very thing you confessed to me back in Nam. You feared it then, why don't you fear it now?"

When Stanley placed his hands on the ledge, at first he thought Stanley was about to get up. But then the hesitation made him think Stanley was close to jumping off.

"I won't be back tonight," Stanley said, and stood up, facing away and started for the dirt path.

He noticed Stanley's shoes—same ones he'd had since he got off the bus nine months ago. Looked more beat up than ever, too, alongside those new threads.

"I'll keep the vow," he said in a wavering voice.

Stanley stopped and looked back over his shoulder. "Thanks." And then went on his way.

So it was every man for himself now. Electronics was no longer in their future. That made him wonder who was the real enemy in Nam and who was it here?

He guessed he wouldn't know, until maybe sometime after he was dead.

# CHAPTER
# THIRTY-SIX

On Thanksgiving Day he stole two bottles even though he knew Stanley wouldn't be home for dinner. He did it to keep in shape, maintain the knack, retain his high level of skill and nerve. He did it for old-time's sake, a remembrance of sorts, though there wasn't much to remember. All Stanley and he had ever done was eat and drink. Oh, sometimes they'd discussed the world situation, but mostly they boasted about the women they never had or about Stanley's plan to make it big, now fading quickly with the seventies only a little more than a month away. But that didn't matter anymore, especially not after drinking two bottles of wine. In fact it was time to celebrate, so he lit a joint, then a second one, and a third.

"Blessed are those whose life is like a motor," he said, holding up the joint. "It just keeps running and running until it runs out of gas."

"Blessed are the meek, for they shall inherit the fucking earth."

Stanley startled him. But to his surprise, there he was, all decked out in a new sport shirt and bell-bottomed leisure suit.

Stanley walked over to the ledge and took the joint from his hand, seemingly avoiding him by looking across the way.

"I suppose you got to work tonight?" he asked. "I mean it's only Thanksgiving. Nothing special or anything."

"Thanksgiving don't mean anything to a black man," Stanley said. "Besides, business doesn't stop because of a holiday, man. It increases if you think about it."

"Yeah," he said. "For Prince."

"Hey, man," Stanley said, "what's eating you?"

"Nothin'. Not a thing."

Stanley shook his head, then looked down into the canal. He thought of asking Stanley for the joint back, or grabbing his leg and throwing him off.

"Something's eating you," Stanley said, still watching the canal.

He looked up at Stanley, then across the canal. "I can't figure out why you couldn't get Thanksgiving off. It's just one fucking day. Shit, man, you don't even come around any more and I'm supposed to hang out here just in case the business falls through. It ain't easy, you know. And it don't help when you do come around acting like this place is too low-life for you. You can't even sit down because you'll get your fancy clothes dirty. Or look me in the eye."

Stanley sighed. "Fuck you, man."

"No, fuck you, man."

"Fuck you, motherfucker," Stanley said.

"Fuck you, motherfucker," he repeated with a little more emphasis.

He pushed on Stanley's leg and Stanley kicked back, hitting his forearm when he tried blocking it. But getting into it while they were on the ledge would be a big mistake. They would both fall and kill themselves and then nobody would win. Besides, he didn't have the strength to start a fight, let alone finish one, and he was sure Stanley was as stoned and drunk as him.

Stanley stepped back from the ledge, then looked at the joint in his hand. It had gone out and he knew Stanley wanted to ask him for a light, like he always did. But the truth was, he felt like throwing the matches down into the canal.

He knew why things had changed. It was cocaine and smack. It was beer, whiskey and wine. It was high-powered pot. It was fast women and slick talking con-artists. It was staying out late at night. It was taking all the risks and getting nothing.

It almost seemed like they had never left the army.

Then, when Stanley finally looked at him, he saw why Stanley had been avoiding him. Dark rings circled Stanley's eyes, his face was drawn and hollow, the skin stretched over bone in a horrible contrast to the neatly ironed shirt, pants and sport coat, as if he hadn't slept or eaten for weeks.

"What's wrong, man?" Stanley said quietly. "I look as bad as you?"

"We never were very handsome," he said, keeping eye contact and trying to smile.

Stanley kept squinting, as if he had something under his lids. "You weren't very handsome," Stanley chuckled. "You were always too skinny, man. Women like meat, something to grab onto. You know what I mean, man?"

"Yeah, I know."

"So get something to eat for Christsake," Stanley said. "You're fading away, man, you look like some kind of troll or something. Get out in the sun for Godsake. Enjoy the world before you die, you son of a bitch."

Tears ran down Stanley's cheeks. He wiped them with his coat sleeve, then looked at the joint in his hand.

"I know," he said softly, wiping his face.

"You got a light?" Stanley asked.

The war didn't fuck him up. About the only thing it did was speed things up. Wars were good for speeding up the process of eliminating the dead weight. But they didn't add any new revelations on suicide. At best they just made the old reasons more obvious. However, war had taught him how to commit suicide, or how not to. That is, it was easier to kill yourself when there were no friends or parents around, when you had no identification on you and when, like Larry, you were in between a couple of garbage cans.

But shit, he could have learned that in college.

After finishing the joint Stanley pulled out a letter from the inside of his sport coat, looked at the envelope, ripped it in two, and tossed it into the canal. Before it hit the bottom, Stanley had left without a word.

It was about an hour later that he realized he was never going to take a nap until he went down and retrieved that letter. So he climbed down the rope, pieced it together and read it. It was from Stanley's aunt, postmarked from last September, just before Larry's death. It said Stanley's mother had died from her year-long bout with cancer.

He stopped reading and placed the letter back into the envelope, then tore it up into smaller pieces, throwing them throughout the canal, kicking wildly to spread them further apart.

He wiped his tears away, wishing he'd asked more about Stanley's life. But he'd fucked that up too. So he went back to the rope, but when he grabbed it and looked up he thought about God for the first time in quite a while.

"Fuck you," he said, out loud but under his breath.

# CHAPTER
# THIRTY-SEVEN

"Stanley says his mother died," Max said. "He says his whole family is dead. He's even dead."

He couldn't decide what look or gesture to give Max back. Max had worked so hard, so long to find him on the street that he felt he should show some concern, at least ask where the hell Stanley was. But his mind couldn't get into gear. He had smoked too much, not to mention drinking, and it wasn't even noon yet, once again.

"You don't look so well yourself," Max said.

Yeah, he'd noticed the same thing in the bar window a few minutes ago. He looked like he hadn't slept for years, but his clothes looked like they'd been slept in for the same amount of time. And he was so skinny, or even past skinny to a stumbling, bumbling, mumbling skeleton. His eyes were baggy and purplish. He had sores in his mouth. So Merry Christmas!

"He's at the bridge," Max said after he didn't answer. "It's a pretty weird scene. He could use some help. He's pretty sick."

"Not today," he said. "I'm fucked up."

"You need help, man?"

"No, I'm okay. I just need some time to get my head straight. I'll go back then, when I can handle it."

He turned his head away from Max. The sidewalk here was full of the usual street people—young and old, black, Chicano and white, long hair, short hair, or none at all, leaning up against buildings or strutting their stuff or stumbling to the oases in their head. He knew that from first-hand experience. Yet, for all the months he'd seen these people he didn't know a one. The fact was, maybe he didn't care to. And didn't care whether they knew him or not.

"Okay," Max said.

When he gazed back at Max's eyes he could tell Max didn't blame him. Max knew the situation with Stanley. Plus Max was the guy who said no one could be there all the time for anybody else. That was why Max said he'd never married and never would. It made perfect sense, didn't it?

But what Max didn't know was that 'not today' also meant not tomorrow or next week or ten years from now. He didn't want to do a fucking thing with Mister Stanley Long! He could go back to his Prince and weather it out wherever Prince in all his generosity sent the downtrodden and ill until they recovered to become efficient workers once again. Wasn't it you, Mr. Long, who said basket cases should neither be seen nor heard? So live it, sucker. Take your due. It's your turn.

From his vantage point against the wall, he watched Max pick his way down the curb side to avoid the stumbling winos and the kids weaving through on their skateboards like it was an obstacle course. He should have said goodbye but he didn't feel like talking. What he felt like instead was biting some heads off. And what pissed him off most was that now, with Stanley at the bridge, he would have to find another place to hang out. No way did he feel like dealing with Stanley. He had to have a life of his own too, no matter how much work it took.

He glanced over at the poster outside the bar he was leaning against. If he got a job as bartender here, for example, he could see 'Miss Lewd-a-Chris' do her thing—and she did plenty of things. For that matter, it might also be a way to keep warm at night.

"My son." A clean shaven wrinkly old man took hold of his arm and looked up at him, squinting as if he needed sunglasses. "You are my son. My step-son," the man corrected himself. "My wife's son who was a son to me as my own son was. My son left home. I remember he left home."

"Not today, old man." He tried to pull away but the old man's grip became tighter. He was amazed by the old man's strength, especially since he looked so frail.

"My son. My son left home because of his mother. His stepmother," the old man corrected himself. "My wife's son who was a son to me as my own son was. He left home. My wife's son."

"That's too bad." He pushed himself off the wall and started down the street. But the old man tagged along.

"My son. My wife's son. My son. He left home. My son."

"Go away, old man," he warned.

"My wife's son. His mother."

"Beat it!" he shouted.

He yanked his arm away leaving the old man standing alone, mumbling about his son, turning in a circle as if he were lost. But when a black hooker strutted by the old man perked up again. He went for her but she straight-armed him in the chest, stopping him dead in his tracks. The old man stood immobile, mouth open, peering down at his chest, trying to touch it with his shaking hand.

But fuck that guy. He wasn't about to have an old coot following him around all day. He had enough problems. Plus he was getting out of this loony bin.

At the next building, an abandoned five and dime, he spotted Max standing inside the alcove with his hands in his pockets, watching a bunch of kids trading baseball cards. Behind Max a plywood board covered the doorway, with words spray painted on it: U.S. out of Vietnam.

He thought it should say: U.S. out of my Life.

He walked past without looking at Max. But he had a feeling all the way down the block Max was watching him. So he took a right turn he hadn't planned on, just to put a few buildings between him and the rest of the world.

Look at it this way: He was lucky to have found a place to sleep. Most people didn't have a brick wall to lean against. Most people didn't have a view of a telephone pole and its various humming transformers. Most people didn't have another brick wall ten feet or so across from them to stare at in the dark, not to mention a dimly lit alley that was also very quiet, a good safe distance from the noisy bars. Then there was the company of all the garbage cans, full of nicely crammed-in trash.

Christ, he felt right at home. It was like all the neighborhood kids were gathered around to listen to his adventures of street life. This particular group would be impossible to bore, even though he would try his best. These cans were here until eternity, like him.

Great. Here he was thinking only of himself, crying over his hard life. He should be with his buddy, pal, blood brother. In fact he wondered what Stanley was doing at this moment. Probably thinking of himself and not his buddy, pal, blood brother. Probably being an asshole just like him.

Fuck. Be a miracle if he got one wink of sleep tonight.

He reached down for his bottle, took a swig, then struck a match to re-light his joint. The reflection off the grimy garbage cans gave him the feeling he was in a cave. At first it made him think of Larry and how he might have felt before he OD'd. Then he was thinking of Stanley again.

Don't you remember the time we danced our hearts out together? Don't you remember those big fat bouncers letting us in free at the back door? The place was way out of our league. We were fucking ripped to the gills. You got that cocaine, remember? I bet you remember there was enough pussy on that lighted dance floor to eat until you died. A man would never have to come up for air again. You're the one who wished he was a flashing light so you could look up at all the ladies' crotches for the rest of your life.

Don't you remember, man?

Didn't we have the biggest hard-ons in the world that night? Didn't we get lost in the rock and roll and dance until our hearts and minds were in some kind of heaven? Yeah, man, that was us, you and me, blood brothers for life. We were in heaven, man. And we were together. Surprised the shit out of ya, didn't it? I could tell. It surprised the shit out of me. Ain't no way in hell that we can get rid of each other, man. We're stuck. I told you we would be. I told you that when we cut our hands and became blood brothers. I told ya we were headed for a world of shit too. But no, you wouldn't believe me.

Goddamn it, man, that was us dancing out there on that floor, laughing so hard we could hardly stand up. You and me, two guys being cool as cool can be. And everyone was happy. They were laughing with us. Even the manager didn't kick us out. We were the main attraction. Everyone loved us.

He looked at the joint in his hand. The truth was, they'd never gone to that disco because he, Mr Closed-Mouth, had never brought it up. And now, like everything else in this fucking hole, the fucking joint was out.

# CHAPTER
# THIRTY-EIGHT

His legs felt weak and his head light as a helium balloon. Although he teetered back and forth, it seemed the motion was only in his mind, like he was standing still while the ground was whirling underneath him. He let the bread drop as instinctively he reached up with both hands for the lip of the girder, but then blacked out before he got a good grip. Next thing he knew he was hanging on with all his weight on his arms. His right foot responded a little but his leg was still without power and his left side was even more like rubber. So he let go of the girder and dropped to his knees and hands.

He knelt there for a moment like a stunned animal. Then he looked up at Stanley lying in the dirt, his head resting on the concrete slope. Stanley was all decked out in his brown cordovan shoes, his light blue pants and sport coat, his colorful shirt, his silk scarf and dark sunglasses. Stanley's arms were out at his sides but his hands should have been folded on his stomach and holding a black rose instead.

Because Stanley was dead. OD'd. He could tell it from here, still a good ten yards away.

His stomach heaved twice in rapid succession. He caught the ball of heartburn in his mouth and swallowed it back down. His forehead broke out in a sweat. The tops of his ears felt frostbit. His heartbeat reverberated all through his body, and sounded like an echo in his head. A good breath was what he needed. But if he took one it would turn his stomach inside out.

He crawled on his hands and knees over to the ledge, and his right hand no sooner reached it than his stomach erupted and the vomit exploded, spraying his arms and hands and splashing the ground. Then another rush catapulted out, and hit the lip of the wall, showered out into the air, or down the wall like thick soup, leaving long sticky strands hanging from his lips and chin, stretching out till they landed on the ledge.

"*Fuck*," he moaned.

Afterwards, his arms jittered and the canal floor rose up and down like he was on a swing. He wanted to move away but feared he might fall into the canal. On the other hand, though, if he stayed the same weakness would cause him to collapse and fall in anyway, eventually. But finally when he took a breath he found it easy to sit back on his legs and feet, though the smell of vomit still clung to him like strong cologne.

But now it was all over. As quickly as it'd started it was done.

No matter how ghoulish it felt he was determined to hold the eyelids shut until they stayed closed. He had done it before, but this was different. This time he could feel his fingertips throbbing in unison with his heart. Only sometimes it seemed not his heart but Stanley's. One moment it was he pumping his life energy into Stanley and then in the next it was Stanley slyly draining him down to his level, inviting him to join the peacefulness and quiet. Everything was free where Stanley was. There was good food, good drink, good dope, fine women. Come my friend and join me. Our utopia is finally here.

But he wasn't that romantic or stupid. Maybe that had been his problem all along. Maybe Stanley had been right about him. Maybe he never gave anybody anything.

He put Stanley's sunglasses back on, making sure they didn't bend Stanley's ears.

Thanks for bringing him back home, Mister Prince, he thought without much anger. Without, so far as he could tell, much of anything at all.

It seemed to get dark quicker than usual but that was okay. He was tired and tomorrow would be a long day. It was best to lie down, to rest, to sleep. Stop thinking about the past, the present, the future. None of that did any good. It never had.

"Yeah," he sighed, settling in next to Stanley. "You were right all along. I did kill Stephens." He laughed some. "Yeah, I killed him. I had to. I was cutting in on his business and he wanted to get rid of me." He laughed again. "So I got rid of him first. Simple business transaction. Nothing more."

Tears wet his eyes, but never built to the point where they would spill over and run down his cheeks.

"I even killed Harmon. But it was for his own good, of course. I really saved his life from drugs."

He pictured Harmon sinking under the water, like the bow of a ship. Then the girl.

"I killed a lot of other people, too. Some supposedly already dead. But I guess it still counts, huh?"

He looked over at Stanley. But Stanley didn't move. Asleep as usual. Always asleep. But it wasn't Stanley's fault. It was his. He never said anything. He never let it all out until it was too late, until no one was around to listen. It had been a fault of his since he could remember, ever since he had first cried alone in his back yard, back behind the garbage cans. And now as usual, once again, it was too late. He still hadn't even told Stanley thank you for being his friend.

"I'm okay," he said to the underside of the bridge. "I'm fine. Really, I am."

It felt so natural pressed against Stanley's body head to toe. They had done it so many times. In their lean-to in Nam. In his hootch. By the dumpster areas, and here under the bridge. Even the smell of his vomit couldn't take that away. But it still bothered him Stanley had failed to make it to the seventies. It wouldn't have mattered if they had become somebodies or not. At least they would have been alive. Which might not seem like much to most people. But most people hadn't killed other people the way he had.

But in any case, the war was only half the story. Again, all it did was speed up the process. For him it was a matter of having a flaw in his personality. He'd had opportunity and squandered it. For

Stanley, being black, there had been little or nothing, no opportunity, identity or support. But now that Stanley was gone, now that there was no more Stanley, what was his excuse going to be from here on in?

# CHAPTER
# THIRTY-NINE

"It's a beautiful day, Mister Long. The sun's shining and there's not a cloud in the sky. Not bad for December, ay?"

Stanley didn't say anything. He lay there with his sunglasses on, all prettied up and ready to go to town.

"It's time to get up, brother. I know you don't want to but time's a-wasting. Now I know," he confessed, "I wasn't an early bird myself. But we all got to do what we don't want to do, so there ain't no excuses today. It's no excuse day, officially. So no more excuses, please."

Stanley didn't disagree. That was something like a first.

"Okay," he vowed. "I won't argue today either. I'll keep my mouth shut, I promise. I'll be a good boy. Agreed?"

Agreed.

"Good." He collected his thoughts, rechecking his mental list of what he had to do. "Well, I guess it's time to go to work."

First he retrieved the extra rope he had stashed in one of the cubbyholes, then threaded the rope under both of Stanley's arms, tying a slip knot on his backside, cinching it down tight and tugging to make sure Stanley wouldn't fall out of it.

"Not the best in the world. But it'll do."

He dragged Stanley by the feet over to the ledge—same fucking old shoes, never did get those platforms—then threw his legs over the side.

"You've taken a fall before, haven't ya, bud? Then this one ought to be a cinch."

The canal floor looked farther down than usual, probably because he hadn't been down to the bottom for quite a while. After this he hoped it'd be a while longer.

"Okay, buddy. This one's on me."

Stanley lay with his arms stretched out over his head as if he were being robbed. Maybe Stanley was. Stanley and he were just late bloomers and they got nailed for it. He guessed the lesson was if you hesitate to jump on the band wagon to a successful career you lose. And if history was right the price could be very high.

In any case, there was still a job to do. No use crying over spilt milk.

He dug his heels into the dirt, bracing them against the backside of the abutment wall, and with his left hand, shoved Stanley inch by inch over the ledge, sometimes using his foot to facilitate the effort.

"See ya in a minute, buddy," he said after a dozen or so good shoves as gravity took over and Stanley's head slipped over the edge.

The bristly rope burned his hands as it slid through. If he'd thought about it he would've used his shirt as a glove. But Stanley was down soon enough and it was over. He sucked his hand to extinguish the burn pain, thinking how Stanley must've gained some weight without him knowing it. Or maybe he was just getting weaker.

Peering down he saw Stanley slumped against the canal wall with his head drooping over to the side, and his left leg underneath him like it was broken, and his right pant leg shoved up to his knee, exposing his sagging navy blue sock.

"Sorry, buddy. We ain't going to the beach today. Maybe some other day."

He stood at attention and saluted the flag passing by in the parade. There was no parade or flag but who was counting? Anyway, it was time to slide down the rope himself. Of course, he'd lowered Stanley right next to the rope hanging off the girder, so he ended up stepping all over Stanley when he reached the bottom, and in the effort to avoid him, tripped over his own feet and went tumbling flat on his ass.

"Ta da!" he proclaimed, holding his arms out to receive the applause.

But Stanley felt differently. He was still asleep, resting his head on his shoulder, though a little dirtier from being stepped on. But then again, who cared?

"Not impressed, ay? You always were hard to please."

He crawled over to Stanley and untied the rope. In doing so he noticed the needle tracks on Stanley's arm—both arms, to be exact.

"I hear it's a pleasant way to go. Got any left?"

No, he'd already promised himself not to check Stanley's pockets.

"I don't suppose you'd care to walk, would you?"

No.

"I figured as much. But we got to do what we got to do. Besides, you're starting to stink." He searched up along the sunny canal. "We got a good day for it though."

He hadn't remembered so many little twisters blowing down the canal, but there were plenty today. He might as well have been in a sand storm in the middle of the Sahara for all the dirt and debris hitting him in the face. Even so, no way he was going to use Stanley's scarf to wrap around and protect himself. He had done some bad things in his life but he was not about to steal from his blood brother. He would carry out his pledge as agreed, no matter how heavy Stanley became on his shoulder, no matter how hot it got, how long it took or how much trouble it got him into, no matter what, he was keeping his word.

On the other hand, if he could make it to the chunk of rock he would rest a little, maybe switch shoulders. He didn't have to go the whole distance in one jump. Besides, he was beginning to hate this canal, every fucking foot of it. When had it grown so long?

"Five more feet," he grunted.

But he didn't make it. He went down on one knee a step or so away, then found he couldn't stand back up.

"I guess this is it for now, buddy."

He slipped Stanley off his shoulder, laying him down on his side. Everything about Stanley was disheveled now, unbuttoned, not tucked in. Even Stanley's collar was standing up.

"I can't take you anywhere, can I?"

He sure could use those sunglasses. It was brighter than hell in this bleached white nothingness, this canal that led nowhere. But a pledge is a pledge is a pledge. No doubt about that.

He sat down next to Stanley, using part of him as a back rest. It felt good to straighten his back and neck, but tomorrow would be a different story. He had a feeling he would be stiff as hell.

"Beautiful weather we're having, don't you think? Oh, yeah, I forgot. You're not talking today. How could I have forgotten? I'll just pretend you're talking. Like I pretended that I liked school once. Like I pretended I liked living in my home town, or living here in this fucking hole," he said, looking up at the fence collecting the blowing debris. "I mean I'm not even here. I swear I'm not. I'm just pretending. I'm up there," he nodded to the broken windows in the warehouse buildings above, "living a normal life. Can ya dig it, man?"

Stanley was zonked out big time. Stanley didn't give a shit. Stanley had problems of his own.

"You sure are a heavy son of a bitch," he said. "I ain't pretending about that. I still like you though. I ain't pretending about that either."

He choked and coughed, feeling slightly nervous.

"I know I'm an asshole," he said. "Ain't no pretending about that either. I am. I admit it." He looked at Stanley and felt the tears reappear in his eyes. "Satisfied now?"

Another twister swept over them like the downwash of a chopper, whipping grit against his face and into his eyes. God, he hated every inch of this canal, every foot of fucking wall. Nonetheless, it was time to go. He had a schedule and today was no excuse day.

"Time to go, bud. Like it or not."

There were lots more rocks in the ravine than he had remembered. His ankles were sore from repeated twistings. Balancing Stanley on his shoulder while wobbling around in these rocks was proving just as hard as carrying him up the hot canal. By this time he could pick out each and every individual tendon and ligament in his ankles, knees and hips. Plus his back hurt like hell, of course. But he was past the point of no return. And besides, this was no excuse day.

He only wished Stanley's legs and shoes would quit hitting him in the shins. Sometimes they got tangled up with his own legs, like a little kid being a nuisance. And he didn't like the feel of Stanley's hands and arms touching the backs of his legs. It was hard enough going uphill without any distractions. He needed to focus his attention on lifting his leg, planting his foot, pushing off, then stepping again, all to raise himself one foot higher. And, more than anything else, he needed a drink of water.

He stopped to look up the last part of the hill, but didn't dare take Stanley off his shoulder or even kneel. Bracing his arms on his knees instead took some of the weight off his lower back and gave him a chance for a breather. He only wished he could work up some saliva, but that had disappeared way back in the canal. By this time he had even stopped sweating, and his once drenched clothes were bone dry. All he could think of was a tall glass of cold water, condensation dripping off it as if it were out in the pouring rain. The glass was jammed with ice, a lemon slice set split on the rim. There was a straw but he would toss it out. He was a gulper from way back.

Of course, none of this was helping him. It was making him want to kill somebody, anybody. All anybody had to do was say the wrong thing, like asking why the hell he was doing this. It was senseless. It was against the law for Christsake. When was he going to get smart?

His muscles were tight when he began again. But it didn't take much climbing to warm up. Or much more climbing before they were burning again. Now he wished he had at least changed shoulders. But stopping now would be sure death. So he kept on and soon found if he side-hilled to the right for a while and then to the left he could rest the downhill leg. Then it became a matter of doing it over and over, again and again. One cycle could be four steps up to the right then four to the left, or it could be six to the right and six to the left. Or for something different, he'd take six to the right and five to the left, or four to the right and six to the left, whatever felt good. Soon he didn't even bother to look up. He knew where up was. It was the only way to go. On top it would be flat and then there'd be only one more mile. He would have reached his plateau.

How poetic.

The flat rock he'd stepped on suddenly slipped out from under him, and he went down on his right knee as Stanley started slipping off his shoulder, Stanley's belt buckle digging into his neck like a dull knife. With all his might he couldn't stop Stanley from falling, his center of gravity had shifted too far to the downhill side. So he let Stanley break free, allowing Stanley to lurch off in front of him like a bag of oats flopping onto the floor. Stanley's head banged against a rock, sending his sunglasses flying partway off, so they ended up being hooked over one ear with the left lens covering Stanley's mouth.

"*Goddamn it!* God fucking damn it! Jesus motherfucking Christ!"

He stood and slung one foot back, aiming at the sprawled-out body. "You son of a fucking bitch! You piece of fucking shit! You owe me, fucker! *You owe me!*" But he still couldn't let the kick go.

Of course, this little temper tantrum did absolutely no good. It just drained him that much more. He was acting as if what he was doing truly meant something to Stanley. What did Stanley care? He was dead. Stiff as a board. Starting to stink real bad. He could give a fuck. Go ahead. Kick him. Get him back. Have the final word. Sort of.

Yeah, right. Listen to the voices in your head. They've always been right, right?

Yeah, right.

The longer he stared at Stanley the more he realized what a fool he was. He couldn't even climb up a hill without tripping over his own feet. He was just one worthless motherfucker. Stanley was probably glad to get rid of him. Too bad Stanley had done it the hard way.

He looked up at the clear blue sky. Not a cloud in sight. Nothing but the fucking sun.

"I hate you," he snarled. "I hate you. I hate you. I hate you."

He flipped the sun the middle finger.

"*I hate you!*" he screamed.

DUES / PART 3

He closed his eyes a few seconds and then looked back down at Stanley lying sprawled-out as if he'd been shot.

"We having fun now?" he asked.

Stanley didn't care.

"You don't give a shit about what I'm going through now, do you? All you want is your fucking dreams. Well, shove them, buddy. Shove them right up your fucking ass."

When Clarence opened the shack door he had a white upper lip and half a gallon of milk in his hand. Inside, on his table, a package of chocolate chip cookies was spread out like dominos in three neat rows.

"I've been wondering when you were going to come by. You want some milk? I got a cup."

"No thanks," he said though he was thirsty as hell and those cookies made his stomach groan.

"It's washed," Clarence assured him. "In hot water."

"No thanks. I'm not hungry." Though even as he said it his stomach was groaning. Still, at the moment, he didn't think he could get anything down.

"I've been real busy," Clarence was saying. "They got me working around the whole county this week. I just haven't been able to keep up with this place. People come in here and throw their junk around anywhere. They don't know certain kinds of trash go certain places. You know what I mean?"

"Yeah, I know." He took a quick scan around the dump. "It looks good though. You do a great job here."

"Thanks," Clarence beamed.

"I was wondering," he said, figuring now or never, "if you could fire up the incinerator?"

Clarence squinted his eyes, moving his head back and forth as if talking to himself, as well as answering. "Well...I'm not supposed to use it. You know, because of the environment and such."

"I thought you said you did use it."

"I do, but only when the wind is right." Clarence wet his finger and held it up in the air outside the doorway. "Yeah, I guess it's okay. What you going to burn?"

"Something that needs to be burned," he said, looking at the ground.

"Dope?"

"No." He couldn't believe Clarence thought that.

"What then?"

The moment of truth had arrived. He was shaking all over and he knew if he waited too long he would cry. But he couldn't turn around now, couldn't quit, he had to keep his word.

"Stanley," he said, looking Clarence straight in the eye.

"Stanley?" Clarence scowled. "Is he dead?"

"Yeah."

"You kill him?"

It sent a lightning shock through his heart. Had he killed him?

"No," he said, again forcing himself to look Clarence in the eye. "He died."

"You're going to cremate him then?"

"Right."

"Okay," Clarence said. "If you think it's all right."

"No," he said, taking a deep breath and gambling on honesty. "It's not all right. It's against the law. But I'm going to do it anyhow. It's what he would've wanted. And unfortunately for him I'm his only friend."

"Okay," Clarence shrugged. "But I'll finish my milk first. Okay?"

"Sure. Take your time."

So, while Clarence finished his milk, he went back to the gate to get Stanley, resting against the fence like any other wino, sound asleep and dreaming away.

"Sounds like a go, buddy," he told Stanley. "Hope you're ready for this. I hate to have you change your mind in the middle of it. I would definitely be pissed."

Clarence met him at the incinerator with two cookies in hand. Clarence offered them to him but he had to refuse. Even a sip of water would kill him now. He just didn't have an appetite.

"How well does this thing burn?" he asked as Clarence stashed the cookies in his breast pocket.

"Right down to ashes," Clarence said. "It's gas operated. All we got to do is keep it stoked and we can burn most anything."

"Good."

He knew things had been proceeding too well the moment they tried to shove Stanley into the pipe-shaped incinerator. It was like trying to load a torpedo that was too large for the tube, then beating it with a hammer because you knew it was supposed to fit.

"You push on the legs when I lift up on the body," he grunted to Clarence.

That might have worked if the incinerator hadn't been so damn high, and if he had any strength left. Eventually he even resorted to using his head to lift Stanley up, but then it was too hard to balance him so Stanley wouldn't catch on the sides. And to top it all off, Stanley's legs wouldn't cooperate. Each time Clarence pushed on them they bent either up or sideways or whatever. Even when he and Clarence switched jobs there was always that certain point where no matter how hard he pushed or how high Clarence lifted, the body refused to go in any more.

"God fucking damn it!" he shouted, and kicked the base of the incinerator. "*Jesus motherfucking Christ!* Why in hell did they build it this way for, for Christsake? It's fucking stupid! Fucking stupid son of a bitches!"

Oh boy, he was ready. He'd fucking kill the first son of a bitch who had ever fucking designed one of these fucking things. He'd fucking kill anybody right now. God fucking damn it! Why in the hell did everything go to fucking shit for him? He couldn't do a Goddamn thing without it fucking up. Oh, he'd just love to kill somebody right now. Especially Mister Stanley fucking Long!

He looked down at Stanley lying on the ground all messed up as if he had been dragged a hundred miles behind a runaway stagecoach. Jesus Christ.

"It's too small to get in there," Clarence said, like the fucking idiot he was.

"No shit," he muttered. He'd already thought about climbing in. And they'd already tried turning Stanley around. But no, that hadn't worked either. In fact it only made things worse.

"We need a board or something," he said.

"I got a board," Clarence said. "I'll go get it."

Watching Clarence run off as if he were in a fifty-yard dash, he wished he had a third of that energy left in him. He was beginning to consider climbing in with Stanley himself. After all, it was all over anyhow, except for the crying.

He knelt down next to Stanley and brushed off the rust and soot smudges on his new light blue sport coat. He even wiped some of the dirt off Stanley's face. It didn't do much but what the fuck. Couldn't have him looking like he was made up for night patrol. The last thing Stanley would want was to look like he was still in the army. Fuck, that would be a fate worse than death.

"I got one!" Clarence yelled, running back.

After two tries they found it was easier to lift up on the board while pushing so it wouldn't dig into the sides. But that demanded more strength. And when they did get Stanley almost in, a soot cloud suddenly decided to billow out of the front that made everything even more of a mess, including Clarence and him.

"Whew," Clarence sighed, falling back on the incinerator. "That was tough."

He went down on one knee, his whole body aching, his head feeling like it was being sucked inside out. "Almost finished," he gasped. "All we got to do now is get the board out."

Famous last words. Even with the board sticking out an extra foot they couldn't budge it. Something inside, down in the dark reaches, was clutching it back with an awesome grip.

"You fucking piece of shit." He didn't even have the energy to scream. He was lucky he could even breathe.

"I think it's caught on something."

"Burn the son of a bitch." He lifted the board up and then slammed it back down as hard as he could. Nothing happened except that Stanley bounced and another cloud of soot rolled out around him.

"Motherfuck."

He started wrestling the board frantically, throwing it wildly back and forth. But all that did was create more soot clouds and exhaust him to the point where he toppled back down to his knees.

"I'll cut it off," Clarence's soft, frightened voice said behind him.

He felt like a little kid. Here was Clarence, the dumb one, being cool and calm, probably feeling embarrassed as hell over his raving maniac behavior. He was quite the winner, wasn't he? The bright kid in school who was supposed to go right to the top. Be somebody. Save the world. Be the pride of his family. If they could only see him now.

"You don't need the board?" he asked.

"I can get another one."

This time Clarence walked back to the shack, looking tired himself. Probably wishing this had never happened, either. Couldn't blame him for that.

"What do you think, Mister Long," he said looking up at the end of the board. "Am I crazy? Are you glad to be rid of me?"

Stanley didn't say a word. It made him think of Doran's visit that last night in Nam. The visit that had really been a punishment for keeping quiet about the girl. Not only had he been wrong for letting it happen, and for shooting her himself, he had been especially wrong for allowing the perpetrators to go free. And now here he was with Stanley, trying to get rid of the evidence. Hadn't learned a thing.

He and Clarence took turns with the hand saw but it was hard going, even with their arms about shoulder height. Plus there was just enough of a breeze to blow the sawdust back into their faces. Nothing like sawing with your eyes closed. But they kept sawing, which overall turned out to be one of the easier tasks. It even had a reward. The door closed without any problem.

"Wait a minute," he said before Clarence latched it, and opened it back up to see Stanley one last time. Also he wanted to make sure he had done it right, that is, gotten Stanley's head pointing east and his feet pointing west. It was supposed to symbolize that Stanley had left Vietnam and was heading on the high road to home, which was supposed to be Chicago and electronics. In truth it wasn't the perfect east-west alignment, but it was close enough.

Any other things you might like to say? He couldn't think of any. "Okay," he said.

"Take care, Stanley," Clarence said as he closed and latched the door.

The first clouds of smoke were black wispy puffs, like diesel exhaust. He figured it must be Stanley's polyester clothes making it so sooty. But soon the black disappeared and the smoke became more light gray and even white. The incinerator rumbled and roared like a volcano. The translucent heat waves radiated off it until the whole contraption appeared to be melting. The heat baking his chest and face would have made him sweat if he'd had any fluids left. Then the stink of burning hair and burning flesh hit, so much like the smell of rotten burning food. It was one of those things you had to experience to understand, but then who would want to? It would make them puke. It would singe their sinuses. It would make their eyes water. It would make them want to swallow their tongues, tighten their fists, squeeze their thumbs. The stink would penetrate no matter how long they held their breath. And it would never go away. The only way to get rid of it was to blow your head off, join the fire and the smell, become one with it and repulse someone else.

Clarence had to leave for the back of the shack, holding his hand over his mouth and nose. He could hear Clarence behind him gagging and vomiting, could envision all the milk and cookies splattering over the ground. But today nothing would make him ill. Not even thinking about Stanley melting and burning away in a pool of boiling blood. He was here for the duration, no matter how gruesome. He would stand here and bless every escaping molecule of Stanley's existence as it rose out of the stack into the evening sky— a sunny, blue sky, the kind Stanley would have liked.

He took out the ceremonial joint he had stashed in his breast pocket, lit up, and held each toke as long as he could. His speech, his toast, his eulogy to a friend.

Once he was done he stood at attention and saluted. Then he lay down for the night.

Later in the night when he woke up, the incinerator was still warm and the stars were incredible. There were millions of them, all so bright, so clear, that each one looked like the North Star. He remembered how amazed he'd been to find stars like this in Vietnam. Yet now, like a switch had been turned off, Nam was the furthest thing from his mind.

"Thanks for the warmth, buddy," he thought somebody might have said. "Thanks for everything."

# CHAPTER FORTY

It was classic how the ashes puffed out around the door as Clarence opened it, as if the two of them were cracking a treasure chest that had been buried for centuries. Only problem was, the door didn't creak.

Clarence peeked in, looking like a bank robber with his handkerchief tied around nose and mouth. But with all the fine dust floating in the air Clarence still had to squint.

"Not much left," Clarence said.

The morning sun lit the inside of the barrel but all they could see was the smoky cloud of ash swirling around in there, making the incinerator look endlessly large.

"Yeah," he sighed.

"We clean it out, right?"

"Yeah. Right."

When he whipped the shovelful of ashes in an arc the heavy material dropped to the ground like fresh topsoil spread over a yard and the lighter dust drifted away, fading into the bright and calm morning.

"Ashes to ashes...," he mumbled.

"Dust to dust," Clarence added, throwing his shovelful in a wider arc.

He wished he knew more of the parable, or whatever it was. But he still had no speeches, no eulogies, nothing. The words just weren't there.

"This ain't all Stanley," Clarence shyly admitted. "I didn't clean it out from the last time. I've been real busy lately and everything."

"That's okay," he said. "It'll make it harder to find him."

"Yeah," Clarence said, in a voice full of relief. "You'd never know this was Stanley."

He gazed down at his shovelful and then at the ground. "No. Not in a million years."

He took a handful from the shovel and let it sift through his fingers. He had kept his part of the deal, removed all evidence of Stanley's existence as agreed upon. Stanley would have done the same for him. It was their way of saying they had never meant any harm to anyone. Yet now that he thought about it, it was the wrong thing to do. Their existence should have been known. They were worth as much as anyone else, even if they were just plodders. They had worked hard. They had suffered. But they had also lived, and maybe more than most.

He looked down at the remaining ash in his palm. Once again, it was too late. No one would ever know. Maybe they were even more expendable than he'd ever wanted to admit.

"You'll be back, huh?"

He looked back at Clarence after he went through the gate. "Probably."

"I'll be here," Clarence said.

Yeah. Right.

# EPILOGUE

It was just another hot December day, so he got fried again on his walk back. Then, when he did get back to the bridge he was welcomed by the sight of the climbing rope coiled like a spaghetti noodle on the floor of the canal, not far from where the chalky remains of his vomiting streaked down the wall. Someone had cut it, but he guessed he could handle that. He wasn't going anywhere. He had no appointments to keep, no job to go to. He was a free soul, single again.

So he sat down. Leaned back against the wall. Took out his last joint. Lit it up. Smoked it.

He realized now the one thing he'd done that was truly wrong. When Max had told him Stanley was sick he should have returned to the bridge. He had stayed away when Stanley had needed him the most. He had stayed away because he felt justified in doing so, but there was no justification. He had fucked it up like he had when he left Nam. If he had simply said thank you, thank you for being my friend, maybe the two of them would have gotten along better. Then he would have come back when Stanley needed him, and today they would still be together. But all that was too late again, and all because he had never said thank you. He shook his head. What a fucking stupid son of a bitch he was. But from now on he wasn't going to leave. He wasn't going to run away, hide, or remain silent. He was going to engage. He was going to get something done. In fact, he was going home, and the first thing he'd do was thank his parents for letting him carve his own path. They had confidence in him. Now all he needed was confidence in himself.

He'd also break the unspoken vow he'd made with Stanley. That no-existence idea was bullshit. On his way to New York he'd go to Chicago and find Stanley's aunt. Then he'd visit Stanley's mother's grave and tell her her son was dead. He didn't expect any forgiveness. It was just time to own up. He had learned about life and his own personality at other people's expense. Now he knew what privilege meant.

He took one last hit on the joint, savored it, then flicked it away to the center of the canal.

From now on it was no excuse day. None for anyone at all from here on in.

**Curbstone Press, Inc.**
is a non-profit publishing house dedicated to literature
that reflects a commitment to social change, with an emphasis
on contemporary writing from Latin America and Latino
communities in the United States. Curbstone presents writers
who give voice to the unheard in a language that goes beyond
denunciation to celebrate, honor and teach. Curbstone builds
bridges between its writers and the public – from inner-city to
rural areas, colleges to community centers, children to adults.
Curbstone seeks out the highest aesthetic expression of the
dedication to human rights and intercultural understanding:
poetry, testimonials, novels, stories, photography.

This requires more than just producing books.
It requires ensuring that as many people as possible know about
these books and read them. To achieve this, a large portion of
Curbstone's schedule is dedicated to arranging tours and
programs for its authors, working with public school and
university teachers to enrich curricula, reaching out to
underserved audiences by donating books and conducting
readings and community programs, and promoting discussion in
the media. It is only through these combined efforts that
literature can truly make a difference.

Curbstone Press, like all non-profit presses,
depends on the support of individuals, foundations,
and government agencies to bring you, the reader, works of
literary merit and social significance which might not find a place
in profit-driven publishing channels. Our sincere thanks to the
many individuals who support this endeavor and to the following
foundations and government agencies: ADCO Foundation,
J. Walton Bissell Foundation, Witter Bynner Foundation for
Poetry, Connecticut Commission on the Arts, Connecticut Arts
Endowment Fund, Lannan Foundation, LEF Foundation,
Lila Wallace-Reader's Digest Fund, Andrew W. Mellon
Foundation, National Endowment for the Arts
and The Plumsock Fund.

Please support Curbstone's efforts to
present the diverse voices and views that make our
culture richer. Tax-deductible donations can be made to
Curbstone Press, 321 Jackson Street, Willimantic, CT 06226